Deadly Little Hearts

Jenna Daring

Published by The Daring Press Cover Design: Artista Grafico

Editors: Creating Ink, Autumn Reed Books& Editing & Messenger's Memos

Printed in Australia.

To the reader clutching this book like it holds secrets—

It does. And some of them bite.

Take a deep breath, darling.

Freya's not done breaking hearts...or rules.

Chapter 1

Lucas

Freya reaches out to me, her face a mixture of pain and worry. I stumble backward, my foot hitting something, and I fall to the ground. My heart rips in two, and it's all her fault. She did this—the only person I've ever let in. The woman I'm falling for.

She killed my mother. She pointed the gun at her chest and pulled the trigger. All for what? Revenge for her brother's death? But is killing my mom going to bring Alec back? No. My chest aches, and I want to rip my heart out.

I've watched Hazen and Gage seek revenge on people countless times, but I'm more of a free love kinda guy. And if she really loved me, how could she kill my mom? How could she make me an orphan?

Do I believe my mother killed Alec LeClair? Yes. Did I believe my father when he said Alec was his son? Fuck. It hurt to find out that Freya and I shared a brother I knew nothing about. I have so many questions that I won't ever get answers to.

Maybe my mother made some mistakes when I was younger. She did everything my father ordered. She helped create the man I am today—someone who sold himself to The Brotherhood, a soldier. But she only did it because she wanted me to make the best out of my situation, to become someone that people respected. She was always someone I could count on, and maybe we didn't have the traditional mother-son relationship, but in our world, having someone believe in your worth felt a lot like love.

I lost my father and mother tonight as I became a leader of The Daring Brotherhood. It's a night to go down in history, when I became one with my brothers Hazen and Gage. Signing away my body, soul, and spirit.

"Lucas!" Freya calls to me again.

I harden my gaze and stare at the dead leaves beneath me on the ground.

What a shit show. I can't even look at her. I need to go. I need—fuck, I have no idea, but I have to do something to take away this pain inside.

I push to my feet, and without looking back, I walk away, my footsteps crunching against the gravel underfoot.

"Take her back to my place and clean up," Gage says from somewhere behind me, and I stop just through the archway, spinning back around.

"The fuck?" I snap.

"What?" Gage asks.

"I don't want to be anywhere near her. Send her back over the tracks. That's where she belongs," I say, watching as Freya's face morphs into an expression of torment. Her lip trembles and her beautiful ocean-blue eyes water. Fuck, I can't be around her. I can't let her bring me back in.

Hazen shakes his head. "Lucas, don't—"

"Don't what?" I say, raising my voice. "She killed a family member of The Brotherhood. I should be pulling her heart out of her chest for this!" *Just like she's ripped mine out*, I want to add, but I don't.

Freya pushes herself to her feet. "I didn't mean—"

"Just fuck off, you good-for-nothing gutter rat." The words ring through the tomb, echoing off the countless graves and right back at us, sounding nothing like me.

I catch a silent tear tracking down her cheek. Part of me wants to comfort her, to hold each other until the pain subsides, but the other part doesn't want to be anywhere near her.

My father was right about one thing—girls are mere distractions and will use you, then dump your ass, taking you for everything you're worth. He said to never let them in. Well, it's too fucking late for that. She's already within me, her fingers clawed around my heart, and now she's pulled it clean out.

The air around me closes in and I can't breathe. I need to escape. My fists clench, and I hate myself for how I feel. I hate that I want to reach out to bring her close. *No, she betrayed me. She killed my family.* Even though my mother has done some terrible things, she always put me first, and to The Brotherhood, family is everything.

Fuck. *Family.* I'll have to break the news to my little sister that both our parents are dead. She's been looked after by her nanny, but this will destroy her. Does this mean I'm like her pseudo dad now? Fuck! I can't deal with this. I need some time to process.

Hazen is standing at the archway next to me. He opens his mouth, then closes it.

"Gather all the members and meet at my place," I say to him, then move through the archway. "We're getting drunk." I push open the heavy doors, and they slam shut behind me.

Darkness surrounds me like a warm blanket. The cool air wraps around my bare chest, and I stare down at the new mark branded there: the famous hourglass with the three skulls inside it, along with the words *Daring Brotherhood*. I'm a motherfucking leader of The Brotherhood now. Holy fucking shit.

But you don't have a mother, or a father. And the woman you thought you loved didn't care for you enough to even blink before she pulled the trigger.

I want to drink a shitload and forget the pain, even for a moment. To bury it all so far down that I won't ever be able to feel it. Hazen better follow my orders.

Freya better not come anywhere near me.

My backyard is filled with members of The Brotherhood—*our* Brotherhood. Fuck. I still can't believe it. That Gage, Hazen, and I are in charge of this now. I've waited my whole life for this moment and now we have it at only twenty-three. To watch as every single soldier looks up at me with respect, like they all want to kneel at my feet and take my cock into their mouth. They probably would if I asked. I scoff, bringing the bottle of vodka to my lips. Fuck using a glass. One less thing between me and drowning myself in liquor.

Music thumps out of the speakers. My favorite band, Dead Glow, rocks away on the stage. The beat of the drums echoes through my chest. I can't believe my boys managed to get them on such short notice, but fuck am I glad. Nothing like live music, a party, and drugs to block out everything else.

Hazen and Gage come through the back door and my heart beats faster, waiting for her to appear, but she doesn't. Thank fuck they respected my word. I need space from her—fuck, we all do. We are now the kings. All that responsibility lands with us, and yeah, I love the sound of that. Tonight, we party and then tomorrow, we take the reins and rule this city.

Everything is about to change here in Daring. The people over the tracks in Daringhood don't know what's coming, and I want to keep it that way. Keep them on their toes because there are new leaders, and we aren't messing around. It's time for change.

Hazen snatches the bottle from my hand and finishes the rest of it in three gulps before throwing it to the ground at our feet, where it rolls away on the grass.

"Thanks, asshole," I spit out.

He reaches into his pocket and dangles a little bag of white powder in my face, and I forgive him, taking it. I rarely indulge in our own supplies, opting for a clear head, but tonight is different. I want to numb everything inside me until Freya's betrayal is a distant memory. Until all I can feel is pure ecstasy.

Hazen places a hand on my shoulder. "You know she didn't—"

I shake my head. "Leave it. Tonight, we don't talk about her or what happened back there. Tonight, we celebrate. Got it?"

"Crystal clear," Hazen says, raising his hands and walking backward across my yard toward the bar set up in the corner, manned by a topless waitress.

Gage stays quiet beside me, and I'm thankful for it. There's no denying that I fell head over heels for Freya LeClair, and so did Hazen and Gage. Although, I'm not sure that Gage will openly admit that yet. I didn't know what the future held for us with her by our side, but now it's all fucked. I don't think we can come back from this. Fuck. Why can't I stop thinking about her?

Taking the bag, I empty half the contents onto my wrist and inhale quickly. The coke hits the back of my throat, and I throw my head back, then pour the rest out and shove my hand in Gage's face.

"Fuck, no. I don't get high on our own supply," he snaps, and I laugh more to myself than him.

"Your loss," I say, before finishing the rest of the cocaine and shoving the bag into the pocket of my jeans.

"What are we going to do about Dominic?" Gage asks.

I run a hand over my face. "No business tonight, for fuck's sake. Let your hair down for once. We are the kings now," I say, and a smile plays on Gage's mouth. Reaching out, I put my arm around his shoulders and pull him closer. He struggles against my hold, laughing, but I maintain the headlock.

"Fuck off," he growls, and I let go, shoving his chest. He stumbles back, glaring at me but grinning at the same time.

I spin around and move into the crowd of our soldiers gathered near the stage. They close in around me, hands pulling and shoving me in every direction. I allow it, moving to the front of the crowd. The music pulses through my body, and fuck, it feels good. The bass is so powerful, it's like the entire ground is trembling beneath me.

This is exactly what I want—a night to forget, and then tomorrow I will deal. One thing I do know?

Freya LeClair is dead to me.

Chapter 2

Freya

The water surrounds my body like a safety net. As I drop my head against the jacuzzi padding, one of the dangling ties of my bikini top wraps around my neck, and I flick it back with a sigh.

"Fucking hell. I can't believe they are officially patched in to lead The Daring Brotherhood," Amirah says from the opposite side of the hot tub. She takes her champagne glass and finishes it before pouring another one.

My stomach twists at the mention of *them*. Tonight's been wild. My hands are still trembling underneath the water.

"You still haven't told me exactly what happened in the graveyard." Amirah side-eyes me and I fall farther into the warm water.

"I don't want to talk about it," I say.

Amirah frowns. "Fine, but you did wake me from my beauty sleep, so naturally, I will want answers eventually."

Music from Lucas's house floats through the early morning air, and part of me wishes I was there. The other wants to give Lucas space.

How am I supposed to tell her that I killed Lucas's mother? That I'm responsible for taking away someone he loved, and he'll never forgive me for this? The way he looked at me in that tomb, his eyes full of hurt and pain—I did that, and I won't ever be able to take it back.

"Lucas and my brother share the same father," I whisper, and for the first time, it really sinks in. Alec and I *don't* share the same father. So he's my half-brother. No, fuck that. He's always been my full brother and always will be.

"Holy shit." Amirah sits straighter, half her champagne falling into the water.

"Yep." I sigh, taking my glass from the side of the jacuzzi and finishing it in one gulp.

"That's messed up. I have so many questions."

So do I.

"Yeah, well, he's dead now, so we won't be getting the answers."

She gasps. "Who's dead?"

"Lucas's father and . . . and . . ." The words lodge in the back of my throat.

Amirah slides across the seat so she's closer to me, water sloshing onto the deck. She pulls me into her arms, and I let her take me. Tears well behind my eyes, and my head pounds, feeling like it's about to explode.

"I killed—" My throat becomes dry, and I whisper, "Nadine."

Amirah sucks in a breath, but she doesn't let me go. She holds me close, running her hand up and down my back. A few minutes later, she pulls back, looking into my eyes. The corner of her mouth lifts slightly.

"Never did like that bitch," she says, and I laugh uncontrollably until the laughter turns into tears once again.

I pull myself out of her arms and fall back against the jets.

The reality of the situation hits me again—I killed someone. And even if she wasn't a good woman, I still pulled the trigger. What gives me the right to play God?

"Hey," Amirah says, bumping shoulders with me as she settles back into the spa. "I know you're beating yourself up about this, but I bet you had a good reason for doing what you did."

I shrug. Is any reason really good enough? Still . . . "She pushed drugs on me and admitted to killing Alec. But I didn't mean to kill her—she was aiming a gun at me, and I snatched it off her. A shot went off, and before I knew what happened, she was dead. You should have seen the way Lucas looked at me tonight," I say, squeezing my eyes shut. "He hates me."

"Lucas couldn't hate you. He's in love with you, but he might need time to heal from this."

"I'm not sure he'll get over it, and if he doesn't, I won't blame him. As much as it kills me, I'll leave him alone. Until he finds his way back to me—or not." My words hang in the air, and I don't know if I believe that I'll ever really let him go. Yet if the roles were reversed and he killed my brother, I don't know if I could ever forgive that.

My heart might be broken in two, but if a relationship between us is meant to be, then it'll happen. I need to hold on to that.

"I have to go back home and sort some things out with Mom, and it's probably for the best," I say, though even I can hear the defeat in my tone. "The boys will have their hands full with The Brotherhood, and Lucas needs space."

Amirah huffs. "You belong over here—you always did. Now you can both come back home."

I laugh and shake my head. "We never belonged here, not really, and Mom isn't better. She still thinks I'm lying about Alec and that he'll come back." A shiver runs down my spine. That's not going to be a fun conversation when she finally realizes he's gone. Will it tip her over the edge?

She can't drop further than she already has.

"You do what you have to, but don't just disappear." Amirah takes another sip of her champagne. "That hood rat will get you back over there and won't let you leave, but I'll fight him."

I frown. "Uh, which one?"

"You know . . . the one who's always following you around with those intense dark-brown eyes."

"Kai?" I ask, and she nods.

"Yeah, Kai—that's it. He's always wearing that leather jacket with the 18hood logo on the back."

"You're paying a lot of attention to a guy from the wrong side of the tracks," I tease, and her cheeks pinken, and I'm sure it's not just from the heat of the water.

"Shut up." She splashes me, and I raise my hands in surrender.

We stay in the jacuzzi until our fingers become wrinkled and the sun begins to rise on the horizon. I'm reluctant to leave, since it means returning to my old life without Alec there. He really is gone now, and nothing will be the same again.

As I leave the warm embrace of the swirling water, the fresh morning air sends a wave of goose bumps across my body. Music from Lucas's house down the street continues to play in the background.

"I can't believe they're still going," I say, grabbing two large towels from a chair on the porch.

"Yeah, it'll go on for days. It's a big deal, new leaders. It doesn't happen every day," Amirah says, taking a towel from my hand.

"Will you join them?"

She shrugs. "Traditionally, girls aren't allowed—only the guys in The Brotherhood."

"For real?" My eyebrows raise. "I'd have thought, being the new king's sister . . ."

"Comes with literally zero special privileges." Amirah sighs until a glint of mischief lights her eyes. "But watch me go and visit, anyway."

I frown, shaking my head. There are so many underlining rules of The Brotherhood that I'm still trying to figure out. Women play such a small role in their world, something that I don't agree with, and I have no idea how I'm going to fit in with them.

I slip into my worn-out jeans and Gage's hoodie. His woodsy scent still clings to the fabric.

"Make sure you keep me updated, and don't be gone long," Amirah says, pulling me in for a tight hug.

"Okay, got it."

One of Amirah's drivers gives me a ride back over the tracks, dropping me off in front of the trailer park. Sunshine pierces the clouds, bathing the trailers in an orange glow. The scraping sound of the dirt beneath my soles is a constant reminder of the distance I'm putting between myself and Gage, Lucas, and Hazen. They've been my anchors since Alec went missing.

Coming back here hurts like hell, because everywhere I look, I see him. Memories flood at every corner, all revolving around Alec. Tears well behind my eyes. I just want him here with me. To go back in time and give him one last hug, tell him I love him more than anything in this world. But I can't, and that's like a knife to my chest. He's really gone.

Rubbing my eyes, I yawn. I just want to get home and go to sleep. To let dreams take me away from reality, even for a few hours.

The screen door to our trailer creaks as I pull it back and twist the knob on the main door. It opens and I shake my head. Doesn't she ever learn? No locks. Anyone could walk straight into our trailer.

Darkness surrounds me, and the smell of something burned lingers in the air. Soft snores come from the couch, and I sigh in relief. I never know what I'll walk in to—she's usually on a bad high or a good one or sleeping it off. Thank God for the latter.

Pulling out my phone, I flick on the flashlight and shut the door behind me, sliding the lock into place. Mom stirs on the couch, her blanket falling to the ground. I move as quietly as I can, picking up the blanket and gently placing it over her.

The light from my phone shines down on her. Sweat beads on her forehead, but her body trembles. She's probably coming down from one of her benders. I hate that she puts herself through this—that the drugs have become her only source of relief. I'll never forgive Lucas's mother for giving her that first hit and kicking off the avalanche that was our family's downfall.

Mom stirs and her eyes fly open. She grabs my wrist, digging in her nails before her eyes soften slightly. The more time that passes, the more I forget who she was before, how much she loved me and Alec and would do anything for us. Before the drugs became her priority and she forgot about her kids.

"Where's Alec?" she asks and my heart twists.

I kneel on the carpet in front of the couch and take a deep breath. *Here goes nothing.*

"Remember, I told you that Alec, he's . . . he's—" My words choke my throat, and I swallow past the lump. "He's dead." Tears slip down my cheeks in a steady stream.

My mother shakes her head. "You're a liar," she hisses, rolling onto her back and looking up at the ceiling.

"I'm sorry," I whisper, my head falling against her chest. I feel its rhythm, a gentle rise and fall with each breath she takes. I wait, anticipating the push, but it never comes.

She breathes, and breathes, and soon her chest shakes as tears spill from the corners of her closed eyes down to the brown fabric of the couch below. Anguish like I've never seen before wrecks her face, and God, I wish we didn't have to do this, but we do.

He's dead. Her first baby. My brother.

I don't know how long we stay like this for—minutes? Hours?—but eventually, when my knees ache from the hard trailer floor and my throat is raw from crying, her sobs subside into choked hiccups, stuttered with silence.

"I want to get better," she says so softly that I think I imagined it.

I lift my head up off her chest and look into her blue eyes, the same as mine. "Really?"

She nods. "For Alec," she says, and I squeeze her hand. I want to believe her, I really do, but I'm just not sure I can. She's got to want this more than she wants to get high.

Her arms wrap around me, and I freeze. My breathing picks up, and I have no idea what to do. I can't even remember the last time my mother hugged me. The last time I felt her warm body against mine. When she presses a kiss into my hair, I'm done for. Tears stream down my cheeks again and soak into her T-shirt.

I move so I'm lying on the couch in front of her. She holds me and I never want her to stop. She may have gone off the rails, but she's all I have left now—and if she does want to change . . . that could mean everything.

She's my mom, and she'll always be my family.

Chapter 3

Freya

In the week I've been back home, I've been helping Mom through her withdrawals, in between the odd shift I've picked up at the diner. It's been hell—watching her as pale as a ghost, her body trembling, and her begging me to give her drugs to help her take the pain away.

My arms are covered in bruises from her assaults, but it's a small price to pay. If Alec was here, he'd be helping me—this is all he ever wanted. For Mom to recover and be her usual self again. For us to have a fresh start. I don't know what the future holds for us, but this is something. I'm praying with everything I've got that she can get through this.

I flip over the eggs, then the bacon sizzling in the pan. Mom's singing nursery rhymes, and the sound makes my ears bleed, but I don't tell her to stop, because it's nice to see her like this.

She hasn't vomited once today, and last night, she slept for five hours straight without waking in a panicked fever.

Day seven, and she's turning a corner, and I couldn't be happier. She's folding our clothes, fresh from the wash, humming along to the radio. I dish up our breakfast and pour us both a cup of coffee.

"Let's eat out front today. The sun's out," she says, taking her mug and plate.

I follow her out the front and fall into one of the chairs on the small patch of dead grass. The crisp, early morning air sends shivers down my arms.

The familiar buzz of my phone breaks through the silence. I pull my cell out and stare at the screen. It's Hazen again. All week, he, Gage, and Amirah have been bombarding my phone with messages. They're begging me to come back, but I've been too focused on Mom to leave. I've been enjoying her company for the first time in years.

Still, I miss the guys. And I hope I get to see them soon.

We eat in silence, watching the sun peek over the trailers.

"Are those boys still calling you?" Mom asks, eyeing me with a raised eyebrow.

"Yeah, they want me to visit. So does Amirah. Is it okay if I go? Will you be okay without me?"

Mom clicks her tongue and doesn't say anything for several seconds. "You're a grown-ass woman, so I'm not going to tell you what you can and can't do." She lets out a heavy breath, placing her plate on the little table between us, and I wait for the *but* because I know it's coming. "But The Brotherhood is dangerous. They want everyone to drop to their knees, to obey their every rule, and if you don't, we know better than anyone what those consequences are."

"I know, Mom, but Lucas, Gage, and Hazen? They're different. Now that they're in charge, things will change in Daringhood. We'll have more freedom and peace. Hazen has always said he's not as against the Hood as his father was," I reply, and Mom snorts.

"Honey, you're beautiful, there's no doubt about that—you get your good looks from your mama—but it won't be enough to convince them to make that kind of change. They've been brainwashed since they were little kids to follow The Brotherhood's guild, and there's no undoing that."

I lean back in my chair, bringing the mug to my lips. I don't want to change the guys. They are who they are. But I want more unity between the two towns, and I'm going to try to convince them of the same.

Dominic may have raised them, but they aren't like him. I wouldn't have fallen for them if they were.

"Why didn't you tell us about Alec's father?" The words fall from my lips before I have a chance to overthink them. It's been on my mind since Nadine dropped the bomb that night a week ago.

Mom says nothing for several long seconds. The air around us tightens and my shoulders tense as I wait for her to flip her shit. Anytime I used to bring up personal things with her, she'd rip my head off.

She exhales, placing her mug down on the table between us. "How'd you find out?" she asks, and I turn to face her. She stares blankly out into the trailer park.

Do I tell her everything that happened that night, or will it just make her worry even more? She's got enough going on with getting clean, and I don't want her spiraling because of this.

"Nadine told me," I declare, giving her a crumb of what happened that night, and Mom grips the arms of her chair.

"That fucking bitch—I hate her. It wasn't her place to tell you that," she hisses.

"Well, you never told me or Alec," I huff.

"I wasn't allowed to. When they banished us, that was part of the reason. Dominic made it very clear that Alec wasn't part of The Brotherhood anymore, even though he had Fox blood running through his veins."

"Why didn't you at least tell me when he went missing? Did you wonder if they'd killed him, thinking someone had spilled the truth about his father?" Dominic was the ultimate villain in Alec's death, but surely information like that could have helped us find him.

Mom shakes her head. "I called George—he swore it wasn't him." A sad sheen glasses her eyes. "And I know he wouldn't lie to me. We may not have made it as a couple, but once, he loved me. That's the only reason I was allowed to leave with my life."

"Why? Why were you asked to leave?" I know full well that we were banished because of her habit, but I want to hear it from her mouth. To see if she takes responsibility for her actions.

"Because . . . because . . . I—" She sighs, dropping her head into her hands. "Don't make me say it, Freya. I know I fucked up. I've been fucking up every day since, and it kills me that now Alec has paid the price for my mistakes. They took him from us, just like they said they would. I want to kill that bitch—everything is her fault."

"She's dead," I say, and Mom whirls around, staring at me. She smiles, and I'm taken aback. I haven't seen her beam like this for years.

"Thank fuck for that, and the world is good again." She leans back in her seat, and I don't want to ask anything more today. I don't want to push her any further, because I'm afraid she'll turn back to the one thing that fucked everything up for us.

I don't feel good about killing Nadine. Hell, I wish I could go back and undo what I've done. But I can't. Besides, she ruined my family, enabled my mother's drug habit, and took my brother from me.

Lucas shared a brother with me, and we never knew. Lucas never had the privilege of really knowing Alec, and that's a shame. All because The Brotherhood believed they could do what they like, take what they like, without consequence.

Yeah. Now that the boys are in charge, something has to change. And if they're not up for it, maybe I can help convince them.

Mom and I stay outside in a comfortable silence, finishing our coffees and listening to the birds sing. Somewhere in the trailer park, a man is yelling at his son, arguing over who'll take the trash out. Stupid shit. I check my phone and curse.

"I've gotta get to work. You good?" I ask, standing and collecting our dishes.

"Yep, I'm just going to stay out here for a bit. Think Jessie is coming over later to keep me company," she answers, closing her eyes, and before I can think twice, I press a kiss against her cheek. My heart thumps against my rib cage, waiting for her to shove me away, but she doesn't. I haven't kissed my mother like that for years.

I move back into the house. A tear slides down my cheek, and I quickly place the dishes into the sink, wiping the tear away. If only Alec was here to see her.

It feels like someone reaches into my chest and pulls my heart out, squeezing it until it pops. It's been almost two months now since I found him, and I thought, with time, it would be less painful, but it isn't. Everything that's been happening makes me wish Alec was here with me, like he should be.

Resting my arms on my knees, I lean forward, waiting for Amirah to show up. Being around my mother this past week has reminded me how much I've missed her. It's also made me realize what our life could be like if we had more freedom—something I need to get the guys on board with. We need change around here, and now that they are leaders, they have that kind of power.

Amirah's pink Bentley Bacalar pulls up in front of me, and I stand up off the sidewalk in front of the diner, brushing the dirt from my ass. Opening the passenger door, I slide in, and Amirah leans over the console, crushing me in a hug.

"I fucking missed you, girl. Next time you're gone for a week, I'm coming to drag your ass home," she declares, before pulling back, and I laugh.

"I missed you too." I click my seat belt into place and fall back against the plush leather seat.

"Now, I want all the details about what you've been doing every hour, minute, and second since you've been gone," she demands, and for the car ride back to her place, I do just that.

She pulls into her driveway and parks in the front of their house. "Holy shit, babe. I can't believe your mom is sober. That's so good!"

"Yeah, I just hope it lasts this time. You know how many times she's tried before, but she hasn't ever gotten this far. Now that she's through the worst of the withdrawals, hopefully she can keep going."

I don't think I can handle another day of cleaning up her vomit and changing the sheets from her excessive sweating.

I follow Amirah into the Ledger mansion, and she moves through the foyer, heading for the kitchen.

"My fingers are crossed, and if I can do anything to help, just let me know. That's what best friends are for." She wraps her arm over my shoulder, and I lean into her. I've missed her this past week. I feel closer to her than ever after the fight with Lucas. Not being around my friends has been hard.

"I was thinking we could watch a movie, eat until our tummies are sore, then pass out?" Her face beams.

"Sounds perfect, but I do need to see the guys first to run some things past them. Is that okay?"

Amirah huffs. "Fine, that'll give me time to get everything ready for our slumber party." She disappears into the pantry.

"Do you know where they are?" I ask.

"When I last saw Gage, he was in his bedroom."

Does he know I'm here? If he did, he'd be with me, not letting me out of sight. It's been a week since they walked away from me, and there's so much I want to say but can't. Not yet.

I follow Amirah into the pantry. "Can I borrow one of your dresses?"

Amirah smirks. "What are you planning?"

"A business meeting."

"With who and what about?"

"The guys and about the future."

Amirah purses her lips, eyes widening. "Fuck, yeah! Give those men some of that woman power. You're welcome to anything in my closet."

I head out of the kitchen and up the stairs, taking them two at a time. The closer I get to Gage's room, the faster my heart beats. I pause outside it, and the faint sound of music reaches my ears. Only the door stands between us. I want to push it open and see him, but I've got a plan.

After continuing down the hall and into Amirah's room, I close the door behind me. Her king-size bed is neatly made with a white-and-pink comforter. Nothing is out of place. I open her closet and there are rows and rows of beautiful garments. It's like walking into a clothing store.

I spend the next several minutes scanning over everything, trying to find something that will work. I want to look smart but sexy. A baby-blue suit jacket hangs neatly in front of me, and I pull it out. Bringing it closer to my body, I note that it sits mid-thigh. This will be perfect. I grab one of Amirah's black lace bodices to go underneath and some knee-high black socks with heart-shaped suspenders. My black cotton thong doesn't really go, but it'll do.

After dropping my clothes to the floor, I get dressed before staring at my reflection in the mirror. I do up the buttons of the suit jacket, so I'm not completely naked from the waist down. I don't want to distract the guys *too* much. Although this is bound to distract them just enough.

To finish off the look, I slide into a pair of Amirah's black Prada heels. This outfit costs as much as I make in at least six months of working at the diner. The difference between me and my best friend is crazy, but I did live like this once. Well, we weren't this well-off, but we were comfortable. We didn't have to worry about money until we did—when my mother developed a habit and everything went to shit.

It'd be better if Mom had never developed her habit, but I'm glad I grew up over the train tracks. Even if we live poor, anything is better than being around Dominic, fearing what he'll do next. I really do hate him. Thank God he's MIA, and I hope he stays gone. But if I've learned anything from Dominic over the years, it's that he won't ever truly disappear. He's been released from jail, and he's out there somewhere. I won't be able to relax until he's dead.

I brush my fingers through my dark-brown hair, and it falls down my back in soft waves. After grabbing my phone from my discarded jeans on the ground, I pull up a group text with Gage, Hazen, and

Lucas. My fingers pause over Lucas's name and my chest squeezes. The last time I saw him, he couldn't even look at me, and I don't blame him. I killed his mother. Even if it was in self-defense, I took away someone who meant so much to him, and nothing can change that.

Still, we have business to discuss. And if I don't put myself out there, nothing will change.

Meet me in the Ledger office in ten minutes.

Without waiting for a reply, I shove my phone into the suit jacket pocket, ready for a business meeting that will either unite us or create a divide we might never come back from.

Chapter 4

Gage

My phone vibrates against my chest and my shoulders tense. I sit up, leaning back against my pillows, and open the text in our group chat.

Meet me in the Ledger office in ten minutes.

She's here? I throw my legs over the edge of the bed and head straight for the bathroom, shooting off a one-word text back, agreeing. What's she doing here, and why does she want to meet in my office? I haven't seen her for a week, and it's been hell.

Freya not being around makes me feel like there's a missing piece in the puzzle of The Brotherhood, and no matter how much I throw myself into work, nothing will distract me enough. I want her back here with us. I have no idea when the lines were blurred to the point that she became all I could think about and want.

Fuck, I hate to admit it—my stubborn ass won't believe it—but she's had this hold over me since she came back into our lives. Every time she walks into a room, I can feel her. It's like our souls are connected, long-lost lovers from centuries ago. I'm drawn to her like a fly to a spider web.

I want to be around her every second of every day, and fuck, that *kills* me. I never wanted a distraction. The Brotherhood is my whole life. I'm devoted, and I can't choose between her and it. No matter how much my black heart wants her, my priority will always be my brothers. It's just the way it is and always has been, ever since I was born. Part of me hates that I don't have a choice in the life that I live, but the other part knows my role. To lead The Brotherhood.

We're going to fucking change things around here, and I'm here for it. It's about time. We need to tighten things up at the docks—with as much work as we're giving those shipping magnates, they could afford to charge us less. And then there's the Hood situation.

Dominic didn't give two shits about the others over the train tracks; he only cared about the power we held over them. Making sure that they obeyed every rule we set and paid their dues. We need to rule with force, but not to the point where they have nothing and we have everything.

Everyone has always played by the rules, but over the past couple of months, things have shifted and there's an uprising. They are getting bolder, crossing the tracks more frequently without permission—and I don't just mean Freya. Some houses in the Ville have gone up in flames, and people suspect the Hood.

They don't want to be ruled anymore; they want freedom, and if we don't do anything about it, then there's going to be an all-out war. It's a sign Dominic would have ignored, believing they wouldn't dare, but only fools think that.

I shower in record time and throw on a pair of black jeans and a dark-gray shirt. Moving through my walk-in closet back into my bedroom, I run my fingers through my wet hair, my curls bouncing back. I can't wait to see her.

After closing my door behind me, I head down the stairs, holding on to the railing. Hazen comes through the front door, shutting it with a soft click.

"Where's Lucas?" I ask, reaching the bottom step.

"He isn't coming," he replies, shaking his head. "He's already half into a bottle of whiskey."

"For fuck's sake. He is going to be the death of me," I grumble under my breath, moving toward my office. For all his big talk at our initiation party, he's not done a thing about our new role as leaders, except to snort and drink our merchandise. Fucking idiot.

Hazen's footsteps follow me down the long corridor. I can't get there fast enough. I want to see her again.

The door to my office is slightly ajar. I push it open and suck in a deep breath through my teeth. Holy fucking shit. She's sitting on the front of my desk with one leg crossed over the other, wearing black heels that could kill someone. The blue suit jacket hits her mid-thigh, and the suspenders attached to her knee-high black socks disappear underneath it.

I stalk into the room, heading straight for her. Her bright-blue eyes clash with mine, and I'm done for. The pull she has on me scares the shit out of me, but I never want whatever this is between us to dull. The flames are ablaze, and I'll be damned if I ever let them burn out again.

As I close in on her, her soft floral perfume surrounds me. I brace my hands on the desk on both sides of her, caging her in. She shuffles slightly, unwrapping one leg from the other. I lean in until her mouth is mere inches from mine. She swipes her tongue across her cherry-red lips and my cock stirs. I want her. I need her now.

I go in for a kiss, but her hand on my chest forces me to hesitate, and I pull back, scowling. She raises an eyebrow.

"This is a business meeting, Gage. No touching," she says with a click of her tongue, and I groan, wanting her even more.

Defying her orders, I push back on her hand, capturing her lips in a forceful kiss. A deep groan escapes her as our tongues meet. She succumbs to my kiss, only to shove me away afterward. I stumble back, raising my hands in surrender.

Hazen chuckles from behind me, sitting down on one of the recliner chairs, and I join him, falling into the seat by his side.

"Good to see you, Freya," Hazen says, and the corner of her mouth lifts.

"You too," Freya says, standing. She flattens the suit jacket and moves around the desk. Her heels click against the marble tiles. I can't take my eyes away from her long legs. She needs to wear suspenders more often—or maybe not, as she's enough of a distraction already.

She pushes back my office chair and sits down. Anyone else would be shot for sitting in my seat, but not her. I'll play along with whatever game she's initiating.

Leaning back, she crosses one leg over the other. "Where's Lucas?" she asks, staring at the closed door.

"Not coming," I say, and her face falls.

"Will he ever forgive me for what I did?" she asks in a soft voice, and I have no idea how to answer.

Lucas just lost both his parents, and as controlling as Nadine was, he loved her. What Freya did was in self-defense, and deep down, Lucas knows that, but it'll take time for him to get close to her again. He doesn't deal with shit. He bottles it all up and pretends he's doing fine until it eventually spills over and turns into a flood.

I'm different. I've learned over the years that I need to deal with shit right when it happens. I can't keep it inside, because it fucking consumes me, everything I do and think. My past with Freya and not being able to protect her taught me that—to never leave anything unresolved. It will fuck with your head until it's fried to a crisp.

As kings of The Brotherhood, we can't afford to leave anything unresolved. Everything must be dealt with, so we can be the strong, decisive leaders our brothers need. We had that drilled into us when we started our initiation all those years ago, but Lucas always struggled with it and clearly still does.

"He'll come around. Just give him some space," Hazen says.

"Now, why are we here, Freya?" I ask, eager to find out.

"I've got some ideas for you and The Brotherhood if you choose to accept." She leans back in my chair, folding her arms over her chest. This is supposed to be a business meeting, but fuck me, she's making it impossible to concentrate when she's dressed like that.

"We're all ears," Hazen says, watching her intently, the corner of his mouth lifted. Looks like he's enjoying this just as much as I am.

"So, it should come as no surprise that I want to talk about the love-hate relationship between Daringville and Daringhood. I want you to change that. To create a new chapter in leveling out the divide for more peace and stability."

Running my finger along my jaw, I don't say anything for several heartbeats, and Hazen remains silent beside me. Her eyes dart between us, as if she's waiting to see how we'll respond.

"And how do you propose that we do that?" I ask.

Her hands land on the desk with a slap. She pushes the chair back and stands, straightening her suit jacket before stalking around the table. She reaches the front before leaning back against it.

My eyes slowly move up her legs, taking in every single curve. She knows what she's doing, and I'm not about to tell her off. I'll entertain her, because why the fuck wouldn't I?

Freya LeClair is being a total boss bitch, and we won't be leaving my office until my cock is deep inside her.

Chapter 5

Freya

Gage's and Hazen's eyes haven't left mine since they walked into Gage's office, and that's exactly what I intended. I want their attention on me, without any distractions, so I can get my proposal across to them.

"Is it getting hot in here?" I ask, my fingers playing with the top button of my jacket. The corner of Hazen's mouth lifts. I slowly pop the first button open. More of my black bodice shows and Gage curses.

"Damn it, Freya, this is meant to be a business meeting, but I can't concentrate when you're over there looking like, like—" He gestures his hand up and down my body.

"Like what, Gage? Cat got your tongue?" I ask with a wink.

Hazen sits back in his chair, watching us with a playful gleam in his eyes.

"Like a damn goddess," Gage huffs, his fingers gripping the side of his chair.

"Aww, thanks, babe," I coo, placing my hands on the desk. "Now, where was I?" I pause dramatically. "Oh, yes, so enforcement in the current state costs The Brotherhood time plus labor to send your enforcers to collect and make examples of those who won't or can't pay." I shake my head. "You're bleeding the poor dry, and it'll only end in war or drought or both. Either way, the Hood can't pay for what they don't have, so maybe develop a plan to invest in them so they can be a cash flow source."

Hazen narrows his eyes. "Invest in them how?"

"Maybe you could offer some education—apprenticeships for the youth, where they pay you back in man hours as they grow. Or perhaps it's about leasing them property so some of them can get proper roofs over their heads in exchange for labor—even if those roofs are on the Ville side of the tracks. After all, if you don't offer, we both know that eventually they'll try to take houses by force." I stop and look pointedly at Gage. "Or do you want more blood to clean up?"

His eye twitches, and he rises from his chair. He looks at Hazen, and something passes between them before Hazen stands, too, joining him. They both turn toward me, and panic swells, threatening to swallow me whole. They stalk forward, their eyes never leaving mine. My shoulders tensing, I grip on to the desk, holding on for dear life.

Did I go too far? Did I overstep my authority? Fuck.

They close in, Gage approaching on my right and Hazen on my left. My gaze snaps to the door. I'm ready to flee to safety, but I remain frozen in place. They won't hurt me. Still, I can taste the fear on my lips, and it tastes too darn sweet to resist. They tower over me, and Hazen's tribal tattoos running down both his tanned arms catch my eye.

"And you think we will listen to you?" Gage growls, and I bite down on my lip, holding in the onslaught of anger that I want to throw back at him. Instead, I nod.

Hazen chuckles, taking another step until his knee hits my leg, and tension clenches like a tight fist around my chest. He reaches out and runs his thumb across my bottom lip, the skull on his hand watching me. I suck in a staggered breath and plead with my eyes for him to claim my lips.

"Lesson number one." Gage joins Hazen, running his fingers up my leg, stopping just below my jacket. Shivers dance along my skin, and I want more.

My eyes dart between them, and I open my mouth, but before I can talk, Gage wraps his fingers around my throat, cutting off my air supply. As my gaze clashes with his stormy green eyes, wetness pools between my thighs. I'm well and truly done for. I'd die happily between these two men. Gage's hair falls just above his eyes, and I want to reach out to push it away, but I can't.

"We don't take orders from people outside of The Brotherhood," Gage says, running his nose from my shoulder up to my ear. My eyes close, and I breathe heavily. When he loosens his hold on my neck slightly, I gulp in a breath.

"What makes you think we'll listen to you?" Hazen claims my lips with force, cutting off my reply, and I push back, our tongues clashing as I fight for power. A deep groan comes from the back of his throat, and I want more.

Gage's hand cups my pussy through my underwear, his fingers brushing against my clit, and I lean forward, begging for another touch. His chuckle is low and deep, and Hazen pulls back, taking my bottom lip between his teeth, the sensation both thrilling and terrifying.

My tongue swipes over my tender lips and Gage removes his hand. They look at each other before stepping away. Their warmth is gone, and I want it back.

"Stand," Gage demands in a deep voice.

My thighs press together, and I obey, pushing off the desk.

"Hazen, remove her underwear." Gage's eyes never leave mine, a mixture of lust and anger swirling in their depths. I swallow hard. Both of these men are killers, and I shouldn't be this turned on by them.

Hazen steps between Gage and me before dropping to his knees. He grips my thighs tightly with both hands, and my legs become weak. He holds me in place, his thumb skirting up the inside of my leg. The intensity of his stare is too much. My chest rises and falls at an increasingly rapid rate.

Gage moves forward, his lips crashing into mine in a demanding kiss. When he pulls back, my breath catches in the back of my throat. He unbuttons my suit jacket, and it opens, exposing the black bodice.

"Fucking delicious. I can't wait to eat you," Hazen whispers, and my underwear soaks.

Hazen reaches my thong. His fingers wrap around the fabric before he pulls it down my legs, and it falls to my feet. He breaks his stare, burying his head between my thighs. I stumble backward into the desk as Hazen's hot breath tickles my clit, his tongue swiping between my folds. Pleasure spikes, and my cunt begs for relief. Gage moves back, watching us with hooded eyes.

My fingers itch to touch something, to hold me in place. I reach out, gripping the back of Hazen's head and pushing him farther into my pussy. He chuckles and bites down against my folds. My hips jolt forward, a twinge of pain darting through me. His tongue slides over my clit, and warmth spreads through my core, replacing the pain with pleasure. He fills me with one finger, then two. My chest heaves as he hits the spot over and over again, his tongue flicking my clit. Holy shit.

I keep one hand clutched to the back of Hazen's head, and my other hand clamps tightly around the edge of the desk, holding on for support. My gaze finds Gage's; his pants are pooled at his feet, his hand wrapped around his erect cock. While watching Hazen eat my pussy like it's his last meal, he tugs his cock back and forth. My God.

"Keep looking at me like that, and I'll jam my cock down your throat until you choke," Gage growls, and Hazen picks up his speed. My eyes roll into the back of my head. My stomach clenches, and I'm on the brink of release.

"Is that meant to be a threat? Because it sounds more like a challenge," I say, panting out the words.

Gage stalks forward, having completely removed his jeans. His fingers wrap around my throat, his thumb pressing down. His green eyes turn dark, but I don't dare look away. Panic swells inside me, but I don't let it show. It's as though he's got me standing on the precipice of a cliff, my feet itching closer and closer to the edge.

"Finish her," Gage growls without breaking eye contact, and Hazen obeys. Putting me right on the edge, he bites down hard against my clit, and I release all over Hazen's face. My legs shake, but Hazen's grip on my thigh keeps me in place.

I don't have a second to breathe before Hazen stands and Gage grabs my shoulders, walking me forward a couple of steps, then pushes me down to my knees. He shoves off my jacket and it falls to the ground. I peer up into Gage's stormy eyes, his cock at eye level.

Hazen brushes his fingers along my shoulder and moves behind me. The sound of his zipper sends thrills through my body.

"Hands on the ground and ass in the air," Gage demands, and fuck me, I'd usually run from this bossy side of him, but in this situation, it's hot.

I obey, pressing my hands to the cool floor, my ass bare, and look up at Gage. He kneels, and his erect cock stares back at me. My tongue swipes across my lips, wetting them. His fingers tangle in my hair, and I take him in my mouth. He hits the back of my throat as I lick a trail along his shaft, and he groans.

Hazen grabs my ass before pulling away. A loud slap fills the office, jolting me forward slightly and pushing Gage's cock farther down my throat. Hazen runs a finger along the inside of my folds before the sound of plastic fills my ears. I have no idea what he's doing behind me, and I can't look, because my mouth is full of Gage's large cock.

"You want to know what he's doing back there, don't you, Freya?" Gage asks with a smile playing on his lips, and I nod.

"He's wrapping up his cock nice and tightly in a condom. He's watching you suck my cock like a good girl, wishing that you had his cock in your mouth too." I bite down gently on the head and Gage growls. "He's lining himself up and is about to slam into your tight cunt."

My pussy clenches at Gage's words. Fucking hell. This is something else, being between these two men, one in my throat and the other about to be inside me. It's all too much but not enough at the same time. Someone is missing, and my heart aches.

Hazen rubs his cock between my folds before he fills me completely, pushing me forward. Gage's cock hits the back of my throat, and I almost gag, pleasure lighting me up like Vegas.

"He's now deep inside that beautiful cunt of yours, hands bracing your hips. His eyes are closed, and he's pushing you forward farther and farther. You're sucking my cock like a good girl, and I'm about to come down your throat." He groans. "And you'll swallow every last drop like the slut you are."

I graze my teeth along his cock again. His grip on my hair tightens, and pain burns across my scalp. Hazen slams into me over and over. Cum hits the back of my throat, and I obey Gage by swallowing every last drop.

The sound of the door handle turning and clicking open catches in my ears, followed by the jarring slam of the door against the wall.

My eyes snap to the entrance—and my heart breaks in two. *Lucas.*

Chapter 6

Lucas

Anger roils through me like a tornado swirling around my chest. Here she is in Gage's office, between my two best friends. One is nailing her from behind and the other is down her throat.

I look at her with so much disgust that her eyes drop. She pulls off Gage's cock and wipes her mouth with the back of her hand. Hazen doesn't stop. He plunges into her, and the loud slap of his hand on her ass feels like it's hitting me right upside the head.

My heart can't take this. Part of me wants to walk over to her and claim her alongside my brothers, but the broken part of me wants to take the knife strapped to my thigh, hold it to her throat, and watch the horror dance between her eyes. Then I want to take that same knife and plunge it into my own heart. I'm fucked up, and the reason for my madness is getting railed by Hazen.

Her moans of pleasure follow me out.

"Lucas!" she yells, but I slam the door between us, the bang ricocheting through me.

Fuck. I need to get out of here. Out of this town. Anywhere away from her. Everywhere I go, she's there. I smell her honey-and-milk body wash. I see her dark-brown hair and how it falls effortlessly down her back. Her cute button nose and full dark-pink lips. Fuck me. I don't want to see her anymore. I don't want to remember her. I just want everything to go away. To forget about her. To move on with my life. Why does she have to make this so goddamn hard?

I storm out through the front door. The sun kisses my cheeks, and I don't dare look over to the cliff and out into the water, because I see her blue eyes in the ocean, and all it'll do is make me want to walk straight back into that office. If I do that, I won't be able to control myself. I can't with her.

She's like heroin—a couple of tastes, and everything else fades away. I'm always waiting for my next hit, and when it rushes into my veins, everything is pure bliss. Everything else fades away, and all that remains is her sunshine breaking through the storm. Then, when she's gone, I'll do anything to have one more hit, one more taste because I'm chasing that high again. I'm always needing that sunshine in my veins.

Why did I have to have one taste? Why did I let her claim my heart? Why am I so fucking stupid? She killed my parents. Now I'm left without anyone, and my sister needs me more than she ever has.

I slide into my car and start her up, then pull out of the underground garage, stopping in front of my place. My gaze snaps to my rearview mirror, and there she is, running out the front door, pulling on a blazer to cover up her naked body.

"Fuck you!" I scream, slamming my fist down on the steering wheel before tearing down the driveway and out onto the road.

My hand presses down hard against the horn when I reach the gates. The security guards run toward the tower and open the door. I glance back using the rearview mirror, and she's watching me drive away. *Fucking hurry up*. My hands shake, and I need something to take this pain away.

Reaching into the glove compartment, I pull out a little bag filled with white dust. Sure, I've been high more than sober these last few days, but anyone who's been left an orphan—who's had to tell their own fucking sister that their parents are dead—deserves it. I need this. After emptying the coke on the back of my hand, I bring it to my nose and inhale. It hits the back of my throat, and a smile plays on my lips. Licking my thumb, I gather the remaining powder and rub it against my gums, then throw the bag at my feet.

Shifting gears, I fly through the open gate and into the street. The midday sun shines through the windshield, blinding me. I drive through the streets of Daringville, down the main drag with design-er clothing stores and cobblestone paths. There are people walking around with bags and bags of pointless shit that makes them feel better about themselves. My mother used to do the same—spend thousands of dollars every day, buying clothes that made her feel good. I want to feel good too.

I speed through the main street, and eyes watch my car suspiciously. When I pull to a stop just outside the checkpoint, my tires screeching against the road, one of the men stationed at the guard tower rushes toward my car and opens my door. I throw him my keys before walking toward the train tracks. I have no idea why I'm drawn here—or maybe I do, but I don't want to admit it. Being on the tracks that divide our two cities brings me closer to her without being close to her.

The loud thumping of my heart bleeds through my ears. If only I could reach into my chest and pull out the stupid, good-for-nothing organ and rip it out. Then all this pain would disappear.

My feet carry me along the train tracks, stepping over every wooden panel and balancing on the crushed rocks, the numbness increasing with each step. Part of me wants her here, to hold her and never let go. *But she killed your mother. She made you an orphan.*

The wanting fades away until it's nothing but a small speck.

My phone vibrates and I pull it out.

Gage: We have matters to discuss about changes in Daringville. Full board meeting tomorrow at Luciano.

Cursing, I shove my phone back into my pocket and kick a rock, watching as it bounces along the track.

A loud whistle cuts through the air, and I look over to the Daringhood side of the tracks. Kai and his two henchmen are walking straight toward me from the edge of their slummy town. Fuck. The only weapon I have is the knife strapped to my thigh. Thankfully, that will be enough to protect myself if need be. I stop and wait for them to come over.

"Well, well, well, what do we have here? Lucas Fox, all alone, looking like a lost little puppy," Bear says with a sly grin.

"Fuck off," I growl, shoving my hands into my jeans pockets.

Bear reaches into the back pocket of his pants and pulls out a knife. He runs the blade along his finger, drawing a mere droplet of blood. He watches me with his weird-as-fuck bright-green eyes. I could run, but fuck that. I'm now the leader of The Brotherhood; they should be the ones running from me.

"You know, lost little puppies are easy to kidnap. They're vulnerable, and one pat, one tickle behind the ear, and they are mine." Bear grins, and I step forward over the tracks until I'm right in his face.

My chest almost touches his, and his green eyes glare at me with so much hate. His knife stands between us—one wrong move, and it'll be in me. I hope it is. I want to feel the burn of the blade sinking into my flesh. I hope he hits my heart so I can feel relief.

"Do it," I growl, and Bear frowns, twisting the knife between us, bringing it closer to my chest. I plead with my eyes, begging him to make it happen.

"Enough. We never strike first!" Kai booms from somewhere close, and Bear doesn't budge for several heartbeats before he finally steps back.

"Fucking coward." I laugh, and Bear lunges forward as I step away. He pulls back his knife, as if he's about to plunge it toward my chest, but Kai reaches him first, shoving him to the side.

"He's Freya's," Kai says to Bear, who shoves his knife back into his pocket, mumbling words under his breath.

It feels like a sucker punch to the heart—the mention of Freya, and me being hers. I want to scream that I'm not, and I fucking hate her, but the words clog in the back of my throat.

She told him about me? No, I don't want to know. I can't let her in again. If she loved me, she wouldn't have killed my mother. She broke my stupid, gullible fucking heart.

"I hear congratulations are in order, leader," Kai says, folding his arms over his chest.

I nod. "Yep."

"You better do something to create better treatment for us and provide us with more, or there's a war coming your way," Kai says.

"Are you threatening The Brotherhood?" I scoff. "It's one thing to threaten me, but The Brotherhood? That's too far, even for you, Kai. We've killed people for less."

Kai raises his hands, taking a step backward. "No threats—just words between enemies. Don't say I didn't warn you." He turns around and Zion follows him.

Bear doesn't move for several seconds before he waves. "See you around, pup."

If anyone talked to me like that on any other day, I'd kill them. But not today. I just can't be fucked.

Kai's words from earlier play on repeat. *We never strike first.*

Something clicks in my mind. Freya didn't make the first move with my mother. She protected herself.

Chapter 7

Freya

I watch as Lucas's car speeds down the driveway, taking my heart with it. Fuck. His expression when he walked in on us with Gage's cock in my mouth and Hazen pounding into me from behind . . . I've never seen him look at me like that. First it was pain, then it morphed into anger and disgust.

He hates me, and I don't blame him after what I did, but I'll be fucked if I'm going to let him go without a fight.

The door shuts behind me, and I glance over my shoulder. Hazen walks over, carrying my favorite band T-shirt and ripped jeans. I look down at my bare thighs, the suit jacket with the buttons undone, and the corset underneath, sans panties. I didn't exactly have time to change before running after Lucas.

I take them from Hazen and follow him back inside the front door, into the foyer, and quickly get changed, tying my top in a knot so it rests just above my high-waisted jeans.

"Give him some time. He's dealing with this in his own fucked-up way," Hazen says.

Gage comes into the foyer with his phone pressed to his ear. He offers me a smile before retreating up the stairs.

I turn back to Hazen. "I'm trying, but fuck, I just want to hold him, shake him, and make it all go away." A tear falls down my cheek, and I wish my brother was here. He always made everything better.

"What the hell is going on?" Amirah yells, storming down the stairs with her hair between her fingers as she ties it into a bun on the top of her head.

"Lucas," Hazen grumbles.

Amirah presses her lips together. "You've got your hands full with these boys, Freya darling. But if anyone can bring them to their knees, it's you!" she says with a playful smile on her lips. She comes up to me and pulls me in for a quick hug.

"Can we rain check movie night?" I ask, and Amirah steps back, keeping her hand on my shoulder.

"Yes, but don't keep me waiting too long." She releases me and moves toward the kitchen.

I turn back to Hazen. "I need to borrow your bike."

"You know I don't let anyone ride my bike, right?"

I step forward, our chests touching, and wrap my arms around his neck, peering into his sparkling blue eyes. He wraps his arms around me.

"But I'm not just anyone, am I?" I ask, raising an eyebrow.

The corner of his mouth lifts. "No, you most definitely aren't."

I reach into his pants pocket and take out the key before pressing a light kiss to his mouth. When I go to step back, his grip tightens around me.

"I'm going to need more than that," he growls before claiming my lips in a rough, demanding kiss. My fingers grip his shirt, holding on before I pull back and rest my forehead against his.

"I've got to go look for Lucas and see my mom. She's still clean, and I don't want her to relapse while I'm not there."

Hazen nods, tangling his fingers in my hair before pressing one last kiss against my cheek. "Message me later," he says, before stepping back.

I shut the door behind me. Hazen's bike is parked in front of the garage. The sun reflects off the sparkling black paint. Taking the helmet from the seat, I place it on my head and swing my leg over, starting her up. She vibrates between my legs. My pussy throbs from Hazen's cock pounding into me not long ago.

I tear out of the driveway, through the gate, and onto the road. I search the street for Lucas's bubble-gum-colored Lamborghini Countach; it's not easy to miss. I whiz past massive mansions as I drive through the streets.

He wouldn't have gone toward the Hood—I'll bet he's not looking for a reminder of me—so I drive farther away, toward the outskirts of town and the docks, a direction I haven't headed in years.

The traffic light turns red, and I stop—I don't want to look over to my right. My gut churning, I give in, glancing over my shoulder. My old house sits on the corner of the street. The large oak tree out front still has a swing on the branch. The one-story brick house hasn't changed much. My chest burns. The loud hum of the bike disappears, and memories take over.

Five years old

A loud bang startles me awake, the bed dips, and I open my eyes. My brother, Alec, is hovering over me, shaking my shoulders.

"It's your birthday, it's your birthday!" he screams, then wraps his arms around me, crashing his head against my chest. I giggle, cuddling him back.

"Come see what the birthday dragon left you." Alec rolls over me and takes my hand, pulling me off the bed. Excitement builds inside my tummy. I can't believe this day has finally arrived. For as long as I can remember, Alec and Mommy have always read stories about the birthday dragon who comes every year, delivering presents and treats. Every birthday, we spend together as a family. It's my favorite day of the year. Not because of the presents, even though they are amazing, but because we get to do fun stuff—just the three of us.

My fingers wrap around my brother's. He tugs me through my bedroom into the hallway.

"Close your eyes," Alec says, and I do. He doesn't let go of my hand, pulling me through the house. There's the sound of a door opening, then a gust of wind kisses my cheeks. Shivers tickle my bare arms, and I have no idea why he's taking me outside, but I trust him.

We stop, and Alec's hand disappears out of my grip.

"Open your eyes, princess," Mommy says, and I do.

I scream and jump up and down. Mommy and Alec are sitting on a large blanket in the middle of our backyard, with all my favorite foods and treats on it. I run up, crashing into Mom. She falls back, wrapping her arms around me.

"Happy birthday, my little princess," she says, tickling me, and I can't stop laughing.

This is the best birthday yet.

A loud horn pierces through the memories. I flip off the Volvo driver before speeding away, letting the wind take the memories with it. My birthdays used to be the best time of the year—until they weren't. Until we were kicked out, and Mom poured all the love she used to have for us into drugs.

I wonder if this year will be different. Will she be able to last until my birthday in a month? But it won't be the same without Alec here. Everything is different now, and I don't think I'll ever get used to the hole he's left.

Spotting Lucas's car in the parking lot near the crossing, I slow down and come to a stop next to it. I peer inside, hoping that I'll find him, but he's not here. The bike hums beneath me. A couple of guards from Daringville start walking toward me, but I'm off before they get to me, heading straight through the checkpoint and over the tracks. What if he's decided to take things into his own hands with Daringhood? Fuck. I need to find him.

I spend several hours searching Daringhood for Lucas, but it's useless. He's not here or doesn't want to be found. If I did find him, what would I even say? *Sorry that you walked in on us having a three-way, and I'm sorry I fucked up and killed your mother, leaving you without any parents?* Fuck.

After easing Hazen's bike to a stop outside our trailer, I cut the motor and remove my helmet. I slide my leg over and land on two feet. My legs wobble slightly and pain shoots up my thighs.

"'Bout time you showed up here. Heard you've been here all week but didn't bother to come see me?"

I whirl around as Kai struts over, pushing his black hood back slightly, and his short brown hair fans out from underneath it. He pulls me in for a quick hug before stepping back.

"Sorry, been dealing with Mom."

"So I heard. She okay?" he asks and I shrug.

"What's up?" I ask, dropping the helmet onto the table next to our front door.

"Ran into your boy today," he says, and my gaze snaps to his.

"What'd you do?"

He scoffs. "Nothing—just had a nice little chat. Told him I wouldn't touch him cause he's yours, but fuck, Freya, when are you going to come to your senses and drop them? You don't need them anymore. You've got your answers about your brother. It's over. Fuck them."

I run my fingers through my hair, brushing out the knots, mulling over Kai's words. Part of me wants to walk away from them, but I can't. I'm in too deep now. Somewhere along the way, they've taken pieces of my heart, and I don't want them back.

"It's more than that, Kai."

He curses under his breath. "We've been best friends for how long?"

"Too long." I laugh.

"I'm not going to make you choose between me and them, because that's fucked up, but this is a bad idea, Freya." He shakes his head. "You do what you got to, but when we're together, don't talk about them and don't tell them shit about me. There's a war coming, kid, and I don't want you stuck in the middle of it. I'd do anything to protect you, but when it comes to them, all bets are off."

The door to our trailer squeals open and Mom steps outside, wearing an apron. She shields her eyes from the setting sun. "Kai, darling boy. You staying for dinner?"

The corner of his mouth lifts slightly. "Nah, I got shit to do, but enjoy. See you soon, Freya."

When he leaves, my mother frowns. "Weren't you supposed to be gone for the night?"

"Change of plans."

She watches me closely, her eyes narrowing, then she looks back at Kai walking away. "When did he grow up into a man? Damn, he's fine."

I roll my eyes and follow her inside, grabbing Hazen's helmet on the way. I just hope the guys take what I put on the table about compromise seriously. It's what we need, and hopefully, it'll stop this war. The Brotherhood has done nothing but fuck over me, my family, and friends, but now I have an opportunity to make changes. With the guys taking over, it's time to start fresh—to not have so much of a divide between our worlds.

The smell of curry wafts from the kitchen, and my tummy rumbles, but I don't think I can stomach anything. I grab a cup of water and head straight for my bedroom.

"Where are you going?" Mom's voice echoes down the small hallway.

I turn my hand on my door handle. "Around," I say, and she shakes her head.

"You can't just come and go whenever you want."

"Okay," I say, trying to keep the peace. I go to push my door open but stop when she continues.

"I need to know where you are at all times if you want to stay under my roof." Her words feel like nails against a chalkboard. She's threatening me now? She's made so much progress this past week, and I love her, but I need a break. Why is she on me when just I need some time alone?

"Since when do you care?" I snap, and her face falls. Maybe I should feel guilty for snapping at her. She's trying, I know, but it doesn't make up for the past fifteen years.

"I'm trying to be better, Freya. But I need to be around people. It helps distract me. I'm glad you came back early."

My chest tightens until I'm sure it's going to explode. "I know you're trying, Mom, and it's really good. Just give me some time to myself, please. A lot's going on with me right now, and I don't want to talk about it."

Her face falls.

"Maybe I will soon," I offer, and that's the best I can do.

She nods, taking the crumbs I'm leaving with grace. "I'll bring you a plate." She disappears back into the kitchen, and I shut my bedroom door behind me before falling backward onto my bed.

When my phone vibrates against my leg, I pull it out, finding a text from Hazen, and I sit up, leaning back on my elbows.

Hazen: Meeting tomorrow with The Brotherhood. Be here at 7:30pm to discuss next steps for your proposal.

He pin drops a restaurant in Daringville called Luciano, and hope blossoms. Are they actually open to discussing my offer for the Hood? Holy shit—this is huge.

The next day passes in a blur as I take another shift at the diner. By the time it finishes, my legs are on fire, and I crash for a few hours, eager for rest before my meeting with The Brotherhood.

My head has barely touched the pillow when my bedroom door flies open, and I jump up off my bed. Amirah stands in my doorway, carrying a large bag over her shoulder.

"What the hell? Warn a girl before you storm in without notice. I could have been busy," I grumble, and she rolls her eyes.

"Oh, please. The only thing you would have been busy with is your own fingers strumming yourself like a bass guitar."

I laugh. "Seriously, what are you doing here?"

"Rescuing you, of course." She drops her bag to the ground and unzips it. "I hear there's a board meeting with The Brotherhood and you're invited. I can't leave my best friend looking unprofessional in her ripped jeans and old tees, now, can I?" She raises her eyebrows and I smile. She's always got my back—and I am so lucky to have her.

"Show me what you've got."

"Heads up—your mom's cooking up a storm out there and insisted that I stay for dinner. She's really trying, isn't she?" She pulls out a gray blazer, a black leather skirt, and a white turtleneck.

"Yeah, she is. I hope it lasts."

"Try these on." She throws them onto my bed, and I change out of my work clothes and into Amirah's.

The skirt sits mid-thigh, and the blazer fits snugly. Amirah pulls out some tights and six-inch black pumps.

I purse my lips at the heels. "Oh, come on, seriously?"

She chuckles. "You want to make a statement?"

I nod reluctantly, biting back any further argument.

"Then you're wearing these."

I roll my eyes but take them from her, along with the tights. "Remember when we'd dress each other up as kids?" I ask, laughing. "We were so innocent back then."

"Those were the best days. No responsibility, no men breaking our hearts—"

"Like anyone's ever broken your heart," I tease Amirah, who's eternally single.

"Still . . . things were simpler then. Just you, me, and Jewel," she says, mentioning the daughter of her nanny we used to hang out with.

"Whatever happened to her?" I frown as I hunt for a clutch in my closet. "She wasn't around when I started sneaking to your parties."

"I grew up." Amirah takes the black clutch I've selected and swaps it for a white one. "You don't need a nanny when you're eighteen, and when her mom left, Jewel disappeared out of my life too. She was probably using me for the closet benefits."

"No one could ever use you." I wrap her in an impulsive hug.

After some trouble getting the tights on, I slide into the heels and stand. Amirah wolf whistles before brushing my hair and letting it fall down my back.

My phone lights up on my bed, and Amirah snatches it before I get a chance.

"Hey, give it back."

"Worried I'll find some sexy messages between you and the guys?" she teases before her mouth opens. "You didn't tell me that mystery stalker person was still messaging you!"

"They haven't been." I frown, grabbing the phone out of her hand.

Unknown: Guess who's back—again. See you soon, Freya LeClair. Board meetings are important. P.S. Don't forget your lipstick.

The phone drops from my fingers, landing on the bed. I move to my window, peering outside, but there's no one there. The trees sway with the wind, and Jessie's light flickers from her trailer.

"Well, tonight just got a hell of a lot more interesting. No one outside of The Brotherhood knows about the meeting. It's classified. That means whoever is sending these messages is someone we know," Amirah says.

I frown, hating that she's right. I have no idea who's sending the text messages, but whoever it is, they are messing with the wrong people. One more mystery to solve.

Chapter 8

Hazen

The table's set and all eyes are on us. Our brothers take up each seat. We only invited the councilors to this meeting. Although major changes have to be run past the board for approval, we have the authority to overrule them. But it'll be easier to rule with their support, especially when our first act of business is to push such a massive change.

Gage pulls out the chair next to me and sits down. One of the waiters comes over and pours him a glass of bourbon. We've booked out one of my favorite Italian restaurants to avoid anything getting outside of these walls.

"Have you heard from Lucas?" Gage asks, checking his phone, and I shake my head. "If he doesn't pull his shit together soon, we're going to come to blows."

"He'll be here," I say, bringing the crystal glass to my lips. He knows how important this is for us. Even though he's been a complete train wreck, he won't fuck this up. We're all he's got.

Chatter fills the room, and I check my watch—ten past seven. Better get this show on the road, with or without Lucas.

"Can you call him?" I ask Gage, just as the door to the restaurant opens and Lucas stumbles in with a lopsided grin. The top three buttons of his white collared shirt are undone, and his hair looks like he's run his fingers through it one—or ten—too many times.

"Sorry I'm late," he says, before dropping into the seat on the other side of me. He clicks his fingers to the waitress and orders a drink.

"Where the fuck have you been, and why do you look and smell like a garbage truck?" I say, gripping my glass tightly.

Lucas huffs. "I'm here, aren't I? Isn't that enough?"

I don't bother replying, because he's right, at least he's here. That's all that matters right now. Freya isn't here yet, but I gave her a later starting time, so we could get settled in first. I gaze at the door, waiting for her to come in. Rules state that no one outside of The Brotherhood is allowed to attend our meetings, especially women, but Freya is more than that to me and my brothers. She's one of us, whether she believes it or not, and family sticks together. This is her idea, and I want her to see it through.

We have to start, or we'll be here all night. Eight of The Brotherhood's most trusted men, our councilmen, fill the seats. As Zeke, Callan, and Brax talk among themselves, Brax catches my gaze. I nod, and he raises his glass my way.

"Have you heard from Dominic?" Brax asks, from a couple of seats down.

"Not yet, but we are keeping tabs on his movements. He's been out for a couple of days."

The charges against him for murdering Alec didn't stick. As soon as the police let him go free, Dominic went underground. No one's heard from him since. I've tried calling, but his phone is switched off—untraceable. There's a rumor he's been seen in town a few times, but nothing concrete. Maybe Dad has finally left us.

That shouldn't make me feel a little funny—abandoned, even—but it does.

Zeke looks around the table before bringing his gaze back to me. "If you want more, I'd ask the dock workers. They always have the intel."

Lucas scoffs but doesn't otherwise comment.

He's always been the one to do the wheeling and dealing down at the docks. Still, it's not for him to question our councilmen when they're trying to help, so I kick his ankle under the table. He shoots me a filthy look but doesn't respond.

I grab my glass, turning back to the table. The deep honey and oak of the bourbon runs smoothly down my throat.

Bringing my fingers to my lips, I whistle, and all eyes cut to us three sitting at the head of the long table.

"You were called here to discuss some changes for Daringhood," I say, and Ronald, one of my father's closest friends, sneers.

"This'll be good. 'Bout time we did another rate rise."

A few yeses fill the room, but I ignore them as the door to the restaurant opens and Freya walks in. My gaze moves up her shapely legs to her skintight leather skirt, up her turtleneck that fails to hide her curves, and then comes to rest on her bright-blue eyes. Fucking hell. All eyes are on her, but she doesn't miss a step. No, she walks with confidence, heads straight to us, and sits down in a chair next to Lucas. He doesn't even acknowledge her, tightening his grip on his glass and staring ahead.

"What the fuck is she doing here?" Ronald pipes up again, staring daggers at her.

"She's one of us," Gage says, and an uproar fills the table.

"No one outside of The Brotherhood is allowed in our meetings. That rule's been around for centuries," Samson says, pushing back a lock of black hair that's fallen over his face, while watching Freya with interest and curiosity.

"This is her idea, and she's here to see it through," I say.

Ronald huffs and rolls up his shirtsleeves, exposing skin pocked with age but still toned with muscle. He mutters, loud enough for her to hear, "Gutter whore."

Freya ignores him, twisting her fingers together on the table.

Lucas pushes his chair back with force, and it falls to the ground with a bang. He grabs a glass and throws it across the table, aiming straight for Ronald. Ronald ducks, and it hits the wall, shattering into many pieces. All eyes are on Lucas, and I don't move.

"What the fuck?" Ronald roars, standing, and Lucas laughs.

"Learn your place, Ronald, or next time, it'll be a bullet into your black heart." Lucas stares down at Freya for a moment before storming off toward the bar. Fucking hell, he's getting out of control. This needs to stop before he fucks everything up.

Ronald shakes his head. "You little—"

"Enough!" I yell, and Ronald falls back into his seat without another word. I've always hated him, especially the way he used to follow my father around, clinging to his every word. I wouldn't be surprised if he'd been sucking his cock behind closed doors.

"As I was saying, we are going to propose some changes in Daringhood and invest in them from a housing and education perspective, so they realize we're ready to form an alliance." I lean forward, resting my elbows on the table.

"Why the fuck would we do that?" Ronald snaps.

I open my mouth, but Freya beats me to it. "To avoid the war that's brewing."

"Pfft. Only way to resolve that is to enforce more power and remind them who's in charge and has been for centuries," Samson says, pushing his glasses up his nose.

"We could, but that's only going to create more divide and bloodshed that we simply don't have enough manpower for right now," Gage says, taking a sip from his glass. "It's a distraction from our business transactions with other towns. If we put all our efforts into a war, then we reduce our own supply chain and money. We'll end up running ourselves dry."

"A few quick beatdowns and some rate rises. That'll shut 'em up," Brax says, running his hand with the lion tattoo over his jawline.

"What are you suggesting, then?" Samson asks, ignoring Brax. Samson's always been about logistics and rules.

"We cut down the tax payments they make to us, reduce their costs, and put some money back into the community. Clean up their side of town, provide them with more opportunities. That should be enough to discourage their violence," Gage says.

"And what about the money we're losing from this little exercise? Where will that be made up?" Zeke asks.

Gage rests his elbows on the table. "We'll tighten up costs with our shipping and supply team."

"So, you're saying we should treat the people who help us live like this like shit, reducing what we pay, and we should give money to the scum across the tracks?" Zeke slams his hand on the table. "I'll tell you who's spending money in my strip clubs. It's the dock workers, not the fucking hood rats."

Ronald is out of his chair in seconds, his hands flying around. "This is an outrage! When's Dominic back? He wouldn't stand for this!"

"Watch your mouth, Ronald. We are in charge now, and it's time for a change," I growl.

Ronald stares us down. "You are weak, the lot of ya, and just children yourselves."

Lucas moves, finishing his drink before dropping it to the ground. Another glass smashes to pieces. Retrieving his knife, he twists it against his index finger as he heads for Ronald, pulling him into a choke hold. As Lucas presses the knife against Ronald's throat, Freya gasps and Gage shakes his head.

"Tell me I'm weak one more time, and you are done," Lucas hisses into Ronald's ear. Sweat runs down the man's forehead, and his throat bobs against the metal. I should tell Lucas to sit the fuck down, but I'm enjoying the show far too much. Ronald needs to learn his place, and calling us weak isn't going to do him any favors.

"You're crazy," Ronald grumbles.

Lucas laughs. "You haven't seen anything yet. Now, apologize."

The room is deadly silent, everyone watching the interaction. Brax covers his smirk with his glass.

"Sorry," Ronald huffs, and Lucas grins before letting him go.

He presses a kiss against his cheek. "See? Wasn't that hard, sweetie."

Ronald swats him away with an angry scowl, and Lucas doesn't wipe the smile off his face. He skips around the table, grabbing a bottle of red wine from a passing waiter and bringing it to his lips.

"The rate reduction will take place next week. After that, I expect they'll drop all talk of war, and we can get back to business." I look around the table. Some men have scowls twisting their lips, while others appear mildly bored. "Any objections?"

Ronald stares at his cutlery. Samson opens his mouth, as if he's about to speak, but a sharp look from Lucas seems to have him thinking better of it.

"Now that's settled, let's enjoy the night with a little more peace. Shall we?" I raise my glass, and everyone around the table, even Ronald, follows suit. "To new beginnings."

As the food is served, Lucas finds his seat again but ignores Freya, who tries to talk to him. I don't know what's going to happen between them, but I hope to fuck that they sort it out—and soon. It doesn't feel right, this tension between them. We aren't whole without Lucas. What happened is ten ways of fucked up, and he needs time to come to terms with both his parents dying. I just hope he doesn't kill himself in the process.

The rest of the night, we drink and eat before everyone leaves. Gage takes care of the bill while Lucas flirts with one of the waitresses. She grabs his arm, leaning in closely and laughing at something he says. Freya is glaring at them with her arms crossed over her chest.

"Jealous?" I ask with a grin

She grunts. "I'm about a second from walking over there and punching Lucas in the face. You gonna stop me?"

I laugh. "That's something I'd love to see."

Freya goes to move, but the door to the restaurant opens, and she freezes, her irritation turning to rage. I follow her gaze, my heart pounding heavily against my chest. What the fuck?

My jaw drops. "Dad?"

Chapter 9

Freya

Dominic Hendrix fills the doorway to the restaurant in a three-piece black suit. His gaze is heavy with hatred as it finds mine, and my mouth becomes dry.

"Jesus, son, I'm gone a few days, and you've caused chaos." He chuckles, moving farther into the restaurant. He grabs a drink from the bar before leaning against it. "Luckily, I'm back now to clean up your mess. Spoke to a few of the men outside as they were leaving. Reducing taxes? Helping with housing? Have you lost your mind?"

Lucas scoffs, bringing a glass to his lips. The waitress he was flirting with disappears around the bar, and I glare daggers into her back. Lucas pushes off the counter, his legs wobbling before he rights himself. Gage, Hazen, and Lucas close in around Dominic, and the air around us gets stuffier. I shuffle closer to the door, ready for a speedy exit if I need it. My chest rises and falls at a rapid rate, like it does every time Dominic is near. Fuck, I hate him and the effect he has on me.

My phone vibrates against my hand, and I open it, finding a text from the unknown number.

Unknown: Don't say I didn't warn you. Let the games begin.

I fight off the urge to roll my eyes. Whoever's sending these messages needs to get a life, instead of stalking mine. My gaze moves around the room, but all the waitresses have gone, except the girl who was flirting with Lucas. I want to approach her at the bar, to say something to her, but I can't move. My feet are cemented to the ground.

"We did what was needed to prevent a war," Gage says, folding his arms over his chest.

I slide my phone back into my pocket, then rub my sweaty palms over my skirt.

Dominic rolls his eyes. "You know the last thing those rats did before your great-great-great-grandfather formed The Brotherhood?"

Gage shakes his head.

"Those bastards raped your great-great-great-grandmother. They chained our women up like dogs and fucked them till they bled, and now you want to give them something?" Dominic laughs. "They would sooner stab you in the back than have peace. Don't trust this slut," he adds, pointing at me.

My fists clench at my sides, and I take a step forward, ready to defend myself.

"Leave her out of this," Hazen growls.

Dominic looks between us with a smirk. "Look, I get it. Her pussy probably tastes like candy, and her tight cunt wraps around your cock like—"

Lucas shoves him, and he stumbles backward into the bar top. My eyes widen. Maybe he does still care about me.

"Enough!" Gage yells, and Dominic chuckles.

"Only one way to fix this mess, kids, and now I'm back, so you can return to being my henchmen. I'll clean it up." Dominic straightens his tie and rolls his shoulders back.

"Sorry to inform you, Dad, but we're the new leaders of The Brotherhood, so you don't have any say in what goes on around here." The words fall from Hazen's lips with a satisfied smile, and Dominic's lip curls back, his face turning an angry shade of red.

"That's an outrage!" Dominic roars. "I've heard rumors that you took the throne, but I refuse to believe it. You need my approval before such a thing happens."

Dominic steps forward, coming face to face with Hazen. My heartbeat skyrockets, and I take a step toward them, but Hazen doesn't back down. He stares at his father with a mixture of anger and uncertainty.

"Actually, my father approved it and held the ceremony, since you were contained." Lucas smirks, and Dominic's mouth opens, then closes.

"Wait until I see your father. He'll pay for this," Dominic snaps.

Lucas laughs. "Good luck with that. He's six feet under."

Lucas grabs a bottle of wine from the bar before storming for the door. I step in front of him, blocking his exit. He doesn't even look at me as he brings the bottle to his lips and finishes half of it.

"Don't go. Please, we need to talk," I say, reaching for him, but he steps back, staring at my hand as though it's a weapon about to stab him. I suppose I did when I killed his mother. I stabbed him right in the heart.

"Move. Now," he growls, and I do. He walks straight out the door and takes my broken heart with him.

Chapter 10

Freya

I roll over, my arms wrapping around a strong chest. My fingers run down the muscles and stop at Hazen's briefs. His hand grabs mine before forcefully shoving my fingers underneath his underwear and against his hard cock.

"Someone's happy to see me." I hum around a yawn.

Hazen chuckles. "Who wouldn't be?"

I wrap my fingers around his length and tug up and down. He groans, covering my hand in his and picking up the pace.

"Fuck, I need you," he moans, releasing my fingers.

He rolls over, and I fall onto my back, my lace pajama top riding up my stomach. Leaning on his elbow, he slowly slides his gaze over my body. Heat pools between my legs, and I want him to fill every inch of me. He stands on the mattress, dropping his briefs. His hard dick stares right at me, and I lick my lips.

"Fucking hell, Freya. Keep looking at me like that, and I won't be able to last."

He kneels over me, his knees beside my shoulders, pinning my hands over my head, and I grip on to the bedrail. He shoves his cock between my lips, and I take every inch of him. As he hits the back of my throat again and again, my hands itch to move, but I keep them in place.

My tongue runs along his shaft and my teeth graze the tip. Hazen's eyes roll into the back of his head.

The bathroom door opens, then slams shut, and my gaze clashes with Gage's, the corner of his mouth lifting into a smirk. "Fucking hell. What a sight to walk in on."

"Join us or shut the fuck up," Hazen growls.

Gage's towel drops to the floor, and my heart thumps louder and louder the closer he gets to the end of the bed. The mattress dips, then his hands are on my knees, forcefully pushing them apart. His fingers curl around my shorts, and he pulls them down my legs, along with my underwear, leaving me bare. I can't see what he's doing, as Hazen's in the way, and that only makes it better. The anticipation of what he's going to do to me . . . I hope he eats me.

Hazen grabs my jaw roughly. "Eyes on me."

My throat bobs, and I take his cock deep, his eyes turning darker as a groan falls from his lips.

Gage's tongue licks a line up my thigh, getting higher and higher. My pussy clenches in anticipation, waiting to be touched, begging to have his lips on her. When he stops just before my cunt, I kick my leg out, and Gage chuckles, his breath tickling the space between my legs. I'd tell him to stop fucking around and tongue fuck my cunt, but my mouth is full. My teeth glide up Hazen's shaft, his cock getting firmer, and a loud pop breaks from my lips as I release his head, then swallow him deeply again.

My legs close in around Gage's head, holding him in place, but he's stronger and pushes them back apart. There's nothing but air until his mouth finally hits its mark, his tongue sliding inside my folds. *Oh my God*. I never want him to leave. His nose rubs against my clit, over and over. As a moan escapes my mouth, Hazen's grip on my jaw tightens. I glare at him, and his eyes turn a shade darker.

"You like being with two guys, don't you, you naughty girl?" Hazen asks, pumping his cock in and out of my mouth faster. He hits the back of my throat with force, and I almost gag. It's too much, but not enough at the same time.

"Answer me, you little whore," he growls, and fucking hell, my pussy drips straight into Gage's waiting mouth. I want to reply, to yell at him, but I can't, and he knows it. "That's right. Take my cock like the little slut you are."

Gage shoves one finger inside, then two. My back arches. He hits my G-spot again and again, and just as I'm about to release, he pulls his fingers out. I growl in frustration, and Gage chuckles, his breath warm against my clit.

Hazen's fingers move from my jaw to my throat. He squeezes a little and moves his cock in and out faster, closing his eyes. A deep growl rumbles from his chest before his cum hits the back of my throat. I swallow every drop, then he pulls out and claims my mouth in a sweet, tender kiss. He shifts back, resting his head against mine, his fingers gone from my throat.

"Now it's your turn," he says, before leaning back on his knees, taking his warmth with him. I need this release so bad.

Gage grabs my ankles. "Roll over."

For once, I actually do as he commands because my pussy is dripping and needs tending to. He's left me hanging, and I'm not leaving Hazen's bedroom until my pussy and I are both satisfied. I roll onto my front, resting on my elbows and lifting my ass into the air. I look back over my shoulder at both of them. Gage smirks and Hazen winks.

A loud slap fills the bedroom. Pain kisses my ass cheek before Gage rubs his hand over it and dips his fingers between my wet folds. Hazen shifts beside me. I lean back slightly, and Gage's finger slips inside my pussy. A loud exhale leaves my lips, and Hazen grabs my hips, lifting and repositioning me to straddle his stomach.

Bracing my hands against his chest, I raise my ass back up to Gage. He pushes his finger in and out, but I want more. I want his cock inside me—or Hazen's. Fuck, how's this going to work?

Gage pulls out, running his finger between my folds. "So wet for us."

"Someone better get inside me now," I growl, and the corner of Hazen's mouth turns up.

"Pass me some lube, Hazen, and a condom," Gage says from behind me, and Hazen reaches over to the bedside table. From the top drawer, he pulls out a bottle and foil packets and throws them over my head to Gage. He takes one himself, opening the wrapper before handing the condom back to me.

"Wrap up my cock, Freya, then spit on it. Make it all wet, and then I want you to sink it into your dirty little cunt," Hazen says, and fuck me, I almost come from his words.

I move backward slightly, leaning down, his head staring back at me, and place the condom over his large shaft. I spit before taking his cock into my mouth once more. My ass remains in the air. Cool liquid is rubbed around my ass crack, and Gage pushes his thumb inside. My pussy clenches, and it takes everything in me not to reach between my legs and take matters into my own hands. I'm so ready.

After sucking Hazen's cock until it's drenched in my saliva, I crawl back up so my hands are on his chest and his cock is at the entrance to my pussy. My gaze catches his, and I don't look away as I sink onto his cock. His chest rises and falls against my palms, his eyes turning a stormy blue.

It takes me a few moments to adjust to his size before I pick up speed, fucking him hard. Gage slaps my ass, jolting me forward.

"Tell me, if Lucas was here with us, where would you want him?" Gage asks me, and my heart burns at the mention. I do want him here with us, but I've fucked that up, and I don't know if we'll ever be the same again.

I slow my pace and Hazen growls. "Answer his question, and don't you dare fucking stop."

"I'd want him on the bed next to us, his cock between my lips," I say, my voice turning husky.

"Such a naughty girl. I'm going to fuck your ass now, and you'll take it, won't you?" Gage asks, like I have a fucking choice. He'll fuck me regardless, and that's why he's got part of my heart.

There's the sound of a wrapper opening, then more cool lube is rubbed around my ass before his head presses against my cheeks. Fucking hell, I don't know if I can take him while Hazen's inside me. I slow my pace while Gage pushes inside my ass and my head falls back. The intensity of two large cocks inside me is too much, and I suck in air through my teeth.

"Eyes on me," Hazen says, and I glance back down, losing myself in his blue eyes as I adjust to them both. My heart races, and it feels like I'm being pulled apart in the best way possible.

I ride Hazen's cock slowly before picking up the pace to match Gage's as he fucks my ass. My head falls backward, and I release a deep moan, my breathing getting heavier and heavier.

"Tell us, how does it feel being fucked by both of us?" Gage asks, his breath warm and teasing against the crook of my neck. A shiver rolls through me, and I stare back down at Hazen, licking my dry lips.

"Like you're breaking me in two," I say, panting.

Gage slams into me, forcing me forward, and I brace my hands on Hazen's chest to keep myself from face-planting. Fuck. Hazen fills me completely, hitting exactly where I want him, and I swear Gage is touching parts of me that have never been touched before.

"Our dirty little slut," Gage praises, and I almost lose it. He pulls out, taking off the condom, then his warm cum is landing on my back. As he presses kisses down my neck, my eyes flutter closed.

Hazen grabs my hips, his fingers digging into my skin. He takes over, fucking me hard and fast. I'm done. My thighs clench around his hips, and I scream out both of their names, creaming all over Hazen's cock.

Hazen finishes seconds later, coming with an animalistic groan. He slows the pace before I collapse onto his chest. He pulls out, and coolness hits between my legs. I roll to the side of Hazen, resting my head over his heart. The loud thump matches my own.

Gage falls next to me, wrapping his arm around my stomach. We stay like this for minutes or an hour—who knows? Time vanishes and I can't move.

"Let's get you cleaned up." Gage takes my hand, lifting me off the bed and grabbing the discarded condom as well. My feet hit the ground and my legs wobble. Gage smirks, pulling me into the bathroom. He throws the used rubber and its wrapper into the trash next to the vanity.

He turns on the shower, testing the temperature before moving inside the door. I follow him in. As the warm water washes over me, my eyes close. Gage wraps his arms around me from behind, pulling me into his body. My head rests back against his chest, the thump of his heart ringing through my ears.

When did the lines become blurred between us? When did the hate turn into lust, then whatever this is I'm feeling for him, Hazen, and Lucas? Everything between us seems so effortless now. I spend every second I can with them, and when I'm not, I'm thinking about them. Since Alec disappeared, they've become my saviors, my protectors.

I would never in a million years have thought I'd fall for the leaders of The Brotherhood. I can't run from them, and I don't want to. They've got my heart locked up in a cage, and I'm still clutching on to the key, afraid of what will happen if I give them everything.

"Penny for your thoughts?" Gage says, untangling his hands and stepping back. I instantly miss the pressure of his body against mine.

"Just thinking about how much we used to loathe each other."

Gage chuckles. "And you think that's changed?"

I whirl around and punch him in the chest. He doesn't budge, a wicked smile filling his face.

"You're right, it hasn't," I say, reaching out to grab the shampoo bottle.

Gage grabs my wrists and takes a step toward me. I falter, retreating the short distance until my back hits the tiled wall. His mossy-green eyes feel like they're staring right into my heart.

Releasing my wrist, Gage closes in. His hands slap against the wet wall, and he leans forward, his lips only inches from mine. I can almost taste him.

His hard cock pressing against my stomach, he says, "I've hated you for as long as I can remember." His eyes stay locked on mine as my heart pounds faster and my stomach twists.

"I hated you too," I growl, and Gage captures my bottom lip between his teeth, biting down. The tangy taste of blood hits my tongue, and Gage licks up every drop before resting his head against mine.

"You know I'll do anything for my brothers, yes?" he asks, and I nod. "You are one of us now, which means I'll protect you against anyone or anything, but I can't protect you against myself. You push every single button. You make me angry, crazy, jealous, possessive, and I can't control myself with you."

"Don't," I whisper, and his eyes turn darker before he claims my lips in a hot, demanding kiss. His tongue swipes against mine. Dropping his hands to my shoulders, he lightly kisses my cheek. "You'll live to regret saying that."

"Probably," I say with a grin.

I've watched Gage with Amirah, how protective he is with her, and how much it confused me over the years. The Gage I knew was an arrogant asshole, and I used to think, how could he be like that with her when he didn't protect me? When he walked away and let us go?

"Why didn't you protect me?" The words fall out of my mouth, and Gage's body tenses against mine.

He pulls back. His fingers rest under my chin, and he lifts my head up until his green eyes clash with mine. "That's the one regret I've lived with my entire life." His throat bobs, his eyes glassing over. "Not protecting you from him."

I nod, licking my wet lips. Nothing he says will make up for the heartbreak I felt back then, and there will always be part of me that can't fully trust he won't do it again. That he won't walk away from me and leave me unprotected—but I don't need any man to protect me anymore. I have myself, and that's enough.

"I'll spend every second of every day protecting you from anyone who dares to fuck with what's mine," he growls, and my stomach twists.

I want to believe him, but I'm afraid to be disappointed when he doesn't keep his promise. Words don't mean shit; actions do.

I duck out from under his arm, and he lets me go.

"I mean it, Freya," he says, and I nod, unable to form the right words. If I open my mouth now, nothing will make sense.

When Gage opens up and brings you into his heart, when he claims you as his, there's nothing he wouldn't do for you, and I know that's how he feels about me.

Still, I haven't given him, Hazen, and Lucas my whole heart, and I don't know if I ever can.

Chapter 11

Freya

My fingers slide around the warm mug of coffee, my eyes heavy from sleep as I sink down into the couch in our small trailer the next day.

A slight frown creases my mother's brow as she moves around our small kitchen. "What time did you get home?"

"Late." I yawn, rubbing the sleep from my eyes.

"I don't understand why you're hanging around The Brotherhood."

I groan. "Mom, we talked about this yesterday."

"And you apparently didn't listen. They aren't good people, Freya. You know what they did to us. I don't want you going over there anymore." My mother squeezes the maple syrup onto my pancakes.

It's too early for this shit. "I'm a grown-ass woman. I'm not getting told what to do with my life," I snap.

"I've already lost one kid to The Brotherhood." Her voice cracks. "I'm not going to lose another."

It feels like she's reaching into my chest and squeezing my heart until it explodes into a million pieces. But even though she's in pain, so am I. I lost a brother, but the number of times I've almost lost her as well is far too high. She's clean now, but how many times have I had to pick up the pieces for her? And who knows how long this new sobriety will last?

"You lost Alec long before that, and you know it," I say, and her face falls.

"Why do you keep punishing me?" she says, defeated. "I'm trying, Freya, I really am." She passes me a plate.

"I know you are, but that doesn't change everything you've put us through. It doesn't take it all away." I pause. I would hate for our fight to be the cause of a relapse. "But I am proud of you, Mom. What you're doing . . . it's really impressive."

"Thank you." Mom brings her mug to her lips and takes a long sip. "I wish I could go back to that day and never touch that shit."

"How did it start?" I ask the one question that's been playing on my mind since that night. I heard Nadine's story, but I want the truth from my mother's mouth.

"Fuck, Freya, do you really want to know?" Her grip around her mug tightens, and maybe I shouldn't have asked her.

I shouldn't push her, but instead of saying no, I nod.

"My memories from back then are a little hazy, but I'll try." She takes her mug and sits down on the couch. I leave my pancakes and join her, my knee brushing against hers.

"Back before all of this started, I'd never touched drugs. Yeah, I knew about them but never had any interest. I had everything I wanted in my life—you and Alec. Even after your father left, I was happy. All

I ever wanted was to be a mother, to raise and protect my babies." She laughs. "And I fucked that up."

Without thinking twice, I drop my hand to her knee and squeeze. Her eyes fill with tears, and I realize going back to that time isn't easy for her, but I need to know. And if she's going to move forward, perhaps talking through her past will be beneficial.

"I remember the night so clearly; it replays in my mind on repeat all the time. We'd just celebrated Alec's ninth birthday, and you were already eight. I'd put you both to bed, and there was a knock on the door. Nadine stood behind the door with a bottle of wine in her hand and asked to come in. I knew something was off, because Nadine never liked me—she always pretended to, but I saw through her bullshit. Even though we never spoke about it, I knew when she looked at Alec she saw her husband, George. She knew but never said anything to me. I wanted to talk about it and what it meant for Alec, but she'd always blow it off. With Fox blood running through his veins, it meant he'd join The Brotherhood and even run it one day, alongside Lucas, Hazen, and Gage."

My poor brother. He'd done nothing wrong, except be fathered by the wrong man. Ultimately, Nadine's concerns about him entering The Brotherhood and taking some of Lucas's power had gotten him killed. Fire blazes through my body, and I force my fists to unclench. That's in the past now.

"Nadine was a good mother—hell, maybe too good. She did anything for her kids. She wanted Lucas to rule more than anything else in this world. He was her trophy, her way to get everything she'd ever wanted."

Mom leans back against the couch, her skin wan against the brown cushions.

"George wasn't a good man. Like all men in The Brotherhood, he put it above all else. He didn't have time for Nadine—but me? Somehow, he always made moments for us, even after you were born. And when I was with him . . ." Mom laughed, a sad little sound that held no real mirth. "It felt like I was the most special woman in the world. They trick you like that, you see. Make you think you're more than you are."

"You're better than them, Mom." I smile in sympathy, and she reaches out, covering my hand with her trembling one.

"Didn't know that then." She blinks away her tears and continues. "He wanted me, and I didn't refuse him. The power they hold, Freya, you have no idea. That's why I don't want you to get caught up with them. You can still walk away, please." She looks at me, her eyes filled with tears, her brows drawn together tightly.

I pull my hand back and shuffle over to the other side of the couch, putting some distance between us. This is all new to me, her being so vulnerable, and I'm not ready to be close to her. Shaking my head, I pull my knees up to my chest.

She wipes away her tears and nods. "Anyway, Alec's birthday. I invited her in, and we sat in our living room for hours drinking and talking about our kids. I needed to go to the bathroom, so I got up and the room started to spin. I held on to the couch for support and Nadine giggled. My head was fuzzy from the alcohol. I couldn't see straight—everything in the room blurred, and I fell back down onto the couch. The room went dark. The next thing I remember is waking up in a strange room I'd never been in before. Nadine was there, lying next to me in the bed. This happened several more times, and each time, I never knew what'd happened the night before. It was fucked up. She used to remind me what I'd do, and I fucking hated it." Mom sighs, running her fingers through her hair, pushing it back behind her ears.

Part of me feels sorry for my mother, but the other part remembers everything she put us through, and at the end of the day, she had a choice. She didn't have to keep seeing Nadine; she could have said no.

"Then, one night, she came over as usual after I put you kids to bed. We were drinking and chatting. I'd come to actually like her company. It was nice having someone to talk to. Sometimes I felt lonely, not having a partner around, and Nadine became a friend. I fucking regret that now, but anyway . . ."

She coughs before crossing her legs, leaning farther into the couch.

"My head was starting to become fuzzy, like it always did, and she pulled out a bag of white powder. She didn't say a word, just emptied it onto the table and created lines with her credit card. She took out a hundred-dollar bill and snorted a line, then passed me the note, and I stared at it for several seconds before I shook my head and told her no way was I touching that. She laughed and told me how much it made your mind clear, how fucking good it felt. So, I gave in and took it. It made me feel like the happiest woman in the world, like I was invincible. The coke wasn't that bad. I didn't get addicted to it—not like the heroine." She pauses and my heart hammers against my chest. Her eyes shut and she just breathes deeply for a few moments.

I remained seated on the couch, unable to move. "We can stop if you want . . ."

She shakes her head. "I need to do this. I have to tell you how it all started."

She grabs her mug from the table and finishes it.

"This went on for weeks. Same thing every night—she'd be at my door at eight. Until, one night, I refused to touch the cocaine. I just wanted to drink. She wasn't happy but she let it go. After I passed out, I woke up in that strange room again at her place. She was sitting up next to me in bed with a needle in her hand, filling it up. I sat up straight. Everything around me shook. I felt the prick of the needle in my arm, and I tried to push it away, but Nadine told me I'd asked her for this, but I didn't remember. I still remember the feeling of the liquid hitting my veins. The power coursing through me. Everything in the room came back to me. All the colors around me turned vivid, and all my thoughts turned off. I felt so fucking good, and ever since that moment, I've been chasing that high again and again." Her eyes light up, and I can't stand the sight.

I jump up off the couch and head straight for the door.

"Freya, wait, please," she pleads, but I can't stay and hear her talk about this anymore. I thought I wanted to hear the story, but it's all too much. *Fuck that!*

My feet carry me out of the trailer park. Although the sun beats down on my back, I keep walking. I don't need to hear the rest of her story because I know it—I've lived it. Once she was hooked, everything changed. I didn't see her as much, and when I did, she wasn't the same. She had this faraway look in her gaze, and no matter how much I cried and begged her to come back, she didn't. She chose the drugs, and nothing can take away the heartache I felt, and still feel, that she chose them over me. That shit is poison, and once it touched her veins, she transformed into someone I didn't know.

She's trying to stay clean, and that's all I've ever wanted—all *we* ever wanted—but it seems too good to be true. Although I want to believe in her, I can't ignore that we've tried this many times over the years, and it always ends up the same. This is the most open she's been with me, and that's something I'm not used to. I just hope it means she's determined to stay clean this time.

I wish more than anything that Alec was here with me. He'd be by my side, helping me through this. He always knew how to best deal with Mom without letting his emotions get the better of him, unlike me.

Without realizing it, I find myself walking over the tracks and into Daringville. The guards don't stop me, and even if they tried, I'd tell them to fuck off. I'm not in the mood. I need to forget everything for a minute. Maybe I'm just like her, my mom, always chasing a high. Well, damn.

As I get farther past the tracks and into town, cars fly past me and the wind pushes my hair around my face. My phone vibrates against my leg. I pull it out, and Hazen's name flashes over the screen. I don't answer. I need to talk to someone who gets it—someone who knows Nadine and my mom, who can help me make sense of it all. The only person I want to talk to hates me, and I don't blame him. I broke his heart that night, and there's no going back.

I hit ignore and turn my phone to silent, shoving it back into my jeans pocket. The streets become busier with people. More cars drive by, and I make it to the main street. I find myself a seat on the corner of the block and watch. Men walk around in suits or pressed slacks, and women strut by in fancy dresses. It's like walking back in time. Mom used to dress me in beautiful dresses, just to go down the street. I remember feeling like a doll. I hated it and never understood why we had to impress everyone.

A young girl around thirteen watches me from across the street. She waves and I wave back. An older lady comes up beside her, looking me up and down before curling her lip back. I cross one leg over the other, the denim rip on my knee more prominent, and the corner of my mouth lifts.

She grabs her daughter's hand and crosses the road, moving farther away from me. I flip her off, and the daughter catches me and she smiles. Her mother took one look at my ripped jeans and band tee and judged me. She knew I wasn't from here—but how wrong she is. This was once my home, and I've got the leaders of The Brotherhood in my back pocket. I could have her killed for looking at me like that, but I won't. Fuck her.

A familiar mop of blond hair rushes past me. My fingers grip the corner of the bench, and I sit up straighter. Lucas storms through the street, his head down, avoiding all the people watching him with interest. He reaches his car parked in front of a café and slides in. I find my feet, looking around for a car to jack or an abandoned bike so I can follow him.

He pulls back out of the parking lot and our eyes meet. He looks right through me before he slides on his sunglasses and takes off. Fuck.

I frantically look around and spot one of those e-scooters across the street. Running over, I press my phone to the sensor, and it starts up. I throw the helmet off the bars. Pulling the accelerator, I fly down the path, then onto the road, following Lucas's car.

I said I'd give him time and space, but things are changing, and I need him to know I'll fight for this—I want this.

We need to talk, and I won't take no for an answer.

Chapter 12

Lucas

Anger boils down to my very core as I white-knuckle the steering wheel and scream into the empty car. Everywhere I go, she's there—she's fucking everywhere. I can't get her out of my head, and I just want to forget her, forget I ever met her. She's like a poison that's seeped into my veins, and no matter how hard I search for the antidote, I never find it. I'm well and truly fucked for life.

Maybe that's what I need to do—to end it, and then she'll be gone. As the thought hits my mind, I shake my head. Fuck that. That's the easy way out, and I'm not giving everything up just because my heart's broken. No fucking way.

Looking through the rearview mirror, I catch her long dark-brown hair flying behind her as she stands on one of those stupid fucking scooters. The look of determination is clear on her perfect face, her eyebrows drawn and her lips pulled tightly together. The corner of my mouth lifts slightly, just for a second, before I remember that I hate her now. That I can't think she's cute. She fucked everything up, and that's on her. I didn't make her pull that trigger—hell, she didn't mean to either, but she still took them away from me.

The traffic light turns red, and I really want to drive through it, to keep going, but I find myself stopping. Freya pulls up next to me and slams her fist against my window. I ignore her, pretending like she doesn't exist, because I wish she didn't. I pull out a bag from my glove box and empty the white substance onto the back of my hand before bringing it to my nose. Maybe this is insensitive, given what she's gone through with her mom, but fuck that. At least she has a mom.

The banging gets louder and louder, but I block it out. As the powder hits the back of my throat, the pain vanishes and my head becomes clear again. Why the fuck did I avoid coke before? It's like a magic potion, giving me that high feeling, like nothing can touch me because nothing can.

The light turns green, and I hit the gas, leaving Freya choking on my fumes. I keep driving until I find myself outside of the cemetery. After switching off the engine, I get out, bringing a bottle of vodka with me, and I move through the gates. My heart beats so loud, it's all I can hear.

I twist off the lid, and it falls to the ground. When I bring the bottle to my lips, the vodka burns a line down my throat, and I don't stop until half of it is gone. I keep moving until I come to a stop outside the tomb.

Memories from that night bleed through my brain. It was the worst night of my life . . . and the best. I became a leader of The Brotherhood, something I've waited my whole life for. The ceremony was everything I'd imagined it would be and so much more, standing beside my brothers and sacrificing ourselves to each other and to The

Brotherhood. Little did I know that wasn't all I would be sacrificing that night.

Footsteps crunch against the gravel road, and I don't bother looking over my shoulder. Her honey-and-milk body wash pervades the air as she stands next to me, her warmth so close. If I were to reach out, I could pull her into my arms and never let her go.

No, I can't. I won't let her in. *She's toxic, remember?* Fuck.

"Lucas, I—"

"Just fuck off back to where you belong." The words feel like poison between my lips.

As the silence stretches between us, I can hear every breath she takes. Bringing the bottle to my lips, I let it wash everything away.

"Please don't do this," she pleads, and I squeeze my eyes shut.

"You don't get any say in what I do," I snap.

"Doing this won't bring them back. Please, just let me—" She reaches for me, and I stumble back.

"Fuck off!" I roar, but she doesn't move.

I meet her eyes, and it's like looking into the bright-blue water of the ocean. Fuck. No. I can't let her draw me back in.

"You're ruining your life with this shit. I've seen how hard it's been for my mother to quit, and I won't let you end up like her." She steps forward, and anger boils inside me. I turn and storm off, marching through the graveyard.

She follows, her footsteps right behind me. I stop and she bumps into my back. When I whirl around, she doesn't move an inch. Our bodies touch. So close, yet so far away.

"Fuck. Off," I hiss through my teeth, and she rolls her shoulders back. The tension is thick in the air, tightening its grip around me, cutting off my air supply. I can't breathe. I can't think.

"I'm not going anywhere," she says, her face only inches from mine. Fuck.

My hands shake, and without thinking, I bring the bottle down hard against one of the headstones. The shards of glass fly around us, and she still doesn't move. I bring the smashed bottle up to her neck. Her eyes stare into my very soul, challenging me, telling me to push harder, to make her bleed. Begging me to do something.

I obey. My hand wraps around her throat, my thumb pressing against her windpipe. The bottle rests just below her ear.

Her eyes swim with darkness, holding all the power, screaming at me to do it. To slice the glass bottle across her throat. And fuck, I want to. I want to make her bleed, just like she made my mother bleed. A line of deep red blood runs down her neck. My stomach twists. God, no!

As much as I want to do this, I can't. Not to her. I release the bottle, and it falls to the ground, shattering into a million pieces.

My gaze doesn't leave hers as I run my thumb over the blood, collecting every drop. I bring it to my lips and run my tongue over the warm liquid. The metallic taste floods my mouth in a bitter, acrid wave. My hands shake with rage as I smear her blood over her plump lips. Her tongue glides gently against my thumb as she opens her mouth. The pressure of my cock against my slacks is impossible to ignore.

"You taste that?" I ask, and she nods.

"Good. I hope you fucking choke on your own blood for taking everything away from me," I seethe, before stepping away.

Her eyes glaze over, her warmth disappears, and I'm left cold. It feels as though she took that bottle and drove it straight into my heart.

I turn and walk away, leaving my heart with her.

Chapter 13

Gage

After sliding the weight onto the machine, I sit on the bench and check my phone for the millionth time, but there's still no reply from Freya. This is the very reason I never wanted to let anyone into my heart, apart from my brothers. Because I end up becoming an obsessed weasel, waiting for her to reply, wanting to know where she is and what she's doing every second of every day. It's fucked up. She's a grown-ass independent-as-fuck woman who doesn't need me breathing down her neck.

I drop my phone onto the ground next to me and lie back. Gripping the metal bar, I bring it, along with the weights, to my chest and back up. Sweat drips down my head, running over my cheeks the harder I push. My muscles shake before I place it on the rack and sit back up.

The door to our gym opens, and Lucas struts in, his eyes bloodshot and his white T-shirt covered in blood.

"What the fuck happened to you?" I ask as Lucas grips the bottom of his T-shirt and lifts it over his head before tossing it to the ground.

"Nothing you need to worry about," he snaps, moving toward the weight stand.

"When one of my brothers needs me, I'm there. But you need to let me in," I say as he stares into the mirror as though he's looking right through the reflection.

That faraway look in his eye is one I haven't seen before. I'm worried about him, but there's nothing I can say that will change his attitude. He's a stubborn fucker like me. He won't snap out of this until he chooses to. I just hope to fuck that's soon.

"You're balls deep in the problem I have. Are you going to get rid of her for me?" He looks at me through the mirror, raising both eyebrows.

"Freya's not going anywhere, and you may hate her now, but she's not the enemy. You either fix it with her or not—it doesn't change anything with us."

Lucas's eyes turn to slits before he picks up some heavy weights and starts lifting them over his head. "Fuck off," he grumbles under his breath, and I ignore him, falling back onto the seat and wrapping my fingers around the metal bar.

He doesn't mean half the shit he's saying. His heart's been torn in half, and I get it, I really do, but he needs to stop using substances to block everything out. The sooner he deals with the pain or shoves it into the depths of his soul, the sooner he can move on and step into his role within The Brotherhood.

The heavy-metal guitars from Bring Me the Horizon start blasting from the speakers in the gym, and I finish my workout without another word to Lucas. I grab a cold towel from the fridge and a bottle of water.

I turn around, and Lucas is running on one of the treadmills against the back wall.

"Meeting in twenty in my office. Be there, or don't. I really don't give a fuck," I say, before walking through the door and into the hallway. Samson and Zeke have requested an audience—and with Dominic lurking around, I'm inclined to give it to them.

Lucas needs to be there, and in the past I'd have said he will, but the way he's been acting this last week, who knows? Over the years, we've learned to not feel anything, been molded into soldiers and to live and breathe The Brotherhood. That comes before all else; we signed away our hearts to it the moment we were born.

I've never been in love or ever felt love before her. My mother never even recognized we were there. She fled the moment our father died, and I haven't seen her since. When my father was alive, he didn't show any affection toward me or Amirah, just treated us like everyone else in The Brotherhood. He respected us when we earned it and punished us when we were weak.

I remember when Amirah fell off her bike as a kid and asked for a hug from our father. He laughed, his hand hitting her face. I gave her a popsicle after he left and hugged her. He saw and punished me, leaving me in a dark room for a week.

That day was a cruel reminder to never open your heart to anyone, even your little sister, but Freya has broken down every wall and reached in, grabbed my heart, and taken it. I fought so hard against the restraints, but in the end, she won.

I get now why my father taught us the way he did, because Freya is a distraction. She's all I can think about, and I want to protect her at all costs. My brothers will always come first, but she's next. She won't ever have my whole heart, but fuck, she's got half of it—and that's all I have to offer her.

Shutting my bedroom door behind me, I head toward the bathroom, where I drop my clothes on the tiled floor. I shower quickly before dressing in black cargo pants and a plain maroon T-shirt. I hope to fuck that Lucas shows up because I'm done with his shit. I don't have time to drag his ass there.

We need to work out how to deal with Dominic, and also how we can tell the people in Daringhood that we're going to change the way things are done. We should also probably put it to an official vote—but how can we do that with some of the councilmen still clearly siding with Dominic?

My mind spins. Fucking hell. Leading is difficult.

There's a knock on my door, and I open it. Amirah stands there in a miniskirt that is way too fucking short and a tight tank top.

"You need to change," I snap, before brushing past her into the hallway.

"Piss off," she huffs, walking in step with me.

"What do you want, Amirah?"

"Can you just stop for a second, please?" She grabs my hand, and I slow my steps before stopping. Pulling free of my grasp, she crosses her arms over her chest. "Now that you've taken over, I want something to do within The Brotherhood. Like a job."

"No," I reply. I shouldn't need to remind her that women aren't allowed any role within The Brotherhood. It's just how it is, and I don't want Amirah getting too close to the action. She's better off hidden away in her room; at least she's safe there.

"Gage, hear me out. I'm good at managing people. I can help if you just give me something to do," Amirah protests.

I roll my eyes. "Go paint your nails." She's being a little brat. She has everything she could ever want.

"I'm capable of this—I've got something going on," she says, and I shake my head.

What could she possibly have going on? A plan for a pyramid scheme with one of those makeup companies? "Yeah, whatever little fashion show you've planned, just do it away from me."

She scoffs. "It's more than that. I—"

I raise my hand to stop her. "Look, Amirah, can we discuss this later? There's a heap of shit I've gotta deal with first. Okay?"

Her eyes fall to the ground before she lifts them again and nods. She stalks back toward her room and slams her door. The rattle echoes through me. I hope to fuck she drops this, because I can't deal with her being bratty. Between loose-cannon Lucas, Dominic, and the changes to Daringhood, I've got too much shit to deal with.

Heading downstairs, I'm met with voices carrying through the hallway just outside my office. I open the door and Lucas is standing by my desk with a glass between his fingers, still in his gym shorts, sweat dripping down his bare chest. Fucking hell. Hazen is resting back in one of the chairs, staring daggers at Lucas. Samson and Zeke are sitting next to Hazen, Samson watching Hazen and Lucas closely.

"Clean yourself up," Hazen snaps, and Lucas flips him off.

I shut the door behind me and Hazen looks over.

"Some hood rats broke into one of my car dealerships last night," Samson says.

"What'd they take?" I grit my teeth. Fuckers.

"Nothing. My security chased them off, but it's the principle of the matter. They're getting more brazen every day." Samson shakes his head. "And you want to give them a tax reduction?"

"Not just him. *We*." Hazen emphasizes the word, gesturing to myself and Lucas. "We're a team."

"And though it's frustrating as shit"—I fucking hate people trying to take what's ours—"they didn't know we were planning this reduction. Maybe this will result in less break-ins."

It better.

"What's the plan?" Samson asks, getting straight to it.

I move behind my desk and fall into the chair, and Zeke sits up straighter.

"We need to have a town meeting to announce the money we are going to put into Daringhood and what we expect from them moving forward," I say, and Samson grunts.

"If you're really going ahead with this, then just send out a mass message to everyone in the Hood. We don't need a fucking meeting with the filth," Samson says, and I shake my head.

"No. If we're doing this, we want to make sure they see it's a genuine offer coming from us. We want to open communication between us and the Hood—treat them with a bit of respect. Bring them together and give them a little rope," Hazen says, before I even have the chance to open my mouth.

"He's right. If we're going to grant them this honor, it's better to get the credit in person. Maybe some of their women will be feeling especially grateful," Zeke agrees, running his fingers through his dirty-blond hair.

Samson pushes to his feet. "This is a bad idea. You give them a little, they will push for more. If Dominic was still in charge—"

I slam my fists on the desk, interrupting him. "Enough. It's done. Remember your place, Samson," I growl, and he pinches his lips together.

Lucas laughs, bringing the glass to his lips, and I look away, not having the patience to deal with him.

"What did Dominic say to you last night?" Zeke asks.

"Don't worry about Dominic. You pledged your allegiance to the new leaders, *us*, not Dominic," I say, and Hazen stiffens.

Zeke nods. "What do you need?"

"Get the town hall ready. Send out a text message to all residents about the mandatory meeting tomorrow at seven."

Samson and Zeke nod before leaving and shutting the door. I fall back into my chair, squeezing my eyes shut.

"Well, that's settled, then," Hazen says.

"This is either the stupidest fucking plan we've had or the best." Lucas chuckles, and he's right.

I hope to fuck this goes to plan and those in Daringhood show up and are fucking grateful for this. If not, then I'm done playing nice.

Chapter 14

Freya

My feet dangle over the edge of the building, and the sun kisses my skin. Rows of trailers line the horizon and the peaks of the roller coaster from the old, abandoned amusement park create shadows in the distance. I close my eyes and breathe in and out. Pictures of Lucas fill my mind. The way he wrapped his fingers around my neck yesterday, cutting off my air supply. The way he held that bottle to my neck. The disgust in his gaze. The cut that will probably scar and leave me with the reminder of his hatred toward me.

Space isn't the answer. He may hate me now, but he won't forever. He can't. There's this magnetic pull between us that will never fade. The more he withdraws, the closer I'll move toward him. I won't let go. There's enough room, and once he lets me back in, we'll deal with our heartache together.

"You going to sit up there and sulk all day or kick my ass in basketball?" Kai's voice bellows from below the building.

I open my eyes, peering down. Kai's in a basketball jersey and shorts, bouncing a ball on the old basketball court. His mousy-brown hair fans out from his black cap as he waves me down.

"You know I'll kick your ass," I yell, and he grins.

I pick up my phone from the ledge and shove it into the back pocket of my denim shorts, then move toward the fire escape. The wind picks up, and the whole structure sways slightly. My grip on the rail tightens and my heart races.

I'm tempted to stay here, to be stuck in this feeling forever, the way my heart races and my mind screams at me to move. Everything is heightened, and I fucking love it. It takes away the pain, the heartache, and replaces it with adrenaline.

"Hurry the fuck up," Kai yells, and I laugh.

With a heavy exhale, I climb down, and my feet hit the gravel. Kai wraps an arm around my shoulder and pulls me in before shoving me away playfully. I grab his arm. A new tattoo snakes along it—a moth with a skull as its head.

"Nice," I say.

His arms are covered in gray-scale tattoos of random things, like guns, knives, and reapers. Almost every time I see him, he's got another one. Soon, he'll be covered from head to toe.

"You itching for more ink?" he asks, moving toward the basketball court.

"Yeah, I want something for Alec," I say, and Kai's shoulders tense.

He tosses the ball back and forth between his hands. "I fucking love you, Freya. We're family, but I just don't understand why you're with them. They killed your brother."

"How many times do I have to tell you? They didn't kill him; it was Nadine, Lucas's mother." I sigh, grabbing the ball from his hand, bouncing it, and taking a shot from the three-point line. It goes in and I grin.

"Do you blame the soldier who pulled the trigger, or do you blame Hitler in World War II? They're the leaders. They're responsible," he says. "It's still them, and there will come a time when you have to choose what side you are on."

"Don't be a dick."

We shoot hoops in silence for a while longer. It's nice to spend time with one of my closest friends again. I wish life was easier, that we could all get along . . . Although, that reminds me. A message went out on social media last night about a meeting today for residents of Daringville and Daringhood—together. The boys are going to share the news of my plan!

"Are you coming to the meeting today?" I ask, and Kai scoffs, bouncing the ball and switching it between his hands.

"Fuck no."

"Come on, please. This was my idea to help us," I say, standing in front of Kai and blocking him from the basket.

He dribbles around me, and I swipe out, trying to grab the ball, but he's too quick. He barges past me, knocking my shoulder before launching into the air and dunking the ball.

"Money isn't going to change much, and you know it," he snaps, retrieving the ball and passing it to me. "You can't trust them. They all need to be killed."

I swallow hard. He's wrong.

"But it's a start. Please come?" I push out my bottom lip, and the corner of Kai's mouth lifts before the smile disappears again.

"Over my dead body will you see me at one of their events. Now, drop it and shoot."

I release a heavy breath but decide not to push it. Kai is my best friend, my chosen family, and if I push too hard, I might lose him too. He's right about one thing, even though I wish he wasn't—there may come a time when I have to choose between my best friend and the guys I love, and I won't be able to.

I shoot the ball, and there's the satisfying swish of nothing but net. We keep playing until sweat drips down my back and my legs start to wobble.

"I've gotta get home and get ready. Last chance to come with me?" I ask, and Kai rolls his eyes, snatching the ball from my grip.

"See you soon, Freya."

I flip him off over my shoulder and his laugh follows me.

Trash litters the sidewalks, along with several tents, and homeless sleeping on the streets—this is exactly why I want to help. Everyone deserves a second chance at life. Yeah, some might fuck it up, but if they aren't given an opportunity for a better life, then they'll continue as they are now.

There's a girl around my age bent over her knees, her eyes closed, her legs tucked under her, and I want to help her. To make sure she's okay. I kneel in front of her and push her arm, but she doesn't move. Her body slumps over, and I shove her more forcefully. I check her pulse and there's a light thud.

"Leave her alone," a deep male voice snaps from behind me, and I jump up. An older guy wearing a black beanie and pushing a trolley stands in front of me, half of his arm wrapped up in a garbage bag, and a shiver runs down my spine. He glares at me, wrinkles creasing his forehead.

I raise my hands up and take a couple of steps back. If I've learned anything from my mother, it's that if someone's on anything laced with ice, they can be unpredictable, ready to snap with one wrong move.

"I was just checking on her," I say, taking a couple more steps back to the road.

He scoffs. "I've seen you before, hanging around with those evil cockroaches. Now, piss off."

The girl slowly raises her head, a manic smile on her face. She looks first at me, squinting, then at the man. "You can't tell Kai's girl what to do."

I blink. "I'm not Kai's girl. We're friends."

"Whatever. She's not to be messed with—he said." The girl shrugs and goes back to hunching over her knees, but her words have power. Angry homeless guy ambles off.

My mind's a blur. Kai's always had people who follow him, and he's had Bear and Zion by his side to help enforce things when needed. But when did Kai get so much respect from the homeless around here?

A thought lurks in the corner of my mind. What if he isn't just against The Brotherhood—what if he's leading the uprising?

I turn away and walk the rest of the way back to the park, constantly glancing over my shoulder. News travels fast around here, and the more time I spend back in Daringhood, the more I feel like it's not home to me anymore. Without Alec here, everything's different.

When I'm with Hazen, Gage, and Lucas, they make me feel protected, even though I've always protected myself. Kai is my best friend, and I want to protect him, too, but now I'm torn between him and my lovers. I won't choose sides—I can't. I've already lost one loved one, and I'm not losing anyone else.

Kai will just have to, one day, realize that me spending time with my boys doesn't mean I care for him any less, and it won't change who I am. I'm still here to shoot hoops and shoot the breeze whenever he'd like.

I just hope that *one day* comes sooner rather than later.

The door to our trailer is ajar, and I push it open and step inside. Cool air brushes against my skin, and I curse under my breath; Mom's left the air conditioner on again.

I move into the living room, grabbing the remote off the kitchen counter before spinning around and aiming it at the unit. Movement catches my gaze, and my whole body locks up as though someone is squeezing me so tight that I can't breathe. My heart angrily pushes against my chest.

My mother's sitting on the couch, her hands resting on her knees, staring at the little table in front of her. No. She didn't. Fuck, I knew this was all too good to be true.

"Mom?" I ask and she looks up.

"I didn't—I want to, but I haven't yet." She releases a heavy sob. "Freya, it's all too much." Her voice breaks, and I drop the remote and move toward her, ignoring the needles and drugs scattered on the table. I want to yell, scream, and kick the table over, but it won't help. It'll make things worse, push her over the edge.

I sit next to her and grab her hands. She doesn't look at me, her gaze moving back to the table.

"This isn't going to bring Alec back. Please don't do this again," I plead, and her hands squeeze mine.

"But I can't feel all this anymore, Freya. I'm not strong enough," she sobs out, and I swallow past the razor blades in my throat.

"You are. But I'm not going to ask you to stop for me or Alec, because you have to want to do this for yourself. Do you really want to continue living like this?" I ask, letting go of one of her hands and reaching out. My thumb brushes over her cheek, taking away her tears.

Her body trembles, and she wraps her arms around my waist, clinging to me. My stomach drops, and I freeze, unsure of what to do. Her hand comes to rest on my chest as she holds me like I'm her lifeline.

She hasn't hugged me like this in years. I can't even remember the last time. My arms eventually drop, and I run my hands over her back.

"I wish I was strong like you," she whispers into my chest, and I have no idea what to say back.

I don't feel strong. I may act like nothing affects me, but inside, I'm a mess. Like a ticking bomb ready to blow at any second. I don't know how to deal with all my emotions, other than by jumping off cliffs or putting myself in reckless situations.

Instead of dealing with all my trauma, I've put Band-Aids over it again and again. I'm too afraid to rip them off because, if I do, I'll drown. There will be no saving me from the tidal waves.

For the first time in my life, I understand why she does this. My mother uses these drugs to numb the pain because it's all too much. She's grown used to numbing everything, to constantly chasing that high and freezing everything else out. Now, it's all coming back to her, and she's drowning. I get it, I really do, but I can't help her unless she wants to help herself first.

I just hope she's strong enough to face her demons. This is the first challenge.

Chapter 15

Hazen

My fingers tighten around the balcony railing of Freya's new bedroom. The last ray of sunlight bounces off the water, reflecting into my eyes. After a few days of negotiations, the old tenants moved out of this place—and now it's mine.

I feel free here, away from my father's house, his hold over me, and the place that holds so many unsettling memories for me and my brothers. Having my own place is a step in the right direction—it means more independence away from him. A space for me, Gage, Lucas, and Freya. It's still on the same street as Lucas's, and Gage's place is just down the road.

All I ever wanted was my father's approval, for him to be proud of me, and now I don't know that I'll ever have that. But do I still really want it?

Ever since Dad left the meeting the other night, guilt has churned in my gut. He messaged me, telling me he was disappointed, and that there was still time to turn things around. But we want different things. He says the councilors will never help us with our new plans for Daringhood. What if he's right? What if the way we're doing things is destined to fail?

All we can do is try.

Thinking of Freya, the life she's led, reminds me of that.

We've been training our whole lives for this, when we'd be in power, and now we're lining up our own connections for allies outside of Daring. Dominic always had his favorites and the people he worked with, but we want to expand, change things up. I hate that I still want him to be proud of me. I don't want to be the son that waits for his father's approval, to be told I've been a good boy.

Although I don't want to believe my father is a threat, I know him; he won't give up that easily, and I won't wait to be stabbed in the back. I want to be one step ahead of him. I've got Brax watching Dominic, keeping eyes on him around town, but Dad hasn't made any moves yet.

The meeting is approaching, and I still have no idea if this is going to work. Half of The Brotherhood is on board with an attempt at more equality and less bloodshed, but the other half—those who are more loyal to my father than us—aren't in favor of change or loosening the power hold.

I get it. It would be hard to get behind young blood coming in and taking over under these circumstances, but they should know better than to question us and our authority. They might need reminding of that.

My phone vibrates from the table behind me. I grab it and find a text from Freya, saying she'll be a little late to the meeting, but she doesn't give a reason. I reply with a simple *okay* and shove the phone into my pants pocket.

I have no idea why she still insists on staying at her mother's place when she's welcome to stay on this side of the tracks. I won't push her because I know she won't listen. She has to want to do it herself, which I respect. Her room's almost ready here, and I can't wait to show her. I've just picked out her bathtub, and some soldiers are here installing it.

A car door slams shut, followed by voices carrying through the air. I lean over the balcony as the last of the sun sets over the ocean. Lucas and Gage are head to head, yelling at each other. Gage shoves Lucas, and he falls back into his car. Oh shit.

Not waiting for them to beat the shit out of each other, I head back through Freya's bedroom, then down the hallway and stairs. Fists are getting thrown. I come to a stop between them, my hands on both their chests. Lucas has blood dripping from his lip, and Gage is glaring at him with so much anger.

"What the fuck?" I ask, staring at Gage with an eyebrow raised.

Lucas pushes against my hand on his chest, and I hold him in place.

"I just saw him with Mia, looking a bit too cozy." Gage's eyes narrow and Lucas scoffs.

"Where?" I ask.

"It wasn't even like that."

"Well, what was it like, then? Because if I hear you're fucking her—" I shake my head with a look of disgust, and he rolls his eyes.

"The sooner you're done fucking yourself up, the better." Gage takes a step back. "We have a job to do, in case you didn't notice."

"I'll be done when I'm good and ready. You don't know what it's like. I'm dealing in the only way I know how."

"What, by turning your back on the one girl you've ever given your heart to?" Gage huffs out a derisive laugh, and Lucas breathes loudly through his nose. His eyes glass over slightly before he blinks and they harden once more.

"She broke my fucking heart the second she took my parents from me," Lucas says so quietly, I think I might have imagined it.

My hand drops from his chest and I step back, giving him space. "You know as well as I do that she didn't mean to kill your mother. She protected herself, and your mother killed your father," I say, and Lucas remains silent. His gaze is stuck to the ground.

"Yeah, well, whatever. It still fucking hurts," he finally says.

Gage releases a heavy breath. "I'm sorry. I just hate seeing you like this. You look like shit, and we're supposed to be leading our brothers with pride, not pity."

Lucas wipes his bottom lip with his thumb, taking away the blood. "I know."

Gage doesn't respond, and it's clear that whatever just happened between them needed to, so we can start fresh. Maybe this is the turning point for Lucas. Maybe this is what he needs to start moving on.

Gage is right. We can't afford to fall apart now, when so much is weighing on our shoulders. If we fall, then the whole Brotherhood falls alongside us. I won't let that happen, not when it's our time to shine—with or without my father's backing.

"Let's go. We've got a meeting to hold," I say, moving toward the garage and checking over my shoulder to make sure Lucas follows. Though he's fucked up, we need him; we need to show united leadership.

One of the guards opens the door as Gage and Lucas follow closely behind me. The lights automatically switch on, and the hair on the back of my neck stands on end. Something isn't right. I scan the room, but nothing seems out of place, except the tires of all my cars are slashed with large holes.

I grab my gun from its holder on my hip and look back at Gage and Lucas. Gage already has his pointed at the nearest Beamer. but Lucas runs his hands over his legs, then shrugs, coming up empty-handed.

Ignoring his incompetence, I move silently through the garage, checking every corner, and once we've done a full sweep, it's clear there's no one else in here. I shove my gun back into its holster and check over each car. The tires are slashed, but nothing else.

"What the fuck?" Lucas spits out, running his fingers over the cut on my newest car, a Bugatti Tourbillon. Anger boils deep inside me.

"Blake!" I scream, and one of the soldiers comes running in.

"Yes, boss?"

"Find out who the fuck broke into my garage. Check the cameras," I yell and reach into my pocket for my phone. It's ten past seven, and we are now fucking late.

I hit the call button on Zeke's name. "We're going to be a few minutes behind schedule. Hold the fort until we're there." I hang up, not giving him a second to reply.

"You're driving," I say to Gage and walk out of the garage, heading straight for Gage's car. I slam the passenger door shut once I'm in my seat.

"Who the fuck would do that?" Lucas asks.

"No fucking idea, but we'll find out soon enough."

"Where's your father?" Lucas asks. "Tires slashed—could it have been him?"

I shake my head. "Not his style. Wouldn't wanna break a sweat. Plus, Brax has been following him. He would have known."

My father wants revenge. He wants his Brotherhood back, but slashing tires would be below him. If he didn't want us to attend the meeting, he'd be the type to shoot first, not slash tires.

"The list of people that it could be is a mile long," Gage says.

"From those who support Dominic to Dominic himself, and of course the fucking hood rats we're trying to fucking help right now."

"But would they be stupid enough to do it?" Lucas asks as we pull to a stop in front of town hall, and he jumps out of the back seat.

Gage and I follow him. The parking lot is packed with a mixture of cars, some shiny and some old bombs, and it's not hard to see that the majority are from our side of the tracks. Samson, Zeke, and a couple of other Brotherhood members are standing in front of the hall, waiting for us.

I move in to step beside Lucas and Gage and spot Freya walking toward us from across the parking lot. My stomach drops and my shoulders tense. Her face is full of emotion and she's looking down at her feet, a million miles away.

Without warning, a thunderous boom cuts through the stillness. What the fuck?

The scent of burning wood fills the air as the town hall is consumed by flames. Freya disappears, and in the chaos, I'm flung backward, crashing onto the hard ground, pain shooting through my back. My ears ring so loud before everything goes up in smoke.

Chapter 16

Freya

An hour earlier

My foot connects with a rock, and it skitters over the road, bouncing along until it stops. People walk around me, but my thoughts are a million miles away from here. Images fill my mind of the needles and drugs covering our table and my mother staring at them like they were a lottery ticket. A way out for her.

I was there to stop her this time, but what if next time I'm not? What if she tries again later tonight? I tried to get her to come with me to the meeting, but instead, after I'd taken the drugs and flushed them, she said she wanted to sleep it off, and I sat with her till her eyes closed.

Sobriety is up to her. I can't make that decision for her.

If she chooses them again, I'm done. I can't go back there. With Alec gone, it's too much to watch my mother drain everything away again. She's been clean for two weeks now, which is the longest stint she's had since I can remember. I'd hoped she'd keep going, but now I'm not so sure.

The restaurant we were at the other night for the meeting comes into view; one of the workers is pulling chairs out to the front patio. I peer through the window and freeze. My heart beats faster, my stomach drops, and I want to flee, to run, but I can't.

Lucas is sitting at the bar with a glass in his hand . . . and what the fuck? Mia's leaning in closer and closer. Her hand rests on his thigh, and my hands begin to shake. Red-hot anger courses through my body. What the ever-loving fuck? She'd better remove her hand, or I'm going to lose my shit.

Though Lucas may hate me right now, he's still mine. Touch what's mine and you die. I've never really understood that popular trope until this moment. Watching Mia touch, laugh, and flirt with someone who's mine? I want to kill her, to storm into the restaurant and slam her face down on the bar. Laugh as blood spills from her broken nose.

I don't understand her. She was supposedly in love with my brother, and the second he died, she moved on to Dominic. Now that he's God knows where, she's all over Lucas? Fuck.

I take a couple of steps back and look around before picking up a large rock from the curb. My chest rises and falls to the beat of my heart as my fingers close around the rock. I move toward the window, watching as Mia pushes off her chair and leans in closer to Lucas, as though she's about to kiss him. My hand continues to shake, and without another thought, I take a step back and launch the rock straight at the window. It shatters into a thousand little pieces, just like my heart, and the broken glass falls to my feet.

Lucas jumps up, shoving Mia away; she falls on her ass and cries, but he ignores her. He grabs his gun, aiming it toward the window, straight at my heart. His stormy brown eyes clash with mine, and I glare at him with so much anger and heartbreak. His face twists from shock to understanding, yet he doesn't lower his gun, and I don't want him to. Anything to prolong this connection between us.

He moves through the restaurant in long, powerful strides until he's right in front of me, his shoes crunching against the shards of glass. I move forward, closer to him, and he shoves his gun into the front of his pants.

"I'm not wasting a bullet on you," he says. He reaches out, and I don't move a muscle. He tucks a strand of hair behind my ear, and a shiver runs down my neck. Memories flood my mind of how good we are together—how he tastes, of how soft his lips are, moving against mine. Fuck.

No, I can't. Fuck.

How could he think about kissing someone else?

"You move on quickly," I say, raising an eyebrow just as Mia walks over, her high heels crunching in the glass.

She wraps an arm around his chest and leans into his ear, whispering something I can't hear. My own ears ring loudly, piercing my soul. I take a step backward, and Mia pulls back. She looks over at me, the corner of her mouth lifting.

"He's mine. Back off," I growl, and Mia opens, then closes her mouth.

"I know," she replies, but her expression is still smug. What's she doing, then?

My hands clench against my legs before I shove them into the pockets of my shorts. I'm done. I want to punch that smug look off her face, but then she'll have won.

Lucas doesn't break eye contact with me. "It's not—"

I bolt.

"Freya, wait!" Lucas yells down the street, but his voice floats away on the wind.

My feet hit the road, my heart burning with a thousand tiny flames. Lucas can hate me all he wants.

I keep running until I reach the dirt track that leads up to the town hall. Cars are lined up everywhere. I stop and lean back against one of the cars, an old Ford with rusted-out rims.

I pull my phone out of my back pocket and my stomach twists. Another message from the unknown number.

Unknown: Peace or war? Make sure you're at the town hall and don't be late. Bring your little hood rat friends. It'll be a date.

My fingers tighten around my phone. Anger boils up from within, and I hastily type a reply.

Me: Who the fuck are you?

I'm so fucking over this stupid asshole, hiding behind a stupid screen and sending cryptic messages. I've got enough shit to deal with besides solving these riddles.

Three dots appear, then disappear. After a minute, I give up on waiting for a response, shoving my phone back into my pocket.

Who could be sending these messages? Who's dumb enough to spend their time fucking with me? I have no idea.

But, as much as I hate to admit it, the sender has a point. I've already asked Kai to come here tonight, but what if this is a big chance for him to speak his mind—to let the boys know what he'd like to see for the Hood?

What if this is a way for Kai to see the boys are more than the arrogant assholes he takes them for?

I glance at my watch. The meeting isn't for another ten minutes. I quickly text Hazen, letting him know I'll be late, then I call Kai.

The line keeps ringing and ringing.

"Don't tell me you're calling to try and convince me to come to the hall, because that would be a waste of precious time." He knows me too well, and the corner of my mouth lifts slightly.

"You sure you don't wanna come? It'll be fun." I lean even more heavily against the Ford, the early evening air cool around my shoulders.

"Ha! Hanging around with a bunch of rich snobs who measure their dicks against one another isn't really my idea of fun."

I chuckle. "Met someone who knows you earlier. Some junkie told a homeless guy not to mess with me because I'm 'Kai's girl.'" I try to make light of it with my tone, but a needle of worry pricks at me. "Are you starting something with The Brotherhood?"

Kai sighs. "You know me, Frey. I never strike first."

"You're not answering the question," I press.

"Look, maybe a lot of the Hood have been coming to me, asking questions, and I'm suggesting answers. But I'm not some leader. I'm not like your guys."

Not yet, I think, but I don't say it.

The line goes silent for a couple of seconds. "Got anything else on your mind, or should I hang up already?"

All humor dries up. He's pulling away and I hate it. All I want is for everyone to come together, to put an end to this divide between our town and create equal status. As much as I want it, I know it'll never happen. The Brotherhood won't allow it.

"Freya, I'm here for you. You can talk to me if you need," he says, his voice gentler now, and I can't help it. I spend the next twenty minutes filling in my best friend on what happened with Mia and Lucas.

"My only piece of advice, coming from someone who doesn't and never will have a girlfriend? Leave now while you can, and your heart will be safe over here."

I take a moment to mull over his words. "It's too late for that."

"You're gonna have to choose us or them—and soon."

The line goes dead, and I rest my head back against the car, releasing a heavy sigh. He's right; I've already got my answer. I'll fight for Lucas until he's mine again.

More cars come down the road. A familiar red Range Rover drives past, and I kick off the Ford, following Gage's SUV.

He parks just outside the town hall, and Lucas exits the vehicle first, his blond hair catching in the streetlight. He turns around. Our gazes clash like a lightning bolt breaking between us. Anger emanates from every muscle in my body. I storm closer to them, ready to tell him he can't treat me this way before a deafening boom rips through the air.

Red-hot flames kiss my skin. Smoke dances all around me. I fall forward, landing hard against the ground, and everything goes black.

Chapter 17

Hazen

My ears ring.

Someone is screaming.

It sounds like Freya.

I have to get to her.

She has to be okay.

My hand runs over the rocky ground before I push myself up. Smoke fills the air. People are yelling, but I can't hear what they're saying through the ringing. Pain rips through my muscles as I move to stand.

Gage groans from the ground, and I reach out. He grabs my hand and joins me on his feet. He pinches the bridge of his nose, his brows pulling together.

"What the ever-loving fuck was that?" he asks.

"No idea, but whoever did this might still be around. Load up," I say, pulling out my gun from its holster on my leg.

The smoke begins to clear, and I look around for Lucas but don't see him. Fuck, he was so drunk he's probably gone up in flames.

Fuck, no. I can't think like that.

"Can you see Freya and Lucas?" I ask, and Gage disappears into the swirling gray smoke.

"Freya!" I scream.

We move closer to the town hall, which is on fucking fire. Flames build higher and higher into the night sky. Shit! People run around frantically, trying to get away from the burning building, but all I care about is our woman. She needs to be okay. I can't think of the alternative, because a life without her in it isn't much of a life at all.

"She's here!" Gage's voice sounds through the acrid haze.

I push forward, shoving past panicked bodies, my pulse hammering in my skull. The smoke is suffocating, thick as a damn wall, blinding me with every step. I squint, scanning the chaos, but am met with shadowed figures—running, screaming, burning. My lungs ache, each breath searing hot, but I don't stop. I can't. I yank my collar over my mouth, rub the fabric against my stinging eyes, and keep moving. She's here. Somewhere. And I'll tear this place apart to find her if I have to.

There, a short distance away, Gage is standing, and Lucas is bent over someone. *Her*. My knees give way as I fall beside them. Lucas has her head in his lap, brushing his fingers through her hair. Her eyes are closed, her face covered in ash. Nasty burns line her arms, and I want to kill whoever did this, but right now, she needs me. My hands begin to shake, my breathing deepens, and I open my mouth, but no words come out. She has to be okay—she will be.

I take Freya's hand in mine. Gage sits opposite me, staring at Freya with a pained look in his eyes. My fingers run over her pulse and push down hard, trying to pick up on the faintest beat. I refuse to believe there'll be anything less.

One small thump, then another and another. My lips part, and I let out a heavy breath. Fuck, I thought for a second we'd lost her. I squeeze her hand, but she doesn't squeeze back.

"Call an ambulance!" I yell at both Lucas and Gage, finally finding my voice.

"They're on their way," Lucas says, brushing his fingers over Freya's cheek, removing some of the ash. "Seeing her disappear into the smoke and then finding her unmoving . . ." He sighs, and a tear falls down his cheek. I've never seen him cry—not even when his mother died. "I thought she was gone forever."

My chest tightens. I know exactly how he feels because I felt it too. I've always been taught that women are nothing but distractions—they only serve one purpose, and that's looking good by our side—but Freya is more than that.

Yes, she's a distraction, not only to me but to my brothers as well, but she's also one of us now. If anything ever happened to one of my brothers, then the doors to hell would open and there'd be no going back.

Smoke clogs my throat, thick and bitter, burning its way into my lungs. The town hall is gone, nothing but a skeletal ruin swallowed by flames. A woman stumbles past us, her dress in shreds, her skin blistered and peeling. She doesn't scream—maybe she can't. But others do. Their cries tear through the polluted air, raw, desperate. The scent of burning flesh turns my stomach, but I don't look away. I can't. My fists clench. This isn't over. Not even close.

Someone threatened my family today, my brothers, and this means war. My first priority is making sure Freya receives the best care, then it's time to clean up this mess and find out who was brave enough to fuck with us. Brave enough to set fire to our town hall, to threaten The Brotherhood.

I squeeze Freya's hand more forcefully before releasing it.

"Do you think she'll ever forgive me?" Lucas says, staring down at her. She looks so peaceful with her head in his lap, her hair falling around her like a halo.

"Yes." Gage nods, placing his arm over Lucas's shoulder. "You two need to sort your shit out, and this is the perfect reminder that tomorrow is not guaranteed."

Lucas purses his lips as he considers Gage's words before focusing back on Freya. Gage is right—they need to clear the air. It just sucks that this is what it's taken to pull him out of the gutter.

Sirens ring through the chaos of the night, getting closer and closer. I stand, and Freya moves her hand over her stomach, her brows drawing together in discomfort before smoothing out.

I wave over two paramedics, and they start tending to Freya. Gage gets up, standing next to me, but Lucas doesn't leave her side.

A thought strikes me. "Amirah wasn't in there, was she?"

"Nah." Gage shakes his head. "She's at home."

"Who the fuck would do this?" Gage asks, staring at the burning building. Fire trucks pull up, and firefighters start putting out the flames. People are lining up at the ambulances. A single raindrop hits the bridge of my nose before more follow.

"Someone who has a death warrant." I huff, crossing my arms over my chest.

People are screaming, with nasty burns covering their skin. A few bodies line the footsteps of the building, and I look away, focusing back on Freya. She's on a bed, and I move next to her, taking her hand in mine once more and pressing a kiss against the back of it before letting go. The paramedics push her into the back of the ambulance and Lucas jumps in alongside her.

"Keep us updated," I yell, and the driver nods before the doors close and they drive off. My heart pounds against my rib cage. I should be with her. Fuck everything else.

A hand slaps me on the back. "She's going to be okay. We've gotta deal with this and find out the damage." Gage walks off ahead, and with a final heavy sigh, I roll back my shoulders and follow him.

Time disappears in a blur as the firefighters put out the fire, and black smoke lifts into the sky. My throat burns as though there's a fire lit there, moving down into my belly. Gage passes me a black-and-red bandanna he got from who the fuck knows where, and I fasten it across my nose, attempting to block out the smoke, but it's a bit late for that. My lungs are scorching.

We move toward the building. The closer we get, the more bodies litter the ground.

"Hey, you can't go in there!" someone yells behind us, but I ignore them. We can do whatever the fuck we want. I need to see the damage, how many we've lost.

We reach the entrance, and anger boils up from within. Five members of The Brotherhood lie unmoving across the steps, mostly soldiers, but Samson's among them, and I see red. Who the fuck would do this?

Samson was one of our most loyal men. He might have been a little skeptical when we took over, but he trusted us and had our backs. Now he's gone. A light ache forms between my eyes, and I squeeze the bridge of my nose. I'm not even in the building yet, and I want to kill any motherfucker I see.

Is my father in there too? Fear grips my heart in an icy hold. I hate him, but I don't want him dead.

Gage silently steps around the bodies and disappears through the half-destroyed door. Pressing the bandanna closer to my nose, I follow him in. The smoke rises into the air, and with each step I take, the more I want to step back. Bodies lie across every seat. Hundreds of people who came to the meeting to hear about the peace treaty are now dead.

"What a fucking mess," Gage grumbles, kicking over one of the burned freestanding chairs.

"Whoever did this is going to pay with their life and the life of everyone they love," I say, letting out a heavy breath.

The stench of burned bodies reminds me of being back in my shed, torturing informants for answers, fucking with their minds until they bitch out and give in. I usually love the smell, but now it's different. I didn't do this. Innocent lives have been compromised in someone's fucked-up plan.

"You know if we weren't late, we would have been in here?" Gage says, staring at something on the ground in front of him. I step up beside him, and my blood turns to ice.

A mother with a young baby in her arms, both their bodies burned. Her face is still half recognizable, but the baby is gone. Only their arms and legs are intact.

I have to get out of here. I stumble backward and practically run to the exit. I kick the last remaining piece of wood from the door, and it crumbles to pieces. Stepping around my soldiers' bodies, I rip off the bandanna. The smoke-tainted air clings to my lungs, and I take several deep breaths. My hands shake at my sides, wanting to reach out and snap something, preferably a neck. To hear bones twist and break at my will.

Footsteps approach. Ronald appears with Zeke by his side, who looks as white as a ghost.

Zeke's got a burn on his arm, but Ronald—he's unmarked. How'd he escape without injury?

What if he knew?

"Fuck, how many?" Ronald asks, glancing over my shoulder.

"I want a body count ASAP, and the name of every single person in there," I snap and glare at him, stepping right up in his face. His breath lingers against mine. "You were against this meeting from the moment we mentioned it. How do I know it wasn't you who did this?"

Ronald's eyes widen. He stumbles back, raising his hands up in surrender. "Jesus Christ, you can't be serious?" He looks between me and Gage, who's joined me. I don't stand down. "I may think your idea was fucking stupid, but I would never put my brothers in harm's way."

I stare at him for several long breaths, his jaw tight and eye twitching, but eventually, I step back. He's right; one of our own wouldn't put our brothers in danger. We protect our own above all else. Ronald leaves in a huff, and I grab my phone from my pants and open a text from Brax.

Brax: Dominic is still alive and getting a haircut at Rebel's. Doesn't seem to have the slightest clue about the blast.

My shoulders relax slightly, and I shove my phone back into my pants pocket.

A car speeds toward us and skids to a stop just in front of us. Dirt fills the air, and I use my hand to block it from getting into my eyes. Ronald moves in next to us, grabbing his gun and aiming it forward.

Car doors slam, and Kai, Zion, and Bear get out. Kai stares blankly at the town hall, his hands clenched at his sides. Bear's jaw tightens, and he glares between Gage and me with hatred. Zion reaches into his pants, and Ronald goes to step forward, but I shoot my arm out, placing my hand over his chest. He growls but stays put.

Bear pulls out a small pocketknife. He flicks it open and closed, watching me with his crazy bright-green eyes.

Kai makes a clicking sound through his teeth. "What the fuck did you do?" His voice is full of anger.

I scoff. "I was about to ask you the same."

"Where the fuck is Freya?" Kai asks, staring behind us and around the parking lot.

"She's fine, and no concern of yours," I say, and Bear laughs.

Kai crosses his arms over his chest. "Killing innocents isn't really my MO, but it is The Brotherhood's—and yours." He steps forward, coming within arm's length of me. He looks me up and down, judgment clear in his eyes.

"Did you set this up? So all these innocent people would die?"

I shake my head. "What makes you think that?"

"Gee, I don't know—we get nothing but terror and oppression from you lot for twenty years, and now, all of a sudden, you're offering peace—only for it to end in fucking murder?" Kai's voice is thunderous. "Why do you fucking *think* I think that?"

"We didn't do it."

"You may not have done it, but you called this meeting. It was your job to keep these people safe." Kai stabs a finger toward me. "You could have saved them."

His words hit me like a knife to the heart. My chest rises and falls at a rapid rate. I can't breathe. Everything around me disappears into darkness. Kai glowers at me, his eyebrow raised.

Those words are exactly what I've said in the past, about that night when I killed the little girl. I took her from this world, and I could have saved her, just like I could have saved everyone inside the town hall.

Kai opens his mouth, but before the words can leave, my fist hits him square in the jaw. There's movement around us, but I can't see anything but Kai.

Zion jumps in front of him, throwing his fist, connecting with my stomach. I keep my legs firmly in place as the wind is knocked out of me.

Kai shoves Zion aside, getting up in my face and gripping the collar of my shirt.

"You don't know shit," I growl, and Kai laughs.

"You're just like your father," he snaps, and I push against his chest hard. He falls back, landing on the ground. Zion rushes to his side, and Bear stares at me, his eye twitching, that knife still flicking in his hand.

Am I like my father? Am I nothing but a killer without a heart? I've been brought up in a bloodthirsty environment. Killing is all I've ever known. Maybe I *am* like him. Look what just happened to all those innocent people inside the building. I arranged this, told them to be here, and now, boom—they're dead. Fuck.

Kai takes Zion's hand and stands back up. Zion whispers something into his ear, and Kai watches me, glaring. He runs his hand across his throat. Is that a threat?

"Do it," I say, and Kai's nostrils flare.

"Nah, that would be too easy. You deserve much worse than a bullet to your broken heart." Kai moves around Zion, coming closer to me, within arm's reach.

"I'm trying to fix this between us—that's what this was all about. Giving you something in return for peace," I say.

Kai laughs, though there's no humor in the sound. "And look what you did! You killed people from the Hood and the Ville. You call yourself a leader? Pfft. You're a destroyer."

I swallow past the thump in my throat. He's right, but I won't be telling him that.

"Daddy would be so proud." Kai smirks, and my fists ball at my side. I'm ready to punch this asshole.

"Enough!" Gage yells, stepping between us. "This isn't the time or place for this. We need to settle this properly."

Zion scoffs. "Only way this is going to get resolved now is by war." He turns around, heading back for their car. "May the odds be forever *not* in your favor."

Bear follows Zion, but Kai stays back, shoving his gun back into the front of his pants. "Whatever happens from here on out, that's on you."

He leaves, and my heart pounds so hard and fast that I can't hear anything else around me. A hand lands on my shoulder, but I don't move. I watch as they leave, dust kicking up behind the car.

Guilt slams into me. Who the fuck am I? Is that all I am, a killer? That's all I know. All I've ever known. Kai is right about one thing. If I'd been on time—if I'd thought to have the building checked by security beforehand, if I'd scanned everyone as they entered—I could have saved them.

Chapter 18

Lucas

Freya's hand looks so small. Her fingers curl around mine, holding on for dear life, like she's afraid I'll let go. Part of me wants to release her and walk away. But the other stronger part can't leave her like this. Lying on the hospital bed with angry burns lining her arms.

The doctor said they will heal without too much scarring, but fuck, I want to take it all away. I want to release the pain that's sewn into that little frown on her forehead. To tell her that everything is okay, that I'm here to protect her. But we're not living in a fucking fairy tale, and I won't spin those lies to her, no matter how much she needs to hear them.

She groans, and I sit up straighter, gripping her hand tighter. The frown on her forehead deepens and her eyes blink open. She sits up and looks around the room, her eyes widening before settling back on me, and her frown disappears. Her stare cuts right into my soul. Begging me to forgive her, to lean forward and claim her plump, pink lips that I've been missing and dreaming about every time I close my eyes.

"What happened?" she asks, her voice all husky, and fucking hell, it's sexy as sin.

"The town hall blew up," I say, and she sucks in a deep breath. She coughs. I reach for the glass of water, bringing the straw to her lips.

She takes in several sips, her throat bobbing up and down. Her cheeks are covered in soot from the smoke, and for the better part of the last thirty minutes, I've wanted to wipe it away. But I can't. She's not mine anymore. Hell, was she ever, really?

"Is everyone okay?" she asks, and I place the cup down on the table next to her, not wanting to burden her with more bad news. "Hazen and Gage?"

"Yes, they are okay, but anyone who was in the town hall isn't. It was packed, Freya."

Her frown deepens, and she sighs. "Fuck."

We stay in silence for several minutes, and I still don't let go of her hand, and she doesn't let go of mine either. There's so much I want to say but don't. I want to yell and scream—hell, even walk away. But there's something holding me back, keeping me here. She could have died today, and that's not something I want to experience again. It felt like someone ripping open the last little bit of my heart, pulling it apart vein by vein until nothing remained.

As much as I hate to admit it, Freya still has her claws in my heart, and I have no idea how to release her grasp. I want to hate her, to walk away and never look back, but I can't, and that pisses me off. I'm so fucked up.

"Has the doctor been in yet?" she asks.

"Yeah, he's been in and said it's nothing critical. Everything will heal."

She smiles, and I don't remove my hand from hers, afraid that if I do, I'll lose the last piece of her I still have.

"I'm really glad you're here with me," Freya whispers, and my gaze locks on to the hospital floor. I stare blankly at the dirty white vinyl while my stomach twists and turns.

"I didn't really have a choice," I mumble, and the bed squeaks as Freya moves away from me. She tries to pull her fingers free from mine, but I hold on tighter before she gives in.

"Are we okay?" she asks, and I finally look back up, her blue eyes staring into my very soul.

"It's not as simple as that," I say.

Freya huffs. "What can I do to get back to the way we were?"

My tongue slides over my dry lips. "When I look at you, all I can see is death. I see you killing my mother and taking her away from me."

Tears well up behind her eyes and her bottom lip wobbles. "When I look at you, I always see life." She releases a heavy sigh.

My pulse quickens. No one has ever said those words to me. I'm not a good person. I'm fucked up, broken, and here she is, telling me she sees life in me?

"You were, and still are, always there to protect me. To help me see the light in the darkness. I'm so fucking sorry I killed your mother, and I'll spend every last second of every day trying to take that pain away from you, but please don't let it ruin us. Ruin what we had." Tears stream down her ash-covered cheeks, and I reach out, wiping them away. She leans into my touch, and without thinking, I close the distance between us, claiming her salty lips in a light kiss.

Butterflies flutter around my broken heart, begging me to open up again, to let her in. Except, I can't. Not yet. But I have hope that one day soon, I'll be able to. She could have died in that blast, and that thought kills me.

The door opens and I pull back. Dr. Phillips walks in dressed in scrubs, with a mask over his nose and mouth. He carries a clipboard and quickly scans it before coming to stand on the other side of Freya's hospital bed.

"Hello, Freya, I'm Doctor Phillips," he says and Freya nods.

He reaches out, removing the bandages one of the paramedics put over her burns. He checks out the marks on her arms, and I finally let go of Freya's hand. Her warmth is gone, and I want it back.

"We'll put some cream on your burns and wrap them up. Keep applying the cream over the next couple of weeks, change the bandages, and they should heal nicely. Come back in two or three weeks for a follow-up to see how they're healing. Any questions?" he asks Freya, and she shakes her head.

"Thanks, Doc," I say, standing, and he nods, following me out the door. He shuts it behind him and moves over to the nurses' station, handing me Freya's cream.

"Hope you don't mind me asking, but what on earth happened? I've got my beds full of burn victims," he says with a frown.

"Explosion at the town hall," I say, bracing my hands on the desk. "Do whatever you can to help the victims, even those from the Hood side. We'll cover the bills."

Dr. Phillips presses his lips together before nodding. I know he wants to ask more, but he won't. He's been our family doctor for as long as I can remember. He knows to never ask any questions, outside of what he needs to know to help us. He gets paid well enough to keep his mouth shut.

I head back into Freya's private room, leaving the cream next to her bed.

Her eyes close, and I turn to leave. I should get back to help Hazen and Gage. "Stay with me, please?"

I want to say no. I should be with the guys, cleaning up the mess and figuring out who the fuck did this. Who put us, Freya, and our people in danger. But I can't leave her. Not when she's looking at me with her puppy-dog eyes. Not when I could have lost her forever. So I settle back into the uncomfortable-as-fuck hospital chair instead.

Freya sleeps on and off for the next hour. Nurses come and go before securing fresh bandages around both her arms. There's a knock on the door and one of the nurses steps inside.

"Your next of kin is here to take you home," she says, and I stand, ready to meet her mother, but Kai Mercer walks in instead.

What the ever-loving fuck?

Chapter 19

Freya

Kai walks through the door, and I sit up straighter, my heart thrashing against my chest. He barges past Lucas, whose fists are tightly clamped.

"Holy shit, Frey, are you okay?" Kai rushes to my side, his fingers skimming lightly over my bandages. The meds are helping, but there's still a slight ache in my skin.

"I'm fine," I say, offering him a reassuring smile. Zion and Bear stand at the door, watching Lucas closely.

"We've got it from here, bro," Bear says, lifting the corner of his mouth.

Lucas's jaw tightens. "Why the fuck is Kai your next of kin?" he growls, looking between us both, and I shrug.

"He's my best friend. It used to be Alec, but when he decided he was going to college early, we changed it to Kai in case I needed someone close by when Alec was gone . . ." My words trail off and silence follows.

Lucas stares at me with a mixture of anger and hurt clear in his widened gaze. I won't apologize for Kai being my next of kin, because he is. He's my best friend and has been there for me through everything, and nothing will change that.

This rift between my best friend and the loves of my life will ultimately break me in the end, because I'll never choose between them. I can't.

Lucas comes closer and leans down. He presses a kiss against my forehead, but he doesn't say another word before walking away. I want to tell him to stay, but he won't. When he kissed me earlier, part of my heart stitched itself back together again. We can't return to the way we were before, and I get that, but there's hope for us yet. I'll hold on to that smallest little lifeline and won't let go.

The nurse injects the last of my medicine before Kai signs off the discharge papers. Zion pushes in a wheelchair, and I scoff.

"There's no way I'm going in that," I say, kicking my legs over the bed.

"Who said you have a choice?" Zion comes to a stop in front of the bed and takes my outstretched hand. I slide my feet into my sneakers, and Zion leans down, tying them up.

"Here's your phone. It's been vibrating like crazy," the nurse says, handing it to me, and I thank her.

There are a million missed calls from Amirah. Fuck. I hit dial on her name, and she answers after the first ring.

"Holy shit, are you okay? Where are you? Fuck. None of the guys are giving me much." She speaks so quickly it takes me a moment to process everything. I'm not sure if it's the painkillers or her.

"I'm fine. I'm getting discharged now from the hospital," I say, standing. My head becomes light and my legs wobble. Zion grabs my waist and lowers me into the wheelchair. I throw him a dirty look, but he ignores me, pushing me out of the room.

"I'm coming to get you," she says, then yells something to someone and curses.

"Amirah, I'm fine. Kai is here."

She huffs. "Fine, but I'm coming to see you. Text me where you go, and I'm there." She hangs up before I can tell her no.

The painkiller kicks in, and my eyes start to droop. I try to keep them open, but darkness takes over.

Voices echo around me. My head throbs as though someone is banging something against my skull over and over. I peel my eyes open to the sight of a familiar dark room, the only light seeping in from under the door. Kai's bedroom. The door swings open, banging against the wall before slamming shut again.

Amirah storms in, her gaze wide as she takes in every part of me. There's an angry scowl twisting her mouth before her eyes glaze over. She rushes toward me and jumps onto Kai's bed.

I groan, sitting up. She takes my hand in hers, looking over the bandages. "Oh my God, this doesn't look good." She breathes out through her nose.

"Looks worse than it feels," I say, then laugh. The painkillers have worn off, and the burns sting, but it's nothing I can't handle. I've been through worse than this.

"This is crazy. I can't believe—" Her words stop as Kai's door flies open, and he walks in with his jaw tight. A shirt no longer hides his chest covered in tattoos, and his muscles flex with each step.

"I don't appreciate your friend breaking down my damn door. She's a psycho," Kai growls out. "How'd you even know where I live, anyway?" he asks Amirah.

"Is it a state secret? Are you upset?" She pouts and bats her eyelashes, mocking him, and I giggle.

"You don't want to see me upset," he mumbles, but I'm sure there's a hint of a smile in his tone.

"Freya's mom told me when I came looking for her. Don't worry—I told your mom you're okay and that you'll be home soon," Amirah says, addressing me.

"She's got ten minutes, then she's gone. Got it?" Kai says, and I nod, mouthing *thank you*.

He leaves and Amirah stares blankly at the door for several seconds. "I have no idea why he's your best friend. He's a pig," she says, then snorts like a pig.

"I saw the way you were checking him out. You've never shown such interest in swine before," I tease, and she rolls her eyes.

"I didn't tell your mom you were hurt—just that you were at Kai's place. Didn't want to worry her," Amirah says.

"Thanks. Have you seen the guys?" I ask, and Amirah purses her lips together.

"Yeah, at the hall—they're on major cleanup. Babe, this is huge and whatever comes from this, fuck. I just hope we all get through it together," Amirah says, joining me back on the bed. She doesn't relax, her back straight, and she looks from me to the door several times. Does Amirah think Kai was responsible?

"Yeah, I need to talk to Kai and ask if he knows anything. He wouldn't have done this. He wouldn't put that many people at risk. That's not Kai's style." I release a heavy sigh.

Kai wouldn't kill people from his side of the tracks—that's just not his MO. And why would the guys, when they were the ones who set it up in the first place? There's no way they were behind it. I won't believe that for a second. This is someone else, and I'll get to the bottom of it, hopefully before an all-out war breaks out.

"Same as the guys—they wouldn't do that. Not after they'd finally accepted my plan to try and lower the divide between us," I say.

Amirah raises her eyebrows. "Equity between hood and ville—but still not men and women."

"Huh?" I ask, confused. What's that supposed to mean?

"Don't you ever wish there was a sisterhood?" Amirah asks, and I guess I'd never thought of that before.

"I mean, sounds pretty cool." In the background, I hear Kai talking on the phone to someone, his voice getting louder. "But I don't want to sleep with the leaders of the sisterhood—just saying."

Amirah swats me with a pillow, and we laugh.

I don't reassure her that we'll all make it through, because after what happened to my brother, I can't promise anyone tomorrow. Our life can be ripped from us in an instant.

Amirah stays for ten minutes, then leaves after I promise her I'll come to her place to rest tomorrow. She wanted me to go with her now, but I can't. I need to talk to Kai first.

Kai kicks open his door, carrying a bag of food in one hand and a bottle of water in the other. He passes me the bag, and I sit up, leaning back against the pillow. I pull out a burger from Jerry's and my stomach rumbles.

"I haven't had one of these in ages." I groan before taking a massive bite. My eyes close and the peppery mayo runs down my chin. My tongue swipes out, collecting every last drop.

Kai laughs, sitting down next to me on the bed. "You're a mess."

After I finish eating the burger, Kai hands me a couple of painkillers. I pop them into my mouth and drink from the water bottle before handing it back to him.

We stay silent for several heartbeats. I can practically feel Kai thinking, and I can't take it any longer. "Just spit it out," I say.

"They killed all those innocent people in that hall, and you're still with them?" Kai shifts on the bed, moving away slightly, and faces me.

"They didn't do it."

"But they organized the meeting, knowing full well how many people from our side of the tracks would be there. They fucked up, and the consequences are going to be deadly." Kai grips the comforter in his fist.

"The meeting was my idea, and you know that. Some of The Brotherhood, and plenty of people from the Ville, died." I choke back a sob.

Kai shrugs. "Still, they organized it. It was no doubt a calculated risk. They were obviously hoping more Hood people would have been there."

"Kai! You don't know that," I say, raising my voice.

He shakes his head and bites into his bottom lip. "Most of the dead were women and children, so they were expendable for The Brotherhood."

"Please don't start a war," I beg, reaching for Kai, but he rolls off the bed and stands, facing me.

His eyes turn a darker shade of brown. "The war's already begun, and you'll have to choose your side."

My stomach drops, and I want to throw up. "You know I can't choose between them and you, and I won't."

Kai grimaces and shakes his head. "Frey, if you don't choose, the choice will be ripped away from you. I can't protect you if you're with them, and fuck, I can't lose you too."

"You won't."

Kai blows out a breath before he turns and leaves. I push my head back farther into his pillow and squeeze my eyes shut. Fucking hell. I'm doomed if I do and doomed if I don't. No matter what I do, I'll hurt someone, and he's right—the consequences will be deadly.

Kai didn't blow up the town hall. The guys didn't either; so, who the fuck did? Could it have been a random from the Hood, unhappy with their lot? Seems unlikely. Usually, when big things happen around here, Kai knows about it.

The guys have been watching Dominic, but I wouldn't put this past him. He doesn't want them leading The Brotherhood; he wants to take back the reins. This is the perfect distraction, but would he risk killing members of The Brotherhood in the process? Although I don't think he would, I can't be sure.

I spend the next couple of hours asleep in Kai's bed before the sun starts to rise and I decide to leave. My mom's been blowing up my phone, and I need to go see her. This is the kind of thing to send her spiraling, unless she's already there. When I left her yesterday, I didn't know if she decided to use or not. It's all too much.

Kai's trailer is quiet as I walk down the hall and out the front door. The early morning sky has an orange hue that's hazier than usual, thanks to the fire. It's just past six, and I'm tired, but I can't sleep with all the thoughts swarming around in my head. How can I save everyone and avoid this war? No matter what, someone always gets hurt. I'm fucked if I do and fucked if I don't.

I take the short walk back to our trailer and push open the front door. It squeals and the lights flick on. Mom rushes toward me, pulling me in for a hug. I bite down on my bottom lip, hissing through the pain as her hands touch my burn marks.

"Oh my God, Freya, are you okay?" She pulls back, inspecting my arms, and when she sees the pain in my eyes, she steps away. "Shit, sorry."

"I'm okay, just a couple of burns, nothing major." I shrug, moving toward the couch and falling back into the seat.

"Fucking hell, what a shit show. I have been worried sick about you. Don't you ever leave me worried like that again," she growls, concern evident in the tone of her voice. "I don't wanna lose another kid. I can't."

She pulls out a smoke from a pack on the kitchen counter and lights it up. Her hands shake before she takes a long drag and puffs out the smoke.

Guilt claws its way through my body at the mention of my brother. She wasn't there for him over the years, but she's still grieving after losing her only son, and I get it. I haven't found a way to process, and I'm not sure if I ever will. I'll never be able to fully accept that he's gone forever.

"Sorry. I'm glad Amirah told you I was with Kai," I say, and Mom nods.

"I hope he fucking gives those dogs what's coming to them."

I don't reply, because no matter what I say, she'll argue until she's black and blue. She'll never forgive The Brotherhood for what they did to her and us, and I don't blame her. There's no choosing for her; she'll back Kai and the Hood until her dying breath.

She fumbles with her phone. "I haven't heard from Jessie. She was going to that meeting. Did you see her?"

I shake my head, and Mom breathes in and out before she snatches her smokes off the counter and walks out the front door without another word. I look around the living space for any sign of drugs lying around, but there's nothing. She's keeping to her word.

Fuck, I hope her friend is okay, because if she loses one more person, that could be the end for her. There's no turning back.

Chapter 20

Gage

S weat drips down my face as we bury the last of the bodies in the large hole. I count a hundred and twenty-three men and women. Eighty from Daringville and forty-three from Daringhood. Twenty of those were our men—councilors or soldiers, distributors or dock workers of some sort. People who help The Brotherhood function. Our lifeblood. Most of them are unrecognizable due to the burns on their faces. We are still processing the DNA records to get names of every single person.

What a nightmare. To see this many people gone and have no fucking clue as to who's responsible? That's what pisses me off the most. I need answers before I lose my fucking mind and kill anybody who questions me or our choices. We've been getting looks from our men as they bury the bodies, as though they are waiting for us to give them answers that we simply don't have yet. I know they suspect someone from Daringhood. How could they not? The numbers are in their favor. And why else would so many of them have refused to come to our meeting if they didn't know something was going on? I won't sleep until I find out who did this.

We buried each body in the same hole out back of the town hall as a reminder of what happened today. Some of the men wanted to stake the members of Daringhood, like we usually do when they dare disobey us, but it's not appropriate this time. No matter what side they are from, they all deserve a proper burial. Everyone who was in that town hall was there because we asked them to be. We didn't ask for this massacre, but fuck do I feel responsible for it.

Hazen drives us back to his new place and we remain silent, my thoughts tangled in a revenge plot against whoever did this. Someone will come forward and claim responsibility—it's only a matter of time. What else would be the point? Killing is power, but there's no point having power if no one else knows about it.

I shoot off a group text message to our councilors to gather all The Brotherhood and meet at Hazen's place. The full moon shines brightly against the dark, clear night sky. The sun has just set over the horizon; it took us all day to sort through the bodies and bury them.

Lucas pulls up behind us, and I step out of the car, expecting Freya to be with him, but he exits his car by himself.

"Where's Freya?" I ask, and Lucas slams his door shut, moving around the front.

"Gone back to the Hood after she was discharged." Lucas storms past me, and I grab his arm. He stops and whirls around, glaring at me.

"For fuck's sake, why'd you let her go back there?" I growl.

Lucas pulls free, scoffing. "You know better than I do that she does what she wants." He walks off toward Hazen's front steps and looks back over his shoulder. "And that dick-tard Kai came to get her. Apparently, he's her next of kin."

Lucas storms inside and my body shakes with anger. He *what?* Fuck me. That kid needs to die. He keeps pushing and pushing, and soon enough, he'll be gone. I can't have Freya in the middle of this fucking war. She needs to be on our side of the tracks and stay here—there's no going back and forth anymore. This is it. She's here or she's gone.

As much as it would fucking kill me, I'd let her go if it meant that she was safe, but fuck that. She'll never be safe in Daringhood with Kai. We can't protect her there, not like we can here. We can't protect her from them.

"I should have killed him when I had the chance," Hazen says, lighting up a blunt, and he passes it to me. The smoke hits the back of my throat and does fuck all to calm my racing heart.

Cars drive down Hazen's driveway, and members follow us inside Hazen's front door. We don't usually have full Brotherhood meetings at our houses, but after what happened, today is different. Our security is our top priority, and I won't be losing any more men if I can help it.

I follow Hazen inside, heading downstairs into the massive open den. There's not much in here yet; Hazen is still setting it up. A large pool table sits to the left, next to a kitchen, and a couple of couches. There's not nearly enough furniture to fill all the space. Lucas is already leaning back against the living area's wall, bringing a bottle of vodka to his lips, and for once, I'm not going to say anything. Hell, even I want a drink to numb everything that's happened today.

Each member comes through the set of double doors and finds their place, sitting on the couches or standing around the den. I stand next to Lucas and Hazen's next to me. He leans back against the pool table, gripping the edge, and I know he's blaming himself for this just as much as I am. We didn't light the bomb, but we organized a group of sitting fucking ducks.

We haven't talked much all day, and there's nothing we can say other than *what the fuck*. I have no idea how this meeting is going to go, but I'll do everything I can to reassure our brothers that we'll sort this out.

Now that we're leaders, everything comes back to us—this is our responsibility, and these men, like us, want answers.

The den's almost full. There should be over seven hundred members here, but with today's losses, there's less. Once this is settled, we need to start recruiting again and get in fresh blood. War is here, and we're going to be ready for it. Not like today. Our first official event as leaders, and look at how well it turned out. It's fucking embarrassing.

I clear my throat and the room goes quiet. "You all know why we are gathered here today—to talk about the events that unfolded at the town hall."

A couple of murmurs travel around the room, and one of the men steps forward—Damon.

"You could have warned us. Why lie?" More *yeahs* are thrown around the room, and I exhale heavily out of my nose.

Hazen scoffs. "If you honestly believe we are responsible for the events that unfolded yesterday, then leave now and run. You'll have twenty seconds before Lucas hunts you down and kills you."

I scan the room, and a couple of people shift uncomfortably, but no one leaves. They know better. Without the protection of The Brotherhood, they will spend the rest of their lives looking over their shoulders and end up dead. There's only one way to leave The Brotherhood, and that's with your life. When you join, you sign away every part of yourself. It's The Brotherhood or nothing. They know the risks, and they do it anyway because of how powerful it is to be part of our world, to be one of us.

"If not you, then who did it?" Brax yells out, standing between Zeke and Callan. One of the other soldiers has eyes on Dominic tonight so Brax could be here.

"Could have been rogue members of the Hood trying to pin something on us to gain extra support for war," Callan says, and a few murmurs go around the room. "They've been getting cocky lately—more break-ins, pushing the limits. Ever since one of their own started crossing the lines on the reg."

Freya. I clench my fists at the insinuation, but I don't make a move. If I'm going to lead us in some kind of war, I can't go around killing everyone who mentions my girl. *Don't let women make you weak.*

"We, like you, want to work out who did this. Who would have the guts to start a war against The Brotherhood?" I say, my voice bouncing off the walls.

"You know Dominic wouldn't have allowed this to happen under his command," Damon says, and before I can open my mouth to reply or punch him in the face, Hazen moves right up to him.

He grabs Damon by the throat, pulls out a knife, and rests it against his Adam's apple. Leaning forward, he rests his head against Damon's, and Damon's eyes go wide.

"Say it again," he growls, and Lucas chuckles next to me. I throw him a look, but he just shrugs, bringing the bottle to his lips once more.

We've spent our whole lives looking up to Dominic. He brought us into this world, training us to become the ultimate weapons. Part of me owes everything I know to Dominic, and the other part hates him for what he put us—and her—through.

I have no idea what Hazen's feeling now that Dominic is back and wants power over us all, but if it's anything like me, then he's battling a war inside of him that's going to end up either killing or saving us all. No matter what, I'll be by his side because that's what brothers do and what everyone here should do—not question us and our authority. Somewhere along the way, a couple of members have forgotten that, namely those who are loyal to Dominic and him only. With a new wave of leadership, it's clear they need a reminder of who's in charge around here.

Damon's body trembles under Hazen's grip. "Got it," he says, and Hazen stares at him for several long seconds before releasing him.

He scans the room. "In case you forgot how The Brotherhood works, let me give you a little reminder. Dominic is no longer in charge—we are. We have been initiated by our ancestors to lead our brothers into the depths of hell, to fight, control our town, and most of all"—he pauses, moving back to stand between Lucas and me—"to protect our brothers against all else!"

Cheers ring out through the room.

"We were attacked by our enemies. Someone from Daringhood dared to go against us, and they will pay!" I yell, and more excitement surrounds us. We haven't figured out who did this, but it has to be one of them. Kai might not have done this, but he's declared a war, so that's exactly what he's going to get.

"Now that's settled, I want to open up to any questions," I say, looking over our men.

A younger member in his mid-twenties raises his hand. "I'm worried about my family and what will happen now. Has war been declared? We have the guns and power, but people in Daringhood have nothing to lose. They will fight like madmen."

"Your family will be protected. We'll set up safe houses and do everything we can to ensure their safety," I say, meaning every word. Family is everything to me. I do whatever it takes to protect Amirah, just like my brothers and their loved ones.

"And, yes, war has been declared by people in Daringhood, and we don't take those threats lightly. Tax reductions and changes we were going to implement will be canceled." I scan the room full of my brothers, staring at each and every one of them. "We are ready to fight, to protect what's ours, and we will annihilate them!"

Cheers erupt, and a fire burns deeply in the pit of my stomach.

A battle is coming, and whoever gets in my way won't be breathing for long—but first, I need to get my girl back.

Then it's time.

Chapter 21

Freya

A couple of days have passed since the explosion, and I've hardly left the trailer. Mom's been by my side, feeding me and playing nurse with my burns. It's been weird as fuck. I can't even remember a time when she did this before. But I'm sick of staring at these four walls. If I have to spend another second here, I'm going to go crazy. I need to escape this trailer.

Gage and Hazen have been blowing up my phone. Hell, even Lucas has, telling me I need to get my ass over the tracks before they come and get me themselves. I've held them at bay, promising I'll see them soon, but I don't know how much more time they'll give me before they're knocking down my door.

I'm scared to take a step over the tracks, because if I do, Kai will think I've chosen them, and I can't lose him too. This whole situation is fucked. I'm certain Kai didn't blow up that town hall and neither did The Brotherhood. Someone targeted both sides, killing over one hundred people. Neither side will back down because they are equally stubborn.

Whoever planted that explosion intended to cause chaos, and they've succeeded. Battle lines have been drawn, and I'm smack-dab in the middle of it. Maybe I should set up a tent in the middle of the tracks and just stay there until this is sorted out. Then I won't be choosing anyone.

A loud wail, then a bang comes from the living room, and I kick the sheets off and roll out of bed. Grabbing my phone, I shove it into my pocket before ripping open my door. I run down the hallway and find Mom bent over the table, her fingers clawing through her short brown hair. Tears stream down her face and she screams. The high pitch bleeds through my ears.

I kneel in front of her, taking her hands in mine, but she won't look at me. My heart hammers against my chest.

"What's going on?" I ask, and more tears flow.

"They killed my friend," she wails.

"Who?"

"Jessie's gone!" she yells, ripping her hands out of mine.

I stumble backward from the force, landing on my ass.

"They did this!" she roars, before kicking the table. It flips over, banging into the wall.

I freeze, afraid if I make one wrong move, she'll snap even more. "You don't know that," I whisper, then her wide eyes are on me.

Fuck, I shouldn't have said anything. She glares at me with so much hatred, my hands begin to shake. I'm unsure of what she'll do next.

She releases a loud exhale through her teeth before she spins around, heading for the kitchen. I could run through the door and leave now, but I can't move. I'm paralyzed, my limbs unable to work.

She rips open a cupboard, and pots and pans fall onto the kitchen counter as she rummages for something inside.

My breathing picks up. She wouldn't. Not again. She's better now. She won't do this.

There's a sparkle in her eyes as she pulls out her dirty old black-and-white-checkered purse. My heart explodes into a million pieces. I can guess what's inside there.

"Mom, please don't," I beg, but she ignores me, her gaze set on the needle and drugs.

She turns her back on me, taking out the heroin from the purse, and as she starts heating it up, then transferring it to the needle, I don't move. I need to because as soon as that touches her veins, she'll be gone, and she'll never come back.

I swore that if she went back, then I'd be done. I can't keep doing this. I've spent the better half of my life hoping she'll pull through after she's stopped, that she won't go back. Time and time again, she does. She always chooses the needle over me, over Alec, over our family.

She plunges it into her veins before dropping the needle to the counter. Her body sags back against the bench, a smile touching her lips.

"Why?" I whisper, more to myself than her, but her gaze reaches mine.

The smile switches to an angry scowl. "You were never good enough for Dominic. I knew he hurt you and it's all your fault. Your brother getting killed, me developing a habit—that's all on you," she seethes, and the ground below me drops, swallowing me whole.

She keeps talking, but my ears start to ring, blocking her out. My mind's screaming at me to move, to get out of here before I do something I'll regret. But I can't. I'm frozen in place, sucked into the depths of hell, and I don't know how to leave.

My mother's words repeat in my mind over and over. She let Dominic touch me. She allowed him to do unspeakable things to me. All for what? So she could get her next hit? Bile rises in my throat, and I want all this to disappear. I want my brother here. I need him. He'd know what to do—he always did. He was my protector, my everything.

Movement catches my gaze, and my mother storms toward me. I start to stand, but my legs give way and I fall back down. Darkness claims me with its sharp claws. I don't want to be swallowed whole, but it consumes me. Red-hot pain pulls through my skull. *Just give in. Let her take you.* I surrender and let go, giving in to the voice inside my head. I'm done. This is it—she can do as she wishes. She can't take anything else from me now.

The one person I loved more than anything else is gone. It should have been me instead. A wave of relief pulses over me. I won't have to fight anymore. Everything will disappear and I'll finally be free. Something hard hits my cheek, and I tumble sideways, my head hitting the carpet. My ears ring like a violin.

A voice breaks through the storm, reaching for me. *Move, Frey, get out now. Save yourself. Run and never come back.*

I can't, I whisper back, and the voice gets louder, clearer.

I need you to move, Frey. Please. My brother's voice is clear in my mind, and I want to get up, but it's all too much. I have nowhere to go, nowhere to run. I'm better off just surrendering to my fate and letting her have me.

No. Move. Now. The voice is stronger, and I exhale loudly. I blink a couple of times, the room coming back into focus. The clouds clear. My mother releases my hair and stares down at me with her dull blue eyes as big as saucers. She's not in there anymore. She's gone, wasted on the drug, and I'm done trying to help her. I can't save her; she can only save herself.

As I push myself up, my head starts to spin and pain radiates through my cheek. Mom reaches for me again, but I shove her back and she falls on her ass. Her chest rises and falls rapidly under her thin shirt. Her eyes turn to slits, and she spits at my feet.

"I'm done. You've not only lost Alec, but now you've lost me too," I say, looking right through her.

Her face drops, and she shakes her head. "Good. Walk away, just like your father did all those years ago. He took one look at you and left. He couldn't stand the sight of you. Everything that's happened is because of you. I'm better off without you or anyone," she says as tears fall down her sunken cheeks. She's telling me to leave, but her eyes plead with me to stay. She's so lost, she doesn't even know what's right or wrong anymore.

It's the first time she's mentioned my father in years. We used to ask about him as kids, but she always shut us down and we learned to never mention him again. In her and our eyes, he never existed.

Without another word, I walk past my mother. She tries to reach for me, but I pull away and head for the door.

"No, Freya, don't go," she begs, and I shake my head, opening, then slamming the door behind me. The full moon casts light around the trailer park.

The door squeaks open, and Mom comes running toward me. "You don't get to fucking leave, Freya!" she yells, and I start running, putting one foot in front of the other, moving down the dirt track. Her footsteps follow me until they suddenly stop.

"Fuck you, you little bitch. Don't you ever come back!"

Her voice follows me, and a smile reaches my lips. She thinks that's a threat to me, not being able to come back here, but it's a relief. Her trailer never felt like home. Home isn't a place—it's about who you're with, who feels like home, and to me that was with Alec. He was my anchor, and even though heaven has him now, he'll always look out for me. He's looking down at me now with a big grin—I can feel it. I'm finally free from her grasp.

I stop running. My lungs heave, and it takes me a second to catch my breath. I keep moving out of the park and onto the road. I have nothing but the clothes on my back and my phone in my pocket, but that's okay. I'm safe and away from her. I don't need anything. I can start fresh and buy what I need. The only thing that matters is that I'm okay. I got out. The rest, I'll figure out.

I have no idea where I'm going, but anywhere is safer than with her. I glance up at the night sky. Twinkling stars stare back at me, and a sense of peace rests inside my heart.

"I love you, Alec," I whisper into the quiet, and I hear him whisper back.

I love you too, Frey.

Chapter 22

Freya

L oud hip-hop music surrounds me, blocking out my mother's words that keep repeating in my mind. I just want to forget about tonight—to move on, to leave her in the gutter. She doesn't deserve to take up space in my head. Never again.

Kai moves through the crowd and it parts. He carries a bag of frozen peas and passes them to me before he sits on the couch by my side. I take them, pressing the cool bag against my cheek.

I didn't realize I was seriously injured until I saw Kai and he lost his shit. He was a second away from storming into her trailer and killing her himself. I told him she wasn't worth it, that she's better off alive, living with the consequences of her actions. Ending it is doing her a favor, and she's well and truly out of favors.

Zion and Bear sit on the opposite couch. Bear flicks his lighter on and off, staring blankly at the wall behind me, as if he's stuck in his own thoughts. Zion shuffles a deck of cards and deals them out on the table between us.

"You're staying here tonight," Kai says, and I sigh, not wanting to argue with him. I'll stay with him tonight, but then tomorrow, I need to see the guys. My phone's been going off, and it won't be long before they come looking over the tracks, and with all the shit that's gone down, that will only spell trouble.

Zion's phone rings, and he answers, putting it on speaker. "Kai's here."

"We've got a contact ready for those guns. I'll send it over," the voice on the other line says, and I glance from the phone back to Kai, frowning. He nods and Zion takes it off speaker, then walks away, talking quietly.

Kai grabs a cigarette from a packet on the table, placing it between his lips. What the fuck is he playing at?

"I know there's going to be a war—but really? You're going to lead it?"

"We are." Kai shoots a glance at Bear, then Zion, who comes back into the room, carrying a beer. "And all we're doing is trying to get a better life for all of us."

"This is just going to end in more bloodshed, please—"

He cuts me off. "I'll give you tonight to rest, but tomorrow you've gotta choose whose side you're on. There's no more coming and going, Frey. You're either with us or them. You're my family, Frey. I care about you, and I want you out of this. Preferably out of Daring altogether," he says, staring at me, his eyes softening slightly, begging me to choose him.

Even if I go see the guys, it doesn't mean I'm picking them over Kai. He's been in my life since we walked over the tracks with just the clothes on our backs. I met him at the trailer park; he helped Alec and me settle in, and we've been best friends ever since. He's like a brother to me, and with Alec now gone, I need him more than ever. But Hazen, Gage, and Lucas have stolen my heart right out of my chest and claimed it for themselves.

The way I feel when I'm with them, protected and loved—it's confusing. They didn't save me when Dominic forced us out all those years ago. They broke my heart then, and now they've wormed their way back in. How did they tear down all the barriers I'd put in place? How did I let that happen?

If you asked me months ago which side I'd choose, I wouldn't hesitate to stay here with Kai, but now everything is different. I've fallen for the enemy, and I can't switch that off. I need them and they need me.

"That's not fair, and you know it," I huff, and Kai picks up his cards, then hands me mine.

I fall back into the couch, pushing the frozen peas against my eye. I'm fucked if I do and fucked if I don't. Maybe setting up that tent on the tracks isn't such a bad idea. That way, I'm not picking anyone. Create my own little town, Daring-Frey-town. That's sounding like the winner in this situation. I'll even make a flag and claim my area.

"I can't protect you if you're with them."

"I don't need to be protected, and I can't choose."

Silence follows my statement, and I cling to my cards, letting the frozen peas fall to the ground. My cheek feels swollen and cool. Kai passes me a cup filled with box red wine, and I take it from him, swallowing down the burned grapes.

"Let's get fucked up. That's tomorrow's problem," Kai says, and the corner of my mouth lifts.

Now, that's the best thing he's said all night. Tonight, I'm going to let go and forget about all this shit.

I reach out, landing my hands on the couch, and push myself up. My legs wobble and my head spins. The room sways like I'm on a boat and the wine threatens to spill from my lips. *Fuck me dead.*

Bear and Zion are talking to each other in low whispers, while Kai is passed out on the couch beside me. We've been playing cards all night, and I'm way too drunk.

My shin smashes against the table between us. Pain shoots up my leg, and I curse.

Bear snorts. "There's a table there, kid. Can't you see?"

"Fuck off," I growl, then chuckle under my breath.

I manage to walk around the table and toward the door. I need some fresh air before I throw up. Kai's trailer is in a hell of a mess. Bottles line every surface, and the smell of smoke tickles my nose. *Fucking gross.*

After taking my phone from my leggings, I find a text from the private number. My stomach drops. When is my stalker freak going to give up?

Unknown: If you think your boys miss you, you're dead wrong. Stay where you belong.

I squeeze my eyes shut and push my phone into my pocket. Fuck them. They don't know shit.

Walking outside, I pull the door closed behind me, and the crisp morning air kisses my swollen cheek. The sun rises over the horizon, casting the sky in a yellow-and-orange hue. It's beautiful.

I stand there for several seconds, or minutes, mesmerized by the sky before I have to pee. Not wanting to go back inside, I move around the trailer to the back. There's a couple of trees back here, and I lean against one, pulling my leggings down. Once I'm finished, I stand and pull them back over my ass.

A twig snaps, followed by the distinct sound of footsteps, and the hairs on the back of my neck stand on end. Fuck, I'm too drunk to deal with anyone. I peek around the tree, looking for whoever's here, but I find no one. The trailer park is quiet, apart from the low birdcalls overhead.

My shoulders relax slightly and then there's a shift in the air. I whirl around, but I'm too late. Hands wrap around my waist and a bag falls over my head. I scream, but it's muffled by the bag. The air around me closes in.

I kick and throw my arms out, hitting someone behind me. They groan but don't let go. The arms around my stomach tighten, and I'm shoved forward. My legs give out, and I fall face-first to the ground. I land with a heavy thud and everything disappears.

Chapter 23

Hazen

Freya's head rests in my lap, her soft snores filling Gage's car. I gently brush my fingers over her swollen cheek, anger coursing through me. Who the fuck did this to her? I'm going to find out and kill that motherfucker.

It wasn't my idea to throw a bag over her head and kidnap her, but here we are, driving through the streets of Daringhood, avoiding any of the major roads and trying to get back over the tracks. It was a risk coming here without more members of our Brotherhood to protect us if shit went south, but Freya wasn't answering any of our calls and we were worried. The piece-of-shit car we borrowed blends in with the streets, so no one recognizes us. Thank fuck.

When she finally wakes up, well, it won't be pretty. I'll take her anger and anything else she throws at us, and I'd do it all over again to ensure she's by our side. Protected. I didn't protect her back when we were kids, and that's my biggest regret. I won't ever make that mistake again.

Lucas looks over his shoulder, staring at Freya with his eyebrows drawn together, then his lip pulls back in a half smile. It's gone just as quickly before he turns back around and grabs his bottle of vodka.

He's still hurting—that much is evident. After the bombing, when he went with Freya to the hospital, I thought they sorted their shit out, but apparently not. He's still drinking recklessly and hardly talks to us. I hate to admit it, and I wouldn't get caught telling him this, but I miss his smart-ass remarks and playfulness. It's weird seeing him like this.

"Think *now* you'll sort things out with her?" I ask, and Lucas freezes with the bottle halfway to his mouth. All I hear are the soft snores coming from Freya in the quiet that follows.

"If you know what's good for you, you'll drop it," Lucas mumbles, and I roll my eyes.

"Not when it affects all of us. We're in this relationship together, and we need to know where you stand."

Lucas lets out a loud exhale before bringing the bottle back to his lips.

Gage stays silent in the front seat as we make our way over the tracks. My shoulders drop just as our back wheels roll over the final track. Home in our own territory. Safe. At least for now.

"I'm not fucking dating you or Gage, unless you want me to stick my dick in your ass?" He pulls down his visor and waggles his eyebrows.

I laugh, then shake my head. Finally, some of the old Lucas coming out to play.

"I'm not having your limp dick anywhere near me, thank you very much."

Lucas chuckles. "Yeah, you wouldn't be able to handle the sheer size of it."

I open my mouth to reply, but Freya stirs in my lap before her eyes fly open. She sits up quickly, smacking me in the nose with her fist. Pain splinters through my head and blood drips down onto my lip. She glances frantically around the car, her gaze snapping to mine. Her eyes are wild with rage.

"What the actual fuck?!" she spits out, balling her fists.

I raise my hands in surrender. "Not my idea," I say, pointing toward Lucas.

She shuffles forward on the back seat and reaches around the passenger seat to grip Lucas's throat. A wicked smirk plays on his lips through the visor's mirror. My cock hardens against my briefs, watching her take control of this situation. Fuck, this girl is my everything.

Though I have no idea how I got so lucky as to claim her heart, I hope I never lose her. I don't think I'm worthy of her or her heart, but fuck do I need it. Fuck do I need *her*. She's not pure. She's broken, just like me. Like all of us.

"You like to kidnap innocent, vulnerable women while they're pissing in the woods?" Freya leans between the two front seats, her face right next to Lucas's.

He doesn't move, still facing forward. "You aren't vulnerable or innocent," he challenges, and Freya releases a heavy sigh.

"When will you forgive me?" Her voice breaks a little, and it takes everything in me not to say something, to yell at Lucas. But this isn't my battle. This is between them. Only they can sort this shit out.

Lucas bites into his bottom lip. His eyes drop, and Freya releases his throat but doesn't lean back. She's stuck between the two seats. Gage eases us into my driveway and pulls the car to a stop.

"We've talked about this before, Freya. I love you, but my heart is still broken into a million sharp pieces, and I don't know when I'll be ready to let you back in fully. Just give me time, please?"

The silence of the car rings in my ears.

Freya presses a soft kiss against Lucas's cheek. "I'll wait for you," she whispers, and Lucas smiles before reaching for the door handle and exiting, heading toward the front door.

Freya falls back into the seat next to me, and I wrap my arm over her shoulder, pressing a kiss into her hair. "Who hurt you?" I ask, running my thumb over her swollen cheek.

"My mom." She sighs, and it takes everything in me not to drive back over the tracks and deal with her mother. Freya needs me, but I hope that woman gets what's coming. I don't want Freya anywhere near her anymore.

Gage gets out, and we follow him into the cool night. I pull Freya closer to me and she snuggles into my chest. We make our way inside my house, up the stairs, and into her new bedroom.

I switch on the light and Freya slowly steps inside.

"Wow," she whispers, her gaze scanning the room, from her large bed to the custom-made artwork of the cliff she loves jumping off.

"You did this for me?"

"Of course. I promised that I'd create a space just for you to escape to," I say.

Freya turns to me, her eyes glassy. "Thank you."

She wraps her arms around my waist and rests her head on my chest. I hold her, bringing my lips to the top of her head. She deserves so much more than this, but it's a start.

Gage falls backward onto her neatly made king bed with a heavy sigh, and Lucas shuts the bathroom door behind him with a soft click.

We stop at the end of her bed, and Gage leans back on his elbows, watching Freya with hooded eyes.

"You're wearing too many clothes," Gage says. "Don't you think, brother?" He raises an eyebrow at me, and I nod, brushing my fingers along Freya's stomach.

"Speak for yourself," Freya says, and Gage chuckles.

He moves forward, lifting his shirt over his head, followed by his pants and underwear that fall at his feet. Freya's breath catches.

My fingers move under her top and lift it higher and higher, then over her head. Goose bumps scatter on her stomach as I move my fingers along the waistband of her leggings. They hug her legs like a glove, showing off every curve, but those legs look even better when it's just her milky skin. They need to come off. I pull them over her tight ass and down her thighs, followed by her lacy underwear.

The bed dips, and Gage pushes back until he's leaning back against the pillows. His hand wraps around his cock as he watches Freya closely. His other hand rests behind his neck.

I slap Freya's ass, and she bends over, her hands gripping the dark-blue duvet cover, her ass pushing back against my throbbing cock.

After reaching for her bra, I unclasp it, and her tits fall free. As I run my finger over her hard nipple, a soft moan falls from her lips. I pinch and her head arches back slightly.

"Touch yourself, Freya. Show us what you need," Gage says, and my heart thuds at the prospect.

"Like this," she says, her hand running down her chest slowly.

I move around her, taking off my clothes as I go. I want to watch her. I need to see her come apart.

"Tell us what you're doing. Paint the picture for us," I say, my cock hard and ready in my palm.

"My clit begs to be touched, sucked," she says, her voice husky. She runs two fingers between her folds, her gaze moving between Gage and me. "I'm wet, so drenched. My fingers slide effortlessly—"

The bathroom door opens, and Freya stops speaking but doesn't stop moving her fingers against her clit. Lucas stares at Freya, a mixture of lust and betrayal evident in his gaze. Water from the shower clings to his chest, a towel wrapped low on his waist.

"Don't stop on my account. Keep going with those dirty words," he says, moving toward the armchair in the corner of the room, dropping his towel along the way.

Freya's cheeks turn a light shade of pink. She clears her throat, moving her attention back to Gage. "Where was I?" she asks, biting into her lower lip.

"You were saying how effortlessly your fingers are gliding through your folds," Gage encourages her, and she cocks her head to the side.

She moves forward, one hand propped on the edge of the bed. Her index finger rubs against her clit, and it takes everything in me not to go to her, to help her. To finish her off. No, she's clearly capable of this. A bead of precum pearls at the tip of my cock, and I rub it off and down my shaft.

"That's right, my clit is begging me to rub harder." She inhales deeply. "Faster." Her fingers match her words.

"How does it feel?" I ask.

She looks over at me, her eyes a wild, bright blue. Licking her deep-cherry lips, she murmurs, "Electrifying. *Fuck*." She jolts forward, her fingers tightening around the fabric. I keep up with her pace, imagining her tight cunt wrapped around my cock. *Fuck* is right.

"Let go. Give in," Gage encourages, and her pace increases until her loud cries fill the bedroom. I follow right behind her, my cum shooting onto the brand-new bedding.

Before she has a chance to relax, I'm up, moving behind her. A wild energy takes over my body, and I want to control her. To fuck her without her approval. To take her cunt, because that's who I am.

My fingers tangle in her hair. I forcefully push her head into the bed, and she lets out a loud shriek. I muffle it by pushing her farther into the fabric.

Her ass rises, rubbing against my ready, throbbing cock that's still rock hard after coming. I slam into her, and she jolts forward.

"Bro—" Lucas tries to say something, but I block him out, slamming my eyes shut as I pound into her, fast and rough. My other hand grips her hip, my short nails digging into her skin.

Her warm cunt wraps around my cock like a second skin. She's addictive, and *fuck*, she feels so good. I want to die inside her, for her cunt to strangle my cock. I'd leave this world a happy man.

I continue fucking her hard until my cum explodes in her sweet pussy. Pulling out, I release my grip on her. The rest of the room comes back into focus after I've sated my need to feel her, to fill her.

I stumble backward, my heart racing so fast it starts to ring between my ears.

Freya turns around slowly, her cheeks red and her hair a tangled mess.

"Fuck, I'm so sorry. I—" I stop as I catch blood running down her hip. She follows my gaze and moves closer to me, but I shake my head, retreating until my back hits the wall.

I'm a monster. How am I this fucked up, hurting her for pleasure? Is this who I am?

Freya hugs me, and I squeeze my eyes shut, unable to look at her. She doesn't deserve the likes of me.

"Shh, look at me," she begs, her finger running along my jaw.

My chest rises and falls against hers, but I refuse to open my eyes. I can't. Because then she'll see me for who I truly am. One fucked-up animal, who preys on broken toys. Who chews them up, then spits them out once I'm done, leaving them panting, bleeding, and messed up. Fuck. I'm just like him.

Freya's hands wrap around my torso, her head resting on my raging heart. My hands ball at my sides, and I want to push her away. To flee and never come back. But I can't move. I can't walk away. I'm stuck, and I fucking hate myself for it.

"I wanted that, and I want you," she whispers, and my damaged soul clings on to each word.

"But I'm broken, fucked up," I say.

She peers at me with her stormy-blue eyes. "Who isn't? I'm the same," she whispers.

"We all are," Lucas says from the corner of the room, but I can't look away from her, afraid that if I do, then she'll be gone.

"That's why we fit together," Gage says.

"Till death do us part," I whisper, and Freya's lips claim mine. Her salty tears are a reminder of what I've got to live for.

She loves me for who I am, and I'll spend every day wondering how my broken soul got so lucky.

Chapter 24

Lucas

The boat comes to a stop, and the workers move down the large dock, securing ropes and pulling out the bridge. They start removing crate after crate full of products, from guns to drugs, that will no doubt destroy families and fuck up people's minds. I should feel bad about it, but I'd rather they get pure shit from us rather than cutters from some low-life scum. At least we know our shit is the purest you're going to get on the streets of Daringhood, but after it's out of our hands, who the fuck knows what those lower drug dealers do with it? Frankly, it's not our problem.

I mean, look what it did to Freya's mother. She hasn't talked directly to me about it yet, but fuck, her mother is a wreck. I shouldn't even call her a mother, because she's not. She's been chasing that high her whole life. She put drugs before her own kids—that much is evident—and it's the reason they got kicked out of Daringville in the first place. At least my mom actually gave a fuck about me, even if it was for her own personal gain. She always made sure we were taken care of. Now that she's gone, I've got to keep my shit together for my sister. I'm all she has. I'm her role model, and that's fucked up. Thank God she's got her nanny looking after her.

I slide my sunglasses over my eyes, pulling the cap farther over my head. I shouldn't be here without telling my brothers, but fuck it. I need answers about the explosion, and we aren't getting any with our dicks in our hands or in Freya. We've sent Zeke, Brax, and Callan in to check the docks, but they haven't given us anything useful, and whoever set that bomb would have had to get it from somewhere—and nothing comes in or out of Daring without going through the docks.

Watching Freya touch herself the other night and get herself off was like watching my own private porn show. The way she worked her fingers over her clit until she made herself come? Jesus. It took everything in me not to move from that seat in the corner of the room and have my way with her. I wanted to keep my distance from her, to not let her in too deep. To take things slow. But watching her come apart . . . fuck, it was hard not to intervene. To stay put with my hand around my own cock, imaging her lips around it. My dick twitches, but it's not the time or place. I've got work to do, and I can't afford to be distracted by her.

It's time to find out who the fuck has big enough balls to blow up the town hall and get away with it.

I push open my door and step out of the car I borrowed from one of our maids, shutting it quietly behind me. Duke, one of our soldiers, watches me closely before glancing back at the crates and writing something down on his clipboard. I hope the ball cap and glasses are enough to fool him into thinking that it's not me, that I'm just a regular member of the Ville. If I'm someone else, I might get more answers—get the crew to talk and find out if they know anything other than what they've told us. I need the gossip because I know for a fact that these men gossip more than some women. If they have heard anything, I'll get it out of them.

Shoving my hands into the pockets of my reflective jacket, I stroll over and stand next to Duke, and he nods in greeting.

"Big shipment?" I ask, and he grunts. "Hey. I heard your boss has been starting trouble in the Ville."

Duke stops writing, flipping the pages of his clipboard closed. "What? You got the wrong end of the stick." He glares at me, then glances around us, but there's no one close. "I'd be looking a little closer to home if I were you." He steps back, pulls out a cigarette from his pocket, and lights it up.

"What's that supposed to mean?" I ask, crossing my arms over my chest. If he thinks we've got something to do with this, I won't hesitate to pull out my Glock from my pants and kill this fuck head.

He raises his hands in surrender. "I know The Brotherhood didn't do it, but I'd be watching—"

Someone yells out from the ship. "Get over here now, Duke!"

Duke takes one last drag from his smoke before putting it out under his boot. "Look, Lucas, I know it's you under those glasses and hat. That shit doesn't fool me. All I'll say is, look closer to home. That's all I know," he says, before walking off toward the ship.

I turn away, with his words playing around in my head. What the fuck does he mean? I know for a fact that my brothers had nothing to do with this, but who else is in our inner circle that would go behind our backs and kill all those people? Possibly one of the councilmen who was unhappy with the proposed changes. Could it have been Samson? But would they really want war, though?

I head along one of the piers, where there's a large shipped docked, and one of the workers drives a forklift off the ship with an empty case.

What the fuck? I move closer, standing in front of him on the jetty. He stops, his eyes widening when I take off my hat and glasses.

"Shit. Sorry, Lucas," he mutters. I haven't seen him around before.

"What's this about?" I ask, waving to the empty crate.

"It's empty. The last few weapons shipments have been short."

Fucking hell, we need to sort this shit out. We can't be losing stock. This isn't good for business. I step out of his way, and movement near one of the rows of shipping containers catches my eye. A shadow rushes into a container before I have a chance to see who it is.

I hurry in that direction, bringing my gun out of my pants, the cool metal resting against my sweaty palm. I come to a stop outside the large shipping container door. It's open, but as I look inside, rows and rows of crates stare back at me.

Moving inside, I hide behind one of the crates and listen. "Come out and play, dead little birdie. This cat is hungry!" I yell into the dark space.

Feet slap against the concrete floor. I peek around the crate and catch sight of a familiar mop of chestnut-brown hair.

What the fuck is she doing here?

Chapter 25

Freya

My heart thumps so loudly I can't hear anything else. I can feel him near, closing in on me. I shouldn't have followed him here, but I didn't have anything else to do. I've been bored shitless the last couple of days, moping around Hazen's mansion. Although my new bedroom feels like a safe haven, even those four walls have started closing in.

Kai's been dodging my messages, and I'm pissed off. If he thinks I've chosen them over him, he's a dickhead. I didn't choose to get kidnapped and taken away from him, but he won't see it that way. I did text him and tell him that, but he's not interested—probably thinks it's an excuse.

Amirah's been preoccupied doing God knows what, so I've been left to my own devices. I spent the first day here online shopping on Hazen's credit card, restocking my wardrobe and getting my skincare essentials. There are only so many places to explore in Hazen's house, since the boys won't let me leave without their approval. That's resulted in more than one argument; they know better than to keep me locked up.

I needed to do something, and when Lucas left, I didn't hesitate to follow him.

My back presses against one of the crates. I don't move a muscle, afraid I'll give away my location. This is what I've been craving—that sensation of my heart exploding out of my chest. The danger of getting caught at any moment. In some fucked-up way, it helps me feel free. It makes me feel alive. Having nothing to do drives me crazy. All the thoughts become too loud, too much. They are silent when I'm on the edge of a cliff, ready to jump, or in a dangerous position like this.

I open my mouth and let out a low, bird-like whistle before moving around the crate with a playful smile on my lips. Lucas said this cat is hungry, and I'll play the helpless little birdie for him. I want to get caught; I want to be punished.

A faint exhale is so close, I shuffle nearer to the edge of the crate and peer around it. Hands wrap around my waist, and I scream. A palm covers my mouth from behind, and I bite down hard into his finger. He curses, shoving me away, and my back hits the crate hard. Pain bites into my skin.

My gaze clashes with Lucas's angry light-brown eyes. "Naughty little birdie, what am I going to do with you?"

I bite into my lower lip. "Punish me?" I ask, but it's more of a beg.

His eyes shift to a darker brown. "You'd like that, wouldn't you?" He steps forward, closing in on me. The air around us shifts, the coolness turning warm. Hot. My skin burns, itching to be touched by him.

He hasn't touched me since before that night, and I want him. I crave him. *Please touch me.*

"What the fuck are you doing here?" he growls, his eyes narrowing.

"Following you because I've got nothing better to do with my time." I shrug and he releases a heavy breath.

"Why is it impossible to stay mad at you?" he asks, like I have the answer.

I don't, but I know what I want, and if he doesn't give it to me, then I'll take it—without his permission.

"Why can't I just walk away?" he whispers, perhaps more to himself than me.

I answer anyway. "Because you know as well as I do that our souls are connected. Drawn together like fire to wood, and no matter how far you try to run, the flame always follows."

I want to run the other way, to put distance between us, but I can't. No matter what I do, I'm always drawn back to him. To them.

As Lucas runs a finger along my jaw, he stares at me, his brown eyes glistening over. He's fighting an internal battle; it's evident in those eyes.

"I hate that I love you," he whispers, and my mouth becomes dry.

I stare at him, waiting for him to take it back—to say that he lied, that he doesn't love me. The one person who truly loved me is now dead. I want to yell and scream, to tell him that he can't. I'm too broken. But the words clog in my throat.

I lower my gaze, staring at the ground. I killed his mother, took away his family. How could he possibly tell me he still loves me?

"You can't," I whisper, and Lucas tucks my hair behind my ear.

"Look at me," he demands, but I don't.

He lifts my chin up until I'm peering back into his soulful gaze. My eyes blur. He presses his forehead against mine. His lips are so close to me, his minty breath clinging to the air around us.

"If I give my heart to you, you'd better fucking claim it, or I'll rip open your chest and shove it right next to yours. Got it, thorn?"

"What if mine is too broken—lost, damaged, and unable to love?" I ask, licking my dry lips. He looks down, following the movement before groaning.

"You think mine isn't?" He scoffs. "That's why we all fit together. Four broken hearts coming together as one fucked-up, jagged heart."

The corner of my mouth lifts, and he softly kisses my lips. I push his hat off, and it falls to the ground.

"There's still so much I don't know about you, and I'll spend the rest of my goddamn life discovering every single thing. Hating and loving you until you take your very last breath," he says, and my damaged heart beats so loud.

"I love you," I whisper, and before I can take my next breath, his lips are on mine.

His hand wraps gently around my throat, his tongue forcefully claiming my mouth. I grip his blond hair, pulling him closer. His body molds to my every curve, but it's not enough. The clothes between us need to go. I want his skin touching mine.

I place my hand on his chest, and Lucas steps back, his breathing heavy. Voices from outside the shipping container echo around us, and they're close. Too close. Fuck, what if they walk in? Actually, who the fuck cares? I want him.

"Take off your clothes," I say in a husky voice.

The corner of his mouth turns up, and he lifts off his safety jacket, followed by his black T-shirt, dropping them between us. The hard ridges of his chest trail down to a perfectly lined V, but then it stops, his stupid pants covering his most prized possession.

He follows my gaze. "Tell me what you want, thorn," Lucas says before biting into his bottom lip.

"Take off your pants."

"You first," he says, raising his eyebrow.

Oh, so we're going to play this game. I unbutton my jeans, pausing on the zipper. Lucas watches me intently, his thumb brushing over his bottom lip. I slowly pull down the zipper, pushing my jeans over my legs, along with my lacy underwear. The cool air sends shivers across my skin.

"You next," I say, pointing to his pants.

He doesn't take his eyes off mine as he pulls them off and they pool at his feet. He steps forward, his fingers disappearing under my top as he traces along my belly. My stomach fills with butterflies.

"Arms up," he says, and I obey.

He pulls my top off, then throws it behind us. He grips the back of my neck and claims my mouth in a hot, all-consuming kiss. Sliding his fingers down my back, he unclasps my bra, releasing my tits from their lacy confines. As he flicks his thumb over my nipple, I groan into his mouth, my legs squeezing together.

He rests his head on mine. "Down on your knees. I want your lips around my cock." His voice comes out all gravelly, and without a second thought, I step away from the crate and sink to my knees.

The concrete bites into my skin, but I ignore it, peering up at Lucas. "What if someone comes in?"

Lucas chuckles, his fingers tangling in my hair as he urges me forward. "Let them watch."

I take the head of his cock into my mouth slowly, flicking my tongue around it before swallowing him whole. A deep groan falls from his lips and my hand grips onto his ass.

"Fucking hell, thorn. Watching you on your knees for me, sucking my cock like a damn queen . . . Jesus. It's taking everything in me not to come down your throat already." He closes his eyes, and I slap my hand hard on his ass. When his eyes fly open, he smiles.

His cock hits the back of my throat, and I breathe through my nose. My other hand fiddles with his balls, rolling the soft skin around. Lucas pushes my head back and forth several times with more speed, then he yanks on my hair. His cock pops out of my mouth and his warm cum shoots against my chest.

"Beautiful," he breathes, staring at the cum running over my tits.

He offers his hand, and I take it, standing back up. Before I can catch my breath, he spins me around and pushes me forward onto the crate. My cheek rests against the plastic covering the crate's contents, and my ass is bare for him. He runs his cock between my folds and my core clenches, wanting him inside me.

Brushing my hair over my shoulder, he leans down and bites my neck. "Hold on," he says, then slams into me without any warmup.

I jolt forward on top of the crate, my fingers gripping on to the plastic wrap covering God knows what. His cock fills every inch of me. It takes me a second to adjust before my pussy loosens around him.

"Rub your clit," he says, wrapping his hand over mine and pushing it between my legs.

My fingers rub against my nub, the friction almost too much but not enough at the same time. He encourages me to go harder, faster, with his hand still in charge. He wraps my hair around his other fist, pulling back slightly. Pain bites into my skull, and it feels so fucking good.

Lucas slams into me over and over, until I'm so close to coming apart. My heart races, and just as I'm about to release, Lucas pulls my hand, and his cock, away. I groan, and he pulls me back by my hair and spins me around so I'm facing him. His cheeks are tinged with a rosy red, and his chest rises and falls in sync with my own.

"I want to see you come apart for me," he says, lifting me up by the ass.

My legs wrap around his waist before he slowly fills me inch by inch, his light-brown eyes never leaving mine. Tears pool in my eyes, threatening to fall. He holds me in place with his hands on my ass.

"Let go, Freya, and soak my cock. I want to feel you dripping down my balls," he whispers, placing his head against mine, and I moan.

He claims my mouth in a sweet, tender kiss. I drop every wall inside, just for this moment, so I can savor every taste and emotion. Because tomorrow is never promised, and today, right here, I'm complete.

The only things missing are Hazen and Gage.

Chapter 26

Hazen

I grip the spatula, watching as the pancake batter bubbles, waiting for the perfect moment to flip it. Cooking has never been something I've enjoyed doing, because I've never had to. We always had a cook that made every meal and did the grocery shopping because, according to my father, that's peasant work.

We didn't have time to waste doing chores; we paid for help and ruled our empire, alongside our brothers. But here I am, making breakfast for Freya. Flour lines every surface of my kitchen, and it's driving me insane. It needs to be sparkling clean again, but I can't leave these pancakes or they'll burn.

"Smells good," Freya says, coming into the kitchen. I glance over my shoulder and pull my bottom lip between my teeth. She's wearing tight workout shorts and a crop top. A bead of sweat runs down the side of her face as she grabs a bottle of water from the fridge and brings it to her lips. Fuck me, she's beautiful.

She comes up behind me, wrapping her arms around my stomach, resting her head against my back. My stomach muscles seize up, and I freeze, fighting the urge to step away from her, not wanting her to be so close to me. I'm not good enough for her; she's too pure. I'm like poison, infecting her.

She's impossible to keep away from, though. When she's gone, I want her back. But then when she's close again, I want to push her away. It's fucking with my head. My father has caused her so much pain. Does she see him when she looks at me? Do I remind her of him? That's my worst fucking fear.

Freya releases her grip and moves backward. As soon as her warm embrace is gone, I miss her.

She hoists herself up onto the island and watches me closely. "You okay?"

My shoulders tense. "Yeah, I'm fine. Just stressed with all The Brotherhood recruiting and picking up the pieces from the explosion," I reply. It's not the whole truth, but it's something.

Once the pancakes are finished cooking, I place them all on the plate and bring them to the island, next to the array of sauces. I'm not sure what Freya likes, so I got everything out.

"Kai didn't do it," Freya says, turning around on the counter to face me.

"I don't want you getting in the middle of this," I say, taking a couple of pancakes and putting them on a plate for her.

She scoffs. "Too late for that once you kidnapped me and took me against my will. Now Kai won't even talk to me—thinks I've chosen you guys."

"Probably a good thing. At least I know you're safe when you're here with us. Under my roof."

Freya rolls her eyes as she squeezes some maple syrup onto her pancakes. "You know I can take care of myself, and just because I'm here doesn't mean I've chosen a side. Kai is my best friend, and I won't be playing against him."

The front door opens and slams shut.

My father walks into the kitchen, and Freya stops with her fork halfway to her mouth. I move forward, stepping in front of the island, between her and him.

Brax runs into the room, looking from Dominic to me. "Fuck, sorry, he got away from me."

I shake my head, dismissing him with a wave of my hand. "What the fuck are you doing here?" I snap, and my father smirks.

"What, no 'Hey, Dad, glad you're alive and well'?" He looks past me to Freya, his eyes lingering a little too long. "Hello, Freya," he says, and she just stares right through him.

Anger boils inside me. I cross my arms over my chest. "I'll ask one last time—what are you doing here?"

He looks around the room, then comes back to me. "Nice place you've got here, son. Such a pity you moved out of the old family house. We could have done amazing things together under my roof."

He watches Freya closely, and it takes everything in me not to punch that smug look off his mouth.

"You've got ten seconds to tell me why you're here before I kick you out," I say, and he finally looks back at me.

He glances between me and Freya. "Let's talk somewhere a little more private, without prying ears."

"Anything you have to say can be said in front of her."

Dominic shakes his head. "Have I taught you nothing? What, a couple of weeks without me, and you're ruining everything? I won't have it," he snaps, before turning and leaving the kitchen, moving into the hallway.

I follow him out but pause, glancing back at Freya. She motions for me to leave.

"I've got some shit to do with Amirah. I'll see you later," she says, continuing to eat her breakfast.

I'm sorry, I mouth, but she shakes her head. Dominic has no respect for women whatsoever. It's surprising that I even know how to talk to a female, let alone date one, after being raised by this asshole.

I pull out my phone and hit dial on Gage's profile, and he answers after two rings. "Yeah?"

"Dominic is here. Meet us in my office."

I hang up before he can say another word. Last time I saw him, he was working out with Freya and Lucas in our home gym. Gage and Lucas practically live here now that Freya is back. It's nice having my family all under one roof—my found family, not my blood.

Dominic's waiting in the hallway, leaning back against the wall with his phone in his grip. I don't bother acknowledging him as I walk past and head down the hall to my office. I scan my phone against the keypad, the door beeps, and I push it open. Dominic follows, his gaze moving around my office a little too intently for my liking.

It's funny how things changed as soon as I was out from under his thumb. Although I thought the control he used to have over me had faded, being back in his presence is jarring. I can't deny that a small, niggling part of me wants his approval, for him to tell me I'm doing a good job, which pisses me off—I don't want him to have that control over me. Yet here we are, in my office, and I'm waiting for it.

I move around my wooden desk and take a seat, motioning for him to sit in one of the chairs.

A smile forms on his lips. "Well, this is very different to how I'm used to carrying out meetings, isn't it?" He takes a seat just as the door beeps and opens.

Gage comes in, with Lucas behind him. Lucas is throwing on a shirt, his hair damp. They watch Dominic closely. Gage sits down next to him but doesn't greet him. Lucas leans back against the wall opposite my dad.

"What do you want?" I ask, ignoring his comment from before. He's trying to unravel me, but I won't fall for his games. I won't let him see how much he affects me. Weakness gets you killed in our world, and he's not in charge anymore—we are.

"I'm so proud of you, son," he says, running his thumb along his jaw.

Heat burns deep under my skin, rising to my cheeks, and my fingers ball into fists in my lap.

"Clock is ticking. You've got one minute before you're gone," I say, and he sits up straighter, his smile replaced with a sinister purse of his lips.

"I am proud. You must feel so bad about what happened, but you've done all that you can, haven't you, son?" He licks his lips. He's taunting me, and fuck, I want to punch that smug look off his face.

"Say what you really want to. I'm not playing your games," I bite out.

"Fine. You've had your fun, but you are too young, too inexperienced to run The Brotherhood. Look at the chaos you've already caused since taking the reins."

I take several deep breaths, trying to calm my racing heart. How fucking dare he come into my house and speak to me, us, like that?

Lucas lifts his gun from its holster, holding it with a playful grin. I watch him carefully, shaking my head. He can't kill him—at least, not yet.

"Is that all you've got to say?" Gage asks, and Dominic shakes his head, looking between Lucas and me.

"I haven't even started yet. How many years did I rule, and in that time, did we ever have this kind of attack against us?"

I shake my head, lowering my gaze to my hands in my lap. Technically, I know what he's saying is true. I mean, when he was in charge, this never happened. We didn't cause this, but fuck do we take responsibility for it.

"We're working on it," Gage says, speaking up for me. My words are lost deep inside me and I'm finding it hard to speak. This is what he wants. The guilt is too much to bear.

"You know as well as I do that the Hood did this to us," Dominic says, anger lacing his voice. "They sacrificed their own. They are trying to create a divide between us, but I won't allow this when I'm in charge."

I rise quickly from my chair, and it hits the back wall with a thud.

"What the fuck did you just say?" I growl, and Dominic stands, followed by Gage.

Dominic steps forward, leaning over my desk until he's right in my face. "You boys aren't ruling The Brotherhood anymore. I won't stand for it!" he yells, his eyes turning into slits.

"We are in charge now, and there's nothing you can do about it. You know the rules have been in place since the beginning. You have two choices," I say, walking around the desk to stand next to him. He turns, rolling his shoulders back. I stare into his ocean-blue eyes that are a mirror of my own.

"You can walk out of here now alive, drop this shit, and never contact me again. You leave Daring and don't ever come back," I spit.

His jaw twitches. "Option two?"

It takes everything in me not to wrap my fingers around his throat and squeeze until he has no air left in his lungs. He's impossible. He brings out the very worst in me. Fuck.

I release an audible exhale. "Or choose to go against The Brotherhood and—"

Lucas kicks off the wall, closing in on us. "I'll put this bullet down your throat. Open wide, princess."

The air around us thickens, making it impossible to breathe properly.

"You disrespectful, fucking—"

Loud banging hits my office door, and Dominic stops. Gage walks over, opening the door to find Ronald, his eyes widening when he sees Dominic.

"What's going on?" Gage asks.

"Sorry to interrupt, but there's been an incident," he says, showing Gage his phone.

Gage curses before saying something to Ronald, then slams the door shut. "There's been another attack. This time at the track crossing," Gage says, and my stomach sinks. "Our guard station has been destroyed. No casualties, but a lot of our comms equipment has been taken out."

Dominic laughs, taking several steps back. "See, like I fucking told you. It's them!" he yells, and before I can open my mouth, he storms out my office door.

"Follow him out," I say to Lucas, and he doesn't argue.

I stumble backward, my back hitting the wall, and my head falls into my hands.

What a fucking mess. Not only do I have to deal with my off-the-rails father, but now there's been another attack against us.

Battle lines have been drawn, and I have no fucking idea if I have what it takes to keep my chosen family safe.

Chapter 27

Freya

I quickly tap out another text. Message after message goes unread. After finding out about the attack on the tracks four days ago, I've been trying to get in touch with Kai, but he's gone MIA. He won't answer any of my calls, either. I'm so close to storming back over to Daringhood, just to punch him in his smug face. I need to talk to him, to explain that I didn't choose them over him. I told him I wouldn't, but now he thinks I have.

I hadn't thought he was responsible for the bomb at town hall. But this train tracks thing? It does seem targeted at Daringville specifically, and Kai said it himself—they're going to war. What if I was wrong about the town hall bomb? What if my best friend is behind . . . everything? What the fuck was he thinking, causing havoc like that? Everything is fucked.

A pillow hits me square in the face, and I look over at Amirah, who's sitting next to me on her bed.

My lip curls back. "What the fuck?"

"I'm so sick of you being glued to your phone. Let's go do something. Anything." She groans, falling back against her pillow.

She's not wrong. I want to do something too.

Maybe we can. Maybe we can help fix things between the two sides. "Let's check out the station. I want to see proof it was the Hood."

Amirah's eyes light up, and she jumps off the bed and scurries into her closet. "This is the best thing you've said all day."

It's risky going there, but Amirah is right. I've been stuck on my phone or at Hazen's place for more than a week now, and I'm itching for an adventure. Sneaking around watching Lucas at the docks the other week gave me that thrill I've been chasing, but since then, the guys have been preoccupied. I've only seen them briefly or when one of them rolls into bed in the early hours of the morning.

Amirah comes back out wearing a black hoodie, leggings, and sneakers.

"They won't see you coming," I say with a smirk, and she rolls her eyes.

"I wanted to look like you," she snaps back, and I glance down at Gage's hoodie, which I practically live in now, and black leggings. She's right—we are matching.

"Twinning!" I sing in a high-pitched voice.

Amirah shakes her head, throwing me a black ball cap. I pull it on over my hair, tucking any loose locks behind my ears.

Amirah opens her door and peers outside, then shuts it quietly. "Gage is at Hazen's with him, but not sure if Lucas is there or not. Have you heard from him?"

I shake my head. "Not since this morning."

"The best way out of here is the balcony. There are guards at the stairs and front door, and I'm sure they wouldn't let Princess Freya leave her castle," Amirah teases.

"I doubt they'll be up for Princess Amirah prancing down to the tracks, either," I retort, and Amirah smirks.

"I'll message Jeremy; he'll turn a blind eye for me." She grabs her phone from beside her bed and types away.

I slide off the bed, push my feet into my high-top Chucks, and follow her out the balcony door. It's dark out here—a quarter moon sits high in the sky—and my shin smashes into something hard. I curse, rubbing down my leg. Amirah turns on her phone light, illuminating the ground and her stupid fucking outdoor lounge chair.

"Bit late for that," I say through gritted teeth.

She chuckles, moving toward the side of her balcony. She passes me her phone, and I shine it toward her.

"When I whistle, you follow me. If I don't, then stay there. Got it?" she asks.

"Yes," I say quietly.

She peers over the railing before hoisting herself over. I lean forward, providing as much light as I can. She scales down the drainpipe like she's done this a million times before, and she probably has.

Darkness takes her and I pull back. There's not much lighting on this side of the house, but that doesn't mean they aren't watching. If I've learned anything from being around The Brotherhood, it's that they have eyes and ears everywhere, even if you can't see them.

My heart hammers against my rib cage and excitement bubbles up inside me as I wait for Amirah's signal. As much as I wanted a life away from Daring with Alec, I would have missed this if we'd gone to college in a normal town. I have missed putting myself in constant danger just to release all my deep, dark, built-up emotions. That's why Gage,

Hazen, and Lucas pulled me in. Danger surrounds them. They weaved their spiderweb, and I was a fly, trapped to them. With them, every day I'll be fighting off some kind of threat, and that's exactly what I crave.

A soft whistle cuts through the otherwise still night, and I move, turning off the light and shoving Amirah's phone into my hoodie pocket. I hoist my leg over the railing, and my feet catch on the little edge on the other side. I cling to the metal of the drainpipe and maneuver myself over, scaling down like Catwoman.

My feet hit the soft ground, and Amirah reaches out to me. I take her hand and pass her phone back.

"Now I get why you do all that weird shit, like jumping off the cliff and putting yourself in danger. This is exciting," Amirah whispers, and I grin, even though she can't see me in the dark.

"Who are you and what have you done with my best friend?"

"There's so much you don't know about me . . . yet," she replies, throwing me off guard. But before I can ask her what she means, she pulls my hand, yanking me around the side of her house, staying close to the shadows.

We reach the end of the house, and Amirah peers around the corner, letting go of my hand. I brush my palm over my leggings, attempting to dry off the sweat.

"When I say go, we run, and we don't stop until we are through the gates to the estate. Got it?" she asks.

"Yep," I reply, and she peers around the wall again.

"Now," she whispers, taking off across the well-manicured grass, and I follow.

We move between the trees until we reach the gate. Amirah lifts out her phone. The light casts shadows around her face. The gate opens, and before I can take another breath, she's off again, running through it. I follow closely behind her as we step out onto the quiet road.

Amirah tears off down the hill to the neighborhood security gate. I look over my shoulder at Hazen's place. Though I can spot his lights in the distance, it's too far up the hill for them to see us down here.

She drops into a walk as we reach the security box and one of the guards comes out and opens the door for us without any question. Amirah waves at him and blows a kiss from over her shoulder and we are free.

As I fall into step next to Amirah, she takes my hand, placing it over her heart. It pounds fiercely against my palm.

"Holy shit, that was even better doing it with you," she says, releasing my hand.

"You do this often?" I ask, and she wraps her arm over my shoulder, pulling me closer.

"Yeah, but don't tell the boys, because it's the only time I'm free from their hold, ya know?"

I nod. I get it. I really do. "It's our little secret. Just because I'm with them doesn't mean I tell them everything."

"Good," Amirah says, before stepping out of my embrace.

The cool night breeze pushes my hair off my shoulders, making me wish I was wearing a beanie, not a cap. It's doing fuck all to protect my ears from the cold. My phone vibrates against my leg, and when I bring it to my face, I'm not surprised to find a text from the unknown number. I really need to figure out how to block them. I've tried, but they keep getting through.

Unknown: Sneaking out when the stakes are high? You really are the deadly kind.

"How are you doing with everything? I hate to ask this, but—" Amirah stops, grabbing my hands and looking me dead in the eye. "Are you okay?"

I lock my phone and ignore the text.

Then I burst into semi-hysterical laughter. Tears fall effortlessly down my cheeks, and I have no idea how to answer. "Is anyone ever truly okay?" I ask instead of replying.

Amirah pulls her bottom lip between her teeth and squeezes my hands. Warmth seeps into my palms. "You're right, but I want you to know I'm here if you need to talk, escape, or just do crazy shit. I'm here, okay?" She doesn't look away. Her mossy-green eyes are very similar to Gage's, although hers have a tinge of brown in them. They glisten against the streetlights.

"I know, and thank you. Now, stop being weird, and let's go before your brother finds us," I say, pulling away and wiping the tears staining my cheeks.

"You think I'm scared of my big bad brother?" Amirah snorts.

"He even scares me, so, yes, Amirah. If you aren't, you should be."

She doesn't reply, and we continue walking through the streets in silence. A few cars drive past us, but none of them have stopped to pick us up, which means The Brotherhood hasn't been informed of our disappearance yet.

We turn off the last street and onto the large open road, sticking to the side in case any cars come past. The bright spotlights that are usually switched on are black; there's nothing but darkness up ahead.

Amirah reaches for my hand, and I intertwine her fingers with mine.

"You scared?" I tease, and she looks around the street before giving me a side-eye.

"No. I just need your hand in case we lose each other."

I scoff but don't reply, focusing on the road ahead. Goose bumps tickle my neck. It's late—well past midnight. I'm not scared of the dark, but here, on the brink of both sides of Daring, you have to be wary of your surroundings. This is the area where people shoot first and ask questions later.

A rustle comes from behind us. Amirah grips my hand harder. I turn around and see nothing but darkness. Footsteps scuffle along the road, and I whirl back to the front, letting go of Amirah in the process. Pulling out my knife, I hold it tightly in my grip.

"Who the fuck is there?" I yell into the night, and a figure emerges from the tree line.

Anger flares inside me. What the fuck is *she* doing here?

Chapter 28

Freya

Amirah flashes her phone light, and Mia walks over, raising her hands in surrender.

"What the fuck are you doing?" I ask.

Mia stops in front of us. "Sorry. I didn't mean to sneak up on you. I saw you leave, and I wanted to come."

I look at Amirah, who's watching her with a frown. "From where? You don't exactly live close," Amirah retorts, crossing her arms over her chest.

"I was with Dominic." Mia glances away, and I want to warn her away from him, but it's not my place.

"So, you followed us?" I ask, and Mia nods.

"You know that sounds creepy as fuck, right?" Amirah says, scanning her up and down with disgust.

Mia bites into her bottom lip, and I notice the dark ring below her eye. Her heavy makeup covers it, but the skin is puffy compared to her other eye.

"What happened?" I ask, pointing at my own face.

Tears fall down her cheeks, and she tucks her straight black hair behind her ear. I may hate her for the way she was too close to Lucas the other day, but I'm still worried about her.

"Your brother would have never treated me like this." She hiccups and my chest squeezes at the mention of him. As much as I hate Mia, she doesn't deserve this. Nobody does.

"Did Dominic do it?" Amirah asks, her fists balling at her sides.

"Yeah." Mia looks down at her feet.

Of course, Dominic fucking did this. He's a monster. The sooner someone kills him, the better. The number of lives he's fucked with, and the number of times he's gotten away with it, is crazy.

Amirah steps forward, taking Mia's hands in hers. "It's no secret that I don't like you, but if you feel trapped, I can get you out of here. Get you a new identity and you can be free."

Can she do that? Here, I thought I knew my best friend, but apparently not. I could have used that info before everything that happened when Alec went missing. I don't want to leave now. Wherever they go, I go.

"Thank you, I'll message you," Mia says, and Amirah drops her hands, coming to stand beside me.

"Look. since you're here now, you can come with us. Just stick behind me and don't say anything. Got it?" I say, and Mia nods. "And for the record, if I see you that close to Lucas ever again, I won't hesitate to ruin you. Understand?" I stare Mia up and down, while Amirah steps up beside me.

Mia licks her dry lips. "I didn't mean anything by it."

I scoff, turning back around. I don't know if I believe her or not, but one thing I do know is that my brother trusted her. He may not have loved her, but he cared for her deeply—and Alec was one of the best judges of character I've ever met.

I owe it to him to be kind.

"Women get the short end of the stick," Mia says, and I glance over at Amirah, who watches Mia closely. "But it was cool that you made some headway with The Brotherhood for change. I'm here for the girl power."

"They are just scared of the power women can hold," Amirah says, and Mia nods.

We continue walking toward the tracks, and as we near, the air changes. Ash clings to my lungs. I cover my nose with my hoodie, trying to filter it out, but it's useless.

The smell brings me back to the town hall. My skin tingles, and fuck, I hope I never have to go through being burned again. My arms haven't healed yet, but the pain has subsided.

Amirah coughs next to me and brings up her arm, covering her mouth and nose. "I've changed my mind. Let's go back home," she says through the sleeve of her hoodie.

"No way. We've already made it this far."

She sticks by my side. We reach the tracks where there once was an outpost with multiple guards; now it's burned to a crisp, with one wall still standing. Broken pieces of bricks are scattered all over the road. Smoke tarnishes the air, clinging to my skin and lungs.

We come to a stop on our side of the tracks, Mia on my right and Amirah on my left. There, written in bright-red paint on the brick wall, are the words:

The Brotherhood is dead.

Amirah grips my wrist and sweat beads down my neck. This isn't good. A war between Daringhood and Daringville is only going to end in one way—death. I'm on both sides, and I can't lose anyone else. I refuse to.

Three figures come out from the tree line over the tracks. The closer they get, the harder my heart pumps in my chest. Kai leads, a cigarette hanging from his lips, the flame casting light around his sharp jawline. He stares right through me, like I don't even exist, and damn, that hurts more than getting burned.

Bear and Zion stand next to him. Bear flicks his knife in and out with his fingers while watching me with a blank expression. He gives me nothing, but that's not completely new. Bear always holds his feelings close to his chest—hell, if he even has any. All the time I've known him, he's never opened up about anything. Nothing ever fazes him—he's deadly like that. He's someone I wouldn't want to be on the wrong side of.

Zion looks at Amirah, Mia, then finally he stops at me. The corner of his mouth lifts slightly, but his smile is gone just as quickly.

"What do you want?" Kai asks, putting out his cigarette.

I take a step forward, praying that he'll look at me. "Kai let me explain—"

He grabs a gun from the front of his jeans, holding it in his grip.

My stomach drops. He would never hurt me.

"You chose them, Freya," Kai says, his voice full of anger.

"No, I didn't!" I yell, taking a step over the tracks.

Amirah reaches for me, but I step out of her way. Kai's grip tightens on his gun, his knuckles turning white. Bear and Zion don't move.

"I love them, and I won't apologize for that. I want to be with them, and if you think that means I've chosen them, then that's on you. Not me," I say, moving closer until I'm halfway over the tracks.

My lungs burn from the smoke lingering in the air. I should be afraid, but I know Kai would never hurt me, even if he hates me.

"We always have a choice. I asked you to choose whose side you're on, and you did. You made your bed, and now you'll lie in it," Kai says, moving forward until he's only an arm's length away.

He finally looks at me, though it's as if he's a different person. Tears prick behind my eyes.

"You're not welcome in Daringhood anymore. You're one of them now." He points toward Amirah, and she stays frozen to the spot with her phone in her hand. "An enemy to us."

"Kai, please, it doesn't have to be this way. You're like a brother to me. Please, don't do this. We can work this out," I beg, stepping closer.

He points his gun at my chest, and I step into it. Fear courses through my body. I'm hyperaware of each breath, each movement—but I have to trust he won't do this. He won't hurt me.

"I'm still with you," I repeat, praying that he won't actually pull the trigger, but I can't leave now because I need to know he doesn't really hate me, that there's hope for us yet.

Kai is stubborn as shit, and when he's decided something, like thinking I've betrayed him, then that's it. His mind is made up, and it takes some serious convincing to tell him otherwise. But I won't stop fighting for him, for our friendship. If he walks away, it'll be like I've lost two brothers these past few months, and I can't handle that pain.

Kai's dark-brown eyes glare into mine. I can see the war he's fighting from within—the voices telling him to do it and not to at the same time.

"My fight isn't with you—it's with them—but now you're caught in the middle. I can't protect you if you're with them," Kai says, his eyes softening slightly, and my shoulders relax.

He won't hurt me. He's pissed off but still cares, and I'll take that. If there's one thing Kai and my guys have in common, it's that they want to protect me from themselves and each other.

"Can't we settle this between us all? We don't need a war," I plead.

Kai takes a couple of steps back, placing his gun into the front of his jeans. "It's too late for that. They had their chance, and they blew it when they blamed us for the town hall. Something we didn't do," Kai explains.

"So you just blew up this?" Amirah says, stepping up next to me and looking around at the destruction.

Kai casts his gaze up and down her body. He pulls out a cigarette from his pocket, and the sparks from his lighter fill the dark night. He inhales, then exhales a cloud of smoke.

"Tell your brother we've got more than just bombs up our sleeves," Kai says, and Amirah shuffles next to me.

"Men, you're all the same. Measuring how big your weapons are." She huffs before checking her phone again. "Uhhh, Freya, we should go. They are blowing up my phone, wondering where we are." Amirah shoves her phone back into her pocket.

Bear chuckles. "Time to go, princess. Your kings await you."

I open my mouth to reply, but Amirah pulls me away. Kai turns around, walking off in the opposite direction. Part of me wants to run over the tracks and be with them, to settle this and make them see reason, but the other part understands that now isn't the time or place. I won't watch my best friend fight my boyfriends. It's going to be a bloodbath—one I don't want to be in the middle of but already am.

Mia stands in front of us, frozen in place, watching them leave. I almost forgot she was even here. Her phone rings. She checks it, and

Her chin wobbles slightly before she answers and walks off ahead of us toward Daringville. Where is she going?

My heart hasn't stopped beating at double its usual speed, and the farther we move away from Kai, Zion, and Bear, the harder it gets. I wish I could just pull my heart out of my chest and be done with the stupid bitch. I'm over feeling so much. Whoever designed us to have all these feelings, I need their number to call and ask for a refund.

"This isn't good at all," Amirah says, and she isn't wrong. Kai isn't bluffing—blowing up the train tracks is just the beginning. "Did you hear me?"

I realize I haven't replied yet. I'm stuck in my head. "Yeah, sorry. It's not, but I'm going to do everything in my power to prevent an all-out war," I say, meaning every word. I have no idea how, but I'll try.

"Fuck," Amirah blurts, pulling out her phone, and she stops in the middle of the road. "We have to get back to the house now. They know we left, and it won't be long until they find us."

"Where's Mia?" I ask, searching the quiet, dark road. I can't see her anywhere.

"Mia?" Amirah yells, but only silence greets us.

"Just leave her. Let's go." I take Amirah's hand, and we walk quickly along the road. I try to watch out for Mia, but she's the least of my problems at the moment. She's a grown-ass woman and can take care of herself.

Headlights illuminate the road, and tires screech to a stop in front of us. Gage rolls down the window to his red Range Rover, with Lucas and Hazen in the backseat. He glares at me before shaking his head.

"Get in the fucking car," he growls, and I scoff.

These guys never learn.

Chapter 29

Gage

"No, we're walking home," Freya replies with a smug smile on her pretty cherry lips, moving past my door.

My fingers grip the steering wheel, and I can't fucking deal with even one more disobedient person today. I'm already exhausted after recruiting new members, and I have a shit ton more to do tomorrow. The last thing I wanted was to come home, expecting to find Freya in my bed, but finding an empty house with no sign of the girls instead.

We've been driving around for the last thirty minutes, trying to find them, and I'm beyond pissed off. I need sleep and my girl in my bed, preferably with her tight cunt around my cock.

"It wasn't an offer," I growl, and she ignores me. "Get her," I say to Hazen.

The back door of my car opens, and Hazen jumps out, grabs Freya around her waist, and shoves her inside onto the backseat. Amirah slides in next to Freya, glaring at me through the mirror.

They should know better than to be sneaking around, especially with the state of things. If I don't know where they are, then how can I protect them? I fucking can't. I might need to buy a lock for my sister's bedroom and for Freya's room at Hazen's—then at least I'd know where they are. We've got enough shit to deal with. Neither of them would be happy with that, and they might try to burn down their doors, but at least it would buy me some time.

We're not ready for a war, and that's exactly why Kai's attacking us now. He knows that, and fuck, I'd actually applaud him for it if he wasn't our enemy. We've just taken over leadership. We're new—fresh meat. Even though we've been training our whole lives as young pups for this, this time, we have to stand tall. We can't afford to look weak—it's fucking embarrassing.

I drive home, the entire trip silent. We move past Dominic's place, and the lights are on.

"Is he still living there?" Freya asks from the backseat.

"Under our watch," I say. "Brax has eyes on him."

We can't afford to have him attacking us too. He craves power too much to sit back, and we can't entertain that fight right now on top of everything else. If he comes for us, we'll end him.

I drop Amirah back at my place. Freya goes to follow her, but Hazen leans over her, pulling the door shut, and I hit the locks. Freya flips me off, falling back into her seat with a huff. I watch her from the rearview mirror, raising my eyebrow, challenging her to bitch at me, but she doesn't. She rubs her eyes and looks back out the window.

I make sure Amirah gets inside, and one of the security guards waves at me before I drive toward Hazen's house. It's quickly becoming a place we all call home.

Hazen, Lucas, and I stay here most nights, as well as Freya since she's been back. It feels like a home—all of us being together under one roof. I've always loved living with family. That's why Amirah and I were so close growing up. Sure, we never had much to do with Mom, since she was overseas all the time, but our nanny, Lillian, was a great substitute mother who we adored.

I pull into the underground garage and switch the car off. Freya rips open her door and slams it shut.

"Well, someone's cranky. Looks like you're sleeping on the couch tonight." Lucas chuckles.

"Piss off," I grunt, sliding out of the car.

I'm sleeping in my bed with Freya, whether she likes it or not.

I follow her inside. She storms up the stairs, and I'm right behind her. When she walks past my room, I reach out, grabbing her wrist to pull her to a stop. She whirls around, yanking her hand free and leveling me with angry eyes. Fuck me, she's beautiful. This is exactly why I want to make her angry. To feed off the anger coming off her. She shows her emotions way too easily.

I need someone who will challenge me—someone who won't just put up with my shit and roll over like a good girl. I want someone who will fight me, disagree with me, and have her own opinions. Who will rise to all the bullshit I throw her way, and fuck me, have I found her. Our relationship isn't normal, far from it, but what I feel for her is like nothing else. I'd gladly step in front of her and take a bullet to the chest if I had to, even though she'd fight me on that and call me a dickhead.

When she came storming back into my life, I hated her. I didn't want to see her again because she broke my heart when she walked away from me that night and chose Amirah. I've never admitted this to her, and I'll probably take it to my grave. She knows how I feel about her.

"You're sleeping with me tonight," I growl, and she rolls her eyes. I'm on her in seconds, forcing her backward into my door. Her back hits the wall with a soft thud, her eyes changing to a stormy blue.

My thumb rolls over her throat, my fingers tightening around her neck. "I don't wanna sleep with assholes who manhandle me into cars," she huffs through her teeth, and the corner of my mouth lifts. She's fucking breathtaking with my hand around her throat and her angry eyes.

I lean forward, pressing my hips into hers. She doesn't move away. She watches me, her eyes daring me to punish her, to make another move.

"I'll chain you to my fucking bed every night just to know you're safe," I say, running my tongue along my bottom lip.

"Do it," she breathes, then my lips are on hers.

She fights me for dominance, my tongue sliding along hers. She pulls back, biting into my lip hard, and a drop of blood trickles down my chin.

"You tease whips and chains, but where are they?" she asks, pressing her lips together in a pout.

"Whips and chains . . . say no more. I'm in," Lucas quips, coming along the hallway. He takes a bite out of an apple while glancing between Freya and me.

"He's all talk," Freya says with a roll of her eyes.

Leaning forward, I twist the door handle, and she stumbles back a couple of steps before finding her feet.

"Take off your clothes and get on the bed," I demand.

She opens and closes her mouth before turning around and doing exactly what I asked. I watch as she removes my hoodie, one that I won't ever get back now. It looks better on her, anyway. Knowing she's wearing something that belongs to me feels right. My clothes are keeping her warm, my scent surrounding her body.

She pulls her top over her head, leaving her in a black lacy bra. Her full tits bounce as she saunters to my bed. She sits down, glancing over, batting her eyes.

"Lucas, will you be a doll and help me out of these pants?" she asks while looking at me.

Lucas barges past me like a dog in heat and drops to his knees in front of her. Freya glances between me and him. Lucas braces his hands on her knees, and I move into the room, shutting the door behind me and leaning against it. I have no idea where Hazen went, and I don't give a fuck.

This is the first time I've seen Lucas be close with Freya, and I want to know how this plays out.

"My bedroom, my rules," I command, and Lucas looks toward me, pursing his lips together. His hands rest on Freya's knees, as if he's waiting for me.

Freya rolls her eyes, and I stride farther into the room until I'm at the end of the bed.

"Did you just roll your eyes at me?" I ask.

"Yes, hurry up with your commands before I just roll over and go to sleep," she says, yawning.

I shake my head at the brat. "Freya, lie on your back. Lucas, roll down her pants, inch by inch."

Freya falls back with a huff, and Lucas wastes no time peeling her pants over her ass and down her legs until they're flying across the room. He didn't exactly go slow like I asked, but seeing Freya in her matching black lace underwear, I'm not complaining. Her creamy complexion, toned legs, and the scars that line her body are perfection.

It takes everything in me not to storm over to them, push Lucas out of the way, and have her. Fuck. How'd I get so fucking lucky?

"Hurry up, bro, or I'm taking things into my own hands," Lucas complains.

"Run your tongue up the inside of her leg slowly," I say, unbuttoning my jeans and lowering my zipper.

Lucas obeys, and as he moves his way up her leg, my hand finds my hard, waiting cock.

Freya turns her head to the side, her gaze fixated on my length. She licks her lips, and my cock twitches in my grip. No one else has this effect on me. This girl, my girl, *our* girl, is royalty. I never thought we needed a queen in our Brotherhood, but fuck, she's changed everything.

Chapter 30

Lucas

Goosebumps rise, peppering her skin as my tongue slides higher up the inside of her leg. Freya watches Gage from the corner of her eye, and I want to tell her to look at me, not him. But I'm not in charge here, and having Gage dictate my next move is surprisingly fun. That tingling feeling of anticipation, of not knowing what's going to happen next, is way better than watching porn.

I haven't fully forgiven Freya, and I don't think I ever will. Have I accepted her apology, and do I want to move on with our lives together? Yes, but that doesn't take away the pain I felt when she contributed to my mother's death.

It's going to take time to heal that wound, but I don't see my life without Freya in it anymore. As much as I wanted to block my heart from hers, I couldn't deny it any longer. She already had her claws in me, and I'll keep them there until my own dying breath. She's my family now, alongside my brothers. I'll do everything in my power to keep her safe, protected, and loved. Because she's mine and I'm hers.

Freya's leg twitches as I reach her inner thigh, so close to her underwear.

"Lucas, stop," Gage says, and I brace my hands on Freya's thighs, pushing up.

"What?" I snap, wanting nothing more than to eat her out. To taste every last drop of her on my tongue.

"Freya, have you been a bad girl?" Gage asks, glancing back at her, his hand still wrapped around his cock. I look at Freya, and she licks her lips before nodding.

"What do we do to bad people, Lucas?" Gage raises his eyebrows.

The corner of my mouth lifts. "We punish them."

Gage kicks his pants to the ground, along with his underwear, and moves around the bed on the opposite side of me. He opens the top drawer to his bedside table and pulls out a pair of handcuffs, then throws them to me. I catch them, and the sound of metal clinking together rings through the room.

He throws a black leather paddle and a choker onto the bed. Freya tries to catch a glimpse of the goodies, but Gage leans over the bed, pressing against her shoulders. I smirk and cock my head to the side at Gage. He just shrugs. I've always known he liked to be in charge, but sex toys? *That* I didn't know, but I'm here for the show.

"No moving unless I tell you to, understood?" Gage demands.

I expect Freya to fight back, but she nods. My cock twitches against my briefs at the submission.

The door handle jiggles before it opens. Hazen stands in the doorway, glancing between the three of us. "Where's my invite?" he grumbles.

"Get in, shut the fucking door, and do as I say or fuck off. Remove your clothes and leave them on the floor," Gage snaps, and Hazen looks back at me, raising his eyebrow. I shrug, gesturing for him to hurry up.

"Okay, well whatever fuckery is going down, I'm not missing out on this," Hazen says, before shutting the door and flicking the lock in place and removing his clothes. He moves past me and sits on the bed next to Freya.

"Help me?" she pleads, her eyes on Hazen, but Gage wraps his hand around her throat, squeezing.

"He won't help you. Lucas, remove Freya's bra, then secure those cuffs around her wrists and hand her to Hazen." Gage removes his grip from Freya's throat, kissing her roughly on the lips before moving away.

Freya's breath hitches as I make quick work of freeing her tits, then place the cuffs around her wrists, and Hazen takes her from me.

"Hazen, fasten her against my headboard," Gage says, and Freya's eyes widen.

I stand to move Freya around so she's in the middle of the bed, and Hazen secures her cuffs to the headrest. Freya pulls against her restraints, helplessly glancing between the three of us. She knows full well that she can't run now—there's no escaping us, even if she wants to.

"Lucas, remove her underwear," Gage demands, picking up a leather choker from the bed with a lead attached to the end.

Fucking hell, here I thought I had toys, but Gage has taken that trophy. Never in a million years did I expect this from him, but then again, it doesn't surprise me entirely. He does like controlling us.

I move to the end of the bed, removing my shirt and throwing it to the ground, followed by my pants and underwear. Freya watches me with interest, a sparkle in her bright-blue eyes.

After bracing my hands on the bed, I crawl forward on hands and knees until I'm leaning over her bottom half. My fingers glide up her legs, hook under her lacy thong, and I pull it down inch by inch until she kicks it off. She widens her legs. Her pussy stares back at me, begging for me to touch it. Fuck Gage and his stupid fucking rules. She wants me, and I'll happily give her what she desires.

I lean forward until I'm breathing in her sweet cunt, only an inch from tasting when two hands grab my chest and shove me backward. I sit up, glaring at Gage.

"Did I say you could do that?" he bites out.

"Enough of your fucking games. I'm hungry and I need her," I snap.

Gage shakes his head before securing the choker around her throat and passing the lead to Hazen.

"One last thing, then you can go at it," Gage says, and I'm about a second away from punching him. *Hurry the fuck up.*

He grabs a piece of black cloth and lifts it off the bed—an eye mask. He places it over Freya's eyes.

"Fucking hell, Gage," Freya grumbles, taking the words right out of my mouth.

"Shut up and be quiet. Naughty girls get punished," Gage growls.

Freya chuckles. "You know I just love being punished."

Before Gage gives me the go ahead, I'm on her, my mouth hot against her pussy, tongue gliding between her folds. Freya groans, pulling against her restraints. Gage doesn't stop me this time, and thank fuck, or I'd have to knock the fucker out.

The sweet tang of Freya's pussy kisses my tastebuds. My cock hardens as she pulls against her restraints. She's at our mercy to do whatever we please with her.

Gage moves around the bed and disappears from view. A loud smack fills the room before pain bites into my ass. I jolt forward, pressing farther into Freya's cunt before pulling back and standing up.

"What the fuck?" I yell, rubbing my ass, feeling little bite marks from the paddle.

"You didn't follow orders, so you, too, shall be punished," Gage says, rolling the paddle around his fingers with a smug look on his face. Asshole.

Freya chuckles, apparently having figured out what happened and enjoying it.

"Fuck off," I grumble.

"Freya, flip over and on your knees," Gage says.

Hazen uncuffs her and rolls her over, so her ass is in perfect view, before re-cuffing her.

"Hazen, move under our girl," Gage says, and Hazen obeys. "Now kiss her."

Hazen claims Freya's mouth in a hot, slow kiss, and *damn*, if she was any other girl I'd be jealous. But instead, I'm even more turned on watching them together.

I'm itching to move, to eat Freya out again, and I not-so-patiently wait for Gage's orders. This is his little fantasy playing out, but next time we're going to my room, with my own rules.

"Lucas, move closer and touch Freya's cunt. Tell me how wet she is for us." Gage stands at the side of the bed, his hand around his cock and eyes glued to Freya.

On my hands and knees, I run my palm over her tight ass, then trail a finger down her crack before sliding between her folds. "She's soaking."

Gage nods. "Make her come."

About fucking time, I want to grumble but don't. I shuffle my hips forward until my hard cock presses against Freya's ass. She pushes back against me, and I groan, running my finger along her inner thigh before coming back between her folds. She's dripping wet for us.

I slide a finger inside her, and she pulls against her restraints, the metal jingling.

"Every time you move, you'll be punished," Gage says, flipping the paddle around in his fingers.

Freya doesn't reply, her mouth glued to Hazen's. I pump in and out of Freya's cunt with one, then two fingers, hitting deep inside her over and over again.

"She's close," I say. She's tightening around my digits.

"Let go, Freya," Gage commands.

I pick up my speed, rubbing my thumb against her clit to increase the pressure. Freya moans before her juices run down my hand. I pull away, placing my fingers inside my mouth, and I lick off every last drop of her tangy sweetness. It's like ecstasy—one taste, and I'm fucking hooked.

"Do you want Lucas inside you, Freya?" Gage asks.

She pulls away from Hazen. "Yes, fuck me, Lucas. Hard," Freya says, and everything around us disappears—the room, Gage and Hazen. My chest rises and falls at a rapid rate. She's such a dirty fucking girl. I'll be replaying those words every time I touch my cock. Fuck, that's hot.

I faintly hear Gage say, "Fuck her."

I line up my cock with her cunt, her juices giving me the lube I need. I don't waste another second before I push inside her. She jolts forward. Her tight cunt wraps around my cock, and fuck, it feels similar to coming home after a long fucking day. Her pussy invites me inside, squeezing around me like a warm hug, but so much fucking better.

I go slow until she loosens around me, then I fuck her hard. My hips slap against her ass over and over. She kisses Hazen, moaning into his mouth. Gage watches us, tugging his cock to the rhythm of me fucking Freya.

"Hazen, move so Freya can place that dirty mouth over your cock," Gage says, and Hazen shuffles around on the bed, lining himself up.

I don't stop pounding into Freya, keeping up the pace. Hazen pulls at Freya's leash until her mouth wraps around his long, hard dick. Jesus, that's hot. Freya's cherry lips take him whole.

I let loose a deep groan as I watch her. I'm imagining her doing the same to me. My fingers tighten around her hips, holding her in place. My eyes flicker between Gage getting himself off and Freya sucking Hazen off, then back to my dick pounding into her cunt.

She tightens around me. She's ready to release, and fuck, I'm not far off. I go harder, faster, and my pulse skyrockets like I'm about to have a fucking heart attack, and it wouldn't surprise me if I did. My balls release inside her along with a deep rumble from my chest, and she moans, coming right behind me.

I pull out, falling back on my heels, and Hazen slides himself from Freya's mouth before his cum shoots onto her lips and cheeks. Fuck me. Gage groans and follows, and I collapse onto my back on the bed, glancing up at the ceiling as my breathing settles down to a normal pace.

"Fucking hell. I think I'll just keep you locked up forever," Gage proclaims to Freya, and if I had any energy left, I'd agree.

"Who's ready for round two?" I ask, and laughter fills the room.

There's no way I'm getting any sleep tonight.

Chapter 31

Gage

The memory of Freya chained to my bed with Hazen's cock in her mouth while Lucas fucked her from behind is all I can think about. My own dick has been rock hard for the past two days, and that's not exactly ideal when I'm observing the new recruits.

I wish I filmed it so I could watch it every night. It'll be happening again, but this time, I'll be the one fucking Freya from behind. My cock strains against my briefs, begging for me to take a break and release this tension.

"How are they doing?" Hazen asks, coming through the office door.

I look out the window. Hundreds of new soldiers are in groups, sparring or shooting targets in the backyard. They are in the practice stage, proving their worth to us. If they can't fight or hit a target, then they won't continue to the next round.

That's when shit gets lethal. We put them through a series of scenarios to test their loyalty to us. To prove they won't go telling shit to anyone in Daringhood.

Being with The Brotherhood is everything. It's protection and a family. Most of the men don't have any family, and that's exactly what we want—men with no ties to anyone else but The Brotherhood. We are their family now.

We've stepped up security since the guard-house explosion, more men on the gate and watching the girls.

"Already lost twenty, but there's some good talent there," I say, moving back around my desk.

"Good. We're going to need it." Hazen watches me closely. "Are we ready for a war?"

It's the exact question I've been replaying over and over again. "No, but we have to be," I reply, leaning back against my office chair.

Daringhood was never supposed to murder our men, women, and children. They've never gone this far before. Yeah, they have mounted small resistances, causing chaos, but those were always quickly shut down. The Hood is to blame for the explosion, so war it is.

Since we've become the leaders, everything's gone to shit, and that fucking kills me to admit. After all these years of training and being groomed to lead, then this happens. I can't help but wonder if what Dominic said is true—we aren't ready to lead The Brotherhood. I mean, look at what's happened since we took the reins. How can we come back from this?

Still, I won't give up on this, on us. We can do better than those leaders before us.

"We will get through this and make everything right again," Hazen says.

I nod. "Have you heard from Dominic since last week?"

Hazen shakes his head, biting into his bottom lip. "He hasn't made any moves yet, and if he isn't causing any trouble, he can stay where he is."

"You're right. Brax has eyes on him, so if he does anything, we'll know about it and stop him." I'd trust Brax with my life; he's never let me down before.

Hazen turns around, staring out the window. "Ah, Amirah is coming, and she looks pissed off."

I pinch the bridge of my nose and sigh. These fucking girls will be the death of me.

A few minutes later, my office door flies open, and Amirah storms in, her hair flying wildly behind her shoulders. Her security detail waits outside the door.

"Yes, Amirah?" I ask, cocking my head to the side.

"So, what, now I can't even go outside our front door without someone glued to my ass?" she snaps, bracing her hands on the edge of my desk.

Fucking hell, just what I need today—another headache to deal with. She's clearly just found out I've assigned a new guard to her this morning. We finally have enough resources with the new recruits.

"It's for your own protection," I say, glancing back at the paperwork scattered over my desk.

"I don't want to be holed up in the house all day. I wanna help," she whines.

I move around the desk, standing in front of her. "Absolutely not," I growl.

There's no way in fucking hell she's helping us—it'll get her killed. She's safer at home, preferably locked up with nowhere to go. As much as I love my sister, this isn't the life for her. The Brotherhood is run by men, and men only. I can't risk her getting hurt. Our enemies will use her to get to us, and I'd murder every last person in Daring before I let that happen.

"Please, let me do something. Anything. I'm going crazy," she says, looking up at me with her puppy-dog eyes. Fuck. She knows exactly how to win me over, much like her best friend, who I'm surprised isn't here in Amirah's corner, egging her on.

"Fine. Get Freya and go train with the new recruits—brush up on your skills. You both need to be able to protect yourselves if, God forbid, we can't," I say, moving back around the desk.

"Thank you."

I look up to find Amirah beaming, and I frown. Normally, she wouldn't be so enthusiastic about self-defense. When I've suggested it in the past, she couldn't care less. I expected more of a fight.

She leaves, and Hazen shuts the door behind her and watches through the window while she crosses the training field with her security detail.

"You know Freya's not going to back down. She doesn't want this war," Hazen says, and I let out an exhale.

"None of us do, but they declared war on us when they blew up our guard station and the town hall. If there was any other resolution, I'd jump at it. But if we back down now, we'll appear weak to our men, and we can't afford that. There are a few who still don't trust us to lead, and I'm starting to question myself too. I won't allow this to overpower us. We need to make a stand and fight back. We'll deal with Freya when she comes breaking down our door."

Hazen nods. "For now, we need to oversee these new recruits."

Fuck, I hope they are strong enough to stand beside us and fight. There's a war coming—whether we're ready or not.

Chapter 32

Freya

Buzz, buzz, buzz.

I groan, rolling over, snuggling back into the pillow. *Shut that thing up.*

Buzz, buzz, buzz.

"Get your fucking phone," Gage grumbles from next to me, before wrapping his arms around my stomach, holding me in place. I relax into his embrace, ready to fall back asleep.

The buzzing continues. My eyes peel open, and I release a heavy breath before untangling myself from Gage and reaching for my phone on the table next to his bed.

The screen lights up, and I roll onto my back. Seven missed calls from my mother. My stomach drops. I haven't heard from her since I walked out and vowed to never come back after she relapsed and said all those nasty things to me. I was done, but now, seeing all these missed calls, I can't ignore her. She might be in trouble.

Without thinking twice, I roll out of bed. Gage's soft snores fill the room, and I hope to fuck he stays asleep. I'm too tired to argue with him about this. I need to make sure she's okay. Even though I want to cut ties with her, leave her and let her ruin her life, there's still part of me clinging to that tiny piece of her that I saw when she was off the drugs. The kindness she showed me. It was so nice to have her care about me and where I was. Yeah, it was also annoying, but at least she gave a shit.

As quietly as I can, I grab my sweatpants and hoodie, put them on, and step into my new Crocs. Lucas insisted that I needed a pair, and next thing I knew, they were on my bed, along with a bunch of other clothes.

Stepping away from the bed toward the door, I check my phone again. I hit dial, and it rings and rings before she picks up.

"I need you, please."

"Mom? What's wrong?" I ask quietly.

"I just need help, I need—"

The line goes dead. Shit. Something is wrong, and I can't ignore her. If something happened and I did nothing, I couldn't live with myself.

It's three in the morning, and the guys will be up in a couple of hours. I need to get moving.

Reaching Gage's door, I open it as slowly as I can before shutting it behind me. Small lights along the baseboard illuminate the hallway, allowing me to see where I'm going. I make it down the stairs and to the front door.

"And where are you off to, little thorn?"

I jump at the sound of Lucas's voice. He's leaning back against the living room door, watching me.

"Out," I reply, reaching for the door again.

"I'm coming," he says, stalking toward me.

"No," I snap, trying to keep my voice down. I don't want to wake Hazen or Gage. I can deal with Lucas—just not everyone. I need to move.

"You've got two choices. I either come with you, or I yell and wake up the house and you're not going anywhere. What will it be?"

I grumble a few choice words under my breath before opening the front door and walking out, leaving it open for Lucas to follow.

He catches up to me, wrapping me under his arm. "Where are we going?"

"My mom needs me," I say, and Lucas steers me in the direction of his car, but I stop.

"We won't get over the tracks with your car. They'll be on us in seconds."

"Fuck, you're right. Walking it is."

I flip up my hood and blend into the dark night. Lucas keeps me warm as I snuggle into his chest. The guards wave us through the gates, and I hate to admit it, but it's easier having him here with me. Otherwise, I'd have to waste time sneaking out. I need to get over the tracks. I have to make sure she's okay.

"Tell me about your mom?" Lucas asks, and my heart aches.

To some, this is a simple question, but for me, it's complicated. It opens so many wounds that I've buried deep inside, and I'm too scared to deal with all those emotions. The truth is, I have no fucking idea how to answer him. On top of that, the subject of mothers is still raw between us—something we haven't talked about since our truce.

It's going to take time for us to get back to where we were, but if we can get through this, then we'll be stronger than ever. I never believed in soulmates before I met the guys, and I never in a million years imagined they'd be mine or that I'd be giving them my whole broken heart, but I am—and I feel lucky that they treat it with such care.

We move through the second gate and out onto the open road. I lift my head from Lucas's chest, but he keeps his arm around me.

"You gonna answer? About your mom?" Lucas prompts.

I shrug. "That's a pretty loaded question. I have no idea where to even begin."

"I met her a couple of times, and she was nice before," Lucas says, and he doesn't have to say the next words because it's clear what he means.

"Before the poison hit her veins and she spiraled out of control?"

Lucas releases a loud exhale. "Yeah."

"I've been trying to erase her from my memory, to move on with my life, but it's impossible. She's my blood, my family. I chose to walk out on her when she relapsed because I just can't fucking go through that again. I don't want to be around her, afraid of what she'll do next or if she'll make it home every night."

Lucas squeezes my shoulder, and it feels good. I actually feel protected. I didn't want him coming with me, but it's nice having him here, knowing I'm not going to face my mother on my own this time. I've got him here—a way out.

"You know you've got us now. We're your family, and sometimes family isn't blood. It's chosen, and that's the best kind."

I lean back into Lucas's chest, resting my ear against his beating heart. He's right, but I still feel responsible for my mother. Especially since Alec isn't here. She has no one to look out for her anymore. I'll never forgive her for what she's done to me, to us, but I still have to help her.

"I just need to make sure she's okay," I say.

"I get it."

We reach the crossroads a couple hundred yards from the security point that's now a pile of ash. It's too risky crossing there. The Daringhood crew have people patrolling on their side, and we do on ours. They will see us the second we step out of the shadows. I just want to get this over with quickly and come back again. Battle lines have been drawn, and I'm not sure we'll come out alive.

We're close to the fence where I found my brother, and I don't dare look to my right, afraid I'll see him again. The picture of him hanging from the fence is still clear as day in my mind, something I wish would go away.

I move out of Lucas's embrace as we reach a little deserted outpost. This is where I used to sneak over, when Amirah would wait for me on this side of the tracks. On the other side, there's no one in sight, which surprises me, but it doesn't mean that no one is watching from the shadows. Kai isn't stupid. He may not have as much financial support as The Brotherhood, but people in Daringhood don't play games. They get the job done, quick and fast, guerilla warfare style.

"Let's go," I say, stepping over the first track.

Lucas grabs my arm. "Fuck this. Maybe we shouldn't without the guys."

I yank my arm out of his, stepping over the tracks toward the fence. "I didn't ask you to come," I say over my shoulder, before breaking into a run. Lucas curses from behind me, then the crunch of his shoes follows me.

I keep running through the field, the grass brushing against my ankles. The cool early morning air pushes my hair out of my face. Lucas pants from somewhere in the distance. He curses and I laugh. We could stop now that we are far away from the crossing, but hearing Lucas struggling is too good.

"Fuck, Freya, stop. I hate running." He groans, and I slow down once we hit the small fence.

Grabbing on to the barbed wire, I kick my leg over and jump, then land on the soft grass on the other side. Lucas trails closely behind me.

I stop at the dirt road, and a wave of sadness slams into me like a freight train, almost bringing me to my knees. Last time I was here, I was with Alec. It feels like a lifetime ago and like yesterday at the same time. When he drove me down this road, we talked about his new girlfriend, Mia. He warned me not to go over the tracks, but told me he still loved me unconditionally.

I'd do anything to bring him back, to have him here for one more day. To hear him laugh, curse me out, and tell me about his plans for college. If Nadine hadn't interfered, he would have made it there, succeeded in doing what he loved. Spread his wings without anything holding him back.

Arms wrap around me from behind, and I lean back into Lucas's embrace. "You okay?" he asks, and I wipe away my tears with my sleeve.

"This is where Alec used to drop me when I'd sneak over the tracks. Just remembering the last time we did."

"I wish I knew him better and found out he was my half-brother before it was too late," Lucas says, and a heaviness falls on my heart.

"You would have loved him."

"Tell me about him?" Lucas asks, moving beside me and taking my hand in his.

We start walking down the road, and I tell Lucas everything I loved about my brother. I, too, wish we were aware of our mother's affair earlier. Things might have been different. Maybe Alec would still be here with us.

Before I know it, we're in front of the trailer.

"You ready?" Lucas asks, and I shake my head. I vowed to never see her again after the last time, but fate had other plans.

The front door opens, and my mother stumbles out, her eyes as wild as her hair. Her skimpy dress flips up in the wind, but she doesn't bother pushing it back down.

"Oh, thank fuck. Where the fuck have you been?" she yells, folding her arms over her chest.

"I told you I was leaving."

She laughs. "I've heard that a million times before, but you never go far or for this long. I needed you."

"What do you want?"

She finally notices Lucas next to me and frowns. "Who's this?"

"I'm—"

I throw up my hand, stopping him. "It doesn't matter who he is. I'm here now. What do you want?" I snap. I'm about ready to walk back. She's seen him before; she's either out of her mind or doesn't remember.

"Come inside—it's freezing out here. Let's talk. I need you with me," she says, and I don't move a muscle. Lucas stays silent beside me, but I feel his shoulder brush up against mine.

"Are you clean?" I ask.

My mother moves from one foot to the other. "Pretty much."

I push my lips together. There's no "pretty much"—she either is or isn't.

"I'm going," I say, taking a step backward.

"No, Freya, please. I need you," she pleads.

"Why?"

"I need money. Please, just to get on my feet again. I'm trying to get better, but I need you. I have no one else."

"Are you serious? This is what you called me here for?" I ball my hands into fists and exhale a heavy breath. "I thought you were in trouble."

"Please, Freya," she begs, and I shake my head.

"You should have thought of that before you treated me like shit for the last time," I say, my voice breaking a little. I'm trying so hard to hold back the tears and anger I want to throw in her face. I want to tell her how much she's hurt me over the years, hurt us both, but she won't get it. It's too late.

"I've got something to give you." She disappears inside.

"You good?" Lucas asks, wrapping an arm over my shoulder, and I shrug.

She comes back out, carrying a journal in her hand. She passes it to me, and I take it, gazing down at the worn brown leather.

"I found it in Alec's room. He would have wanted you to have it."

I stare blankly at the journal, unable to move or talk. I remember giving this to him for his sixteenth birthday. I'd stolen it, wanting the perfect gift for him. He'd cherished this, writing in it every night.

Fuck, this is too much.

"Thank you," I rasp. "Once you get clean and stay clean, call me, but until then, I can't help you anymore," I say, before turning away.

Fuck, I hope she gets better, but I can't save her. She needs to save herself first.

I cling on to Alec's journal like I'm holding on to him, because this is part of him, and giving it to me is the best thing my mother's ever done for me.

Chapter 33

Freya

We walk in silence until we reach a park not far from the trailer. I sit down on the park bench and open Alec's journal.

"Should we do this back at home?" Lucas ask, glancing around the park.

"Just give me a few minutes, please?" I ask, and he nods.

Using the light from my phone to see the pages, I run my fingers over the words I wrote all those years ago.

To Alec,

May you find peace through your thoughts.

All my love,

Frey xx

Tears run down my cheeks, falling onto the paper. I flick through the pages until I reach the last one. My heart runs wild in my chest. Alec's messy handwriting is hard to read, but thankfully, I'm used to it. A week before he left this world, he wrote an entry.

It's nearly time to leave this town, and I can't fucking wait. The best part will be getting Freya out to give her a chance at a new life, one where she can be anything she desires. To get Mom the support she needs to stay clean and be the mother I once knew.

I don't hate living here. Hell, if things were different and we had more peace, more opportunity, more money and freedom, then I'd stay, but I don't see that happening in my lifetime. My job is to get us out of here alive, and I'll do whatever it takes to make that happen, even if I lose myself in the process. Anything to see Freya smile, to watch Mom cook us dinner and dance around the house to her favorite music once more.

I'm doing things that I vowed to never do, but it will all be worth it once we are out and safe, together.

I run my finger over the black ink. My heart aches, and I wish Alec was still here more than anything in this world. Lucas places his hand on my shoulder and squeezes.

"He wanted us to stay here if things were different for the people of Daringhood," I say.

Lucas sits down next to me, his knee brushing against mine. "If I had known everything I do now, I would have brought you back over to our side, protected you both."

I shake my head. "That's not what he meant. We didn't want rescuing. We wanted more freedom, more opportunities, better living conditions." I turn to face Lucas. The sun is starting to rise behind him, coloring the sky in bright orange and yellow, turning his face into a silhouette.

"I'm sorry you had to live here, but I won't apologize for everything else. Yeah, maybe we could have given the Hood more, but look at how well that's turned out so far." He brushes his fingers through his blond hair, pushing it out of his eyes.

"We need to try harder. I can't lose someone else who means so much to me. Please?" I beg, reaching for Lucas, caressing his cheek.

His light-brown eyes soften. He wraps his hands around my waist and pulls me up, placing me on his lap. My legs wrap around him, my forehead resting against his. The soft rhythm of my heart beats against his.

"I know what it's like losing someone you love," he whispers, and my heart breaks even more.

"I'm sorry," I whisper back, tears falling down my cheeks. Lucas swipes his tongue along my cheek, collecting my tears. My fingers grip his hair, holding on to him tightly.

"Can we try one last time with the Hood to give Alec his wish?" I ask, and Lucas's eyes bore into mine.

"They've already done so much damage." His tone is soft, even as he subtly refuses to give me what I want.

"I know, but Kai is the leader now, so maybe I can create peace. Maybe it's as simple as getting the two groups of men I love to meet. Please?"

"Fucking hell, when you look at me like that, how can I say no?"

"Thank you." I choke on a sob before my lips melt into his.

I can taste the saltiness of my tears as I claim Lucas's mouth. His tongue swipes along mine, and my fingers grip his hair hard, angling him exactly where I want him. He grinds against my core, his hard cock evident. I groan into his mouth, deepening the kiss even further.

Lucas runs his hands up and down my back, holding me in place. He reaches the waistband of my sweatpants and starts to tug them down my ass. Pulling back, I rest my head against his, my breaths coming in and out at a rapid rate. I stand on the park bench seat, and Lucas pulls my pants down. I glance around. The sun is rising between the trees in the distance, and there's no one in sight. This is stupid, fucking reckless, but I want him—hell, I need him inside me.

The crisp morning air kisses my bare pussy before Lucas's hot mouth is on her, eating like a starved man. He bites into my clit and my legs wobble. His hands grab my hips, holding me in place. My fingers tangle in his short hair, gripping on to anything to keep me from falling.

His tongue flicks my nub, running between my folds. He cups my pussy with his hand and slides one finger inside. My stomach burns with desire, and I can't get enough of him—of them all. The way they touch my body, the way it reacts to them is like nothing I've experienced before. I'm addicted to them. They are my drug of choice, and fuck, I'd overdose on them time and time again just to feel this.

Our souls have known each other before, that I'm certain of, because no one's ever made me feel like this. The connection I feel with them is like nothing else. No one has gone to the depths of hell with me like Lucas, Gage, and Hazen. We're one fucked-up relationship, and there's no going back.

I vowed to never give anyone my whole heart, but they have it: Lucas, Hazen, and Gage.

Lucas continues to finger fuck me out in the open until my legs clench around his head and I pant out his name.

"I fucking love you!" I cry out as I orgasm, and before I can inhale my next breath, Lucas pulls me down onto his large cock and fills every inch of me. I gasp, slamming my eyes shut.

"Say that again," he growls, gripping the back of my neck.

My gaze clashes with his, and if I were standing, I'd crumple to the ground. Tears well up in his eyes as he looks at me with so much adoration I can hear my heart pounding between my ears.

"I love you," I whisper, and he smiles, his white teeth on full display.

"I love you too."

I claim his lips in a sweet kiss and pray that this never ends, that I live every day with his cock buried inside me.

Chapter 34

Freya

My pussy aches with every step I take, but it was worth it. I didn't plan on screaming those words to Lucas, but in that moment, it felt right, and I'm so glad I did. It wasn't the first time I've said those words to him, or him to me, but I feel it stronger every time I do.

I don't want to lose him—I can't. If I lose anyone else at this point, I'll crumble, and I just don't know if I could continue living. I'm still wishfully praying that Alec will come back, but I'm starting to realize this is my new reality. The pain is still raw, and it fucking hurts. Having the guys and Amirah with me helps, but with this drama with Kai, things don't feel right. There's so much we need to say and fix.

"Fuck, I hope this meeting between them and us pays off," I say.

Lucas squeezes my hand in his as we reach the train tracks. "You can only try, but please, for the sake of my sanity, don't do anything reckless."

I nod, but both of us know full well that reckless is my middle name.

Kai agreed to meet me here, and so did Gage and Hazen, but none of them know that the other is coming. It had to be this way, or they wouldn't have come. I need to try one last time for a peace treaty. The battle lines may have been drawn, but I'll do everything in my power to stop this war from kicking off.

Footsteps crunch against the rocks behind us. Kai, Bear, and Zion move toward us. Kai gives me a brief look before his dark, stormy gaze pins to Lucas.

"What the fuck is he doing here?" he snaps as they reach us.

Zion gathers up his dirty-blond hair, putting it into a ponytail, and Bear reaches for his knife, flicking the blade with his eyes glued on Lucas.

"Chill, he was with me, and we need to chat," I say, stepping in front of Lucas, but he sidesteps, standing beside me.

The shriek of tires coming to a halt fills the air as Gage's black Bentley Mulliner Batur pulls up on their side of the tracks, and he exits the driver's seat. The sun rises over the skyline, and I have to shield my eyes from the brightness. He's wearing black cargo pants, his gray-scale tattoos peeking out from his white T-shirt.

Hazen hops out of the passenger seat, pulling his black cap over his head. He winks at me, and I smile.

"Freya?" Gage growls in question, and they all look at me.

My heart hammers inside my chest. I stand in the middle of the tracks between them both. Lucas moves, so he's on the Daringville side.

"Fuck you, Freya," Kai spits, and before I can take my next breath, he's moving, running over the tracks, with Bear and Zion right beside him. Lucas races faster, and fists fly between them all.

Fuck! No, this can't be happening. I enter the fray, grabbing on to Kai's waist, trying to yank him back, but he doesn't budge. I reach into the back of his pants, pulling out a gun. My hands tremble against the cool metal, and before I can think better of it, I lift it to the sky and pull the trigger three times.

My ears ring and everyone stops.

"Stop!" I scream, pushing my way between them.

Kai, Bear, and Zion step backward. Hazen grips his arm, blood seeping through his fingers. I grab his forearm, where a nasty cut reaches from his wrist to his elbow.

I whirl around, glaring at Bear, who shrugs, wiping the blood from his knife onto his shirt.

I feel Hazen, Gage, and Lucas at my back, and I release a loud exhale. "I won't allow this shit."

Kai scoffs. "You've got one minute," he bites out.

"Thank you. Now, look—I don't want anything to happen to any of you. Can we please just be adults and sort this out between us?" I ask, and Bear bites into his bottom lip, shaking his head slightly.

"We already tried that and look what happened. Hundreds died because of them," Kai says.

"Fuck off, that wasn't us—it was you," Gage yells, pushing against my back. I hold him off, raising the gun once more.

"Bullshit. We don't kill innocents," Kai says, and I believe him.

"Neither do they," I say.

"You chose them," Kai snaps, and I roll my eyes.

"Fine, I did, but I've always been your sister. What happened to 'we don't strike first'? What happened to family loyalty?" The words burn a long line down my throat. It's a soft blow, but fuck him if he won't accept a peace offering to avoid this war.

"Loyalty?" Kai scoffs. "You wanna talk about family loyalty? Where do you think we got these guns from?" Kai points behind me at Hazen.

Hazen's warmth from my back is gone. He pushes past me, getting right up in Kai's face. "The fuck you say?" he growls, and Kai steps back, grinning.

Bear moves again, knocking his fist into Lucas's jaw. He stumbles back, completely caught off guard. Before I have a chance to react, Bear wraps an arm around my neck and pulls me back against his body. I struggle against him but eventually stop. Bear is unpredictable, at best; he likes me, but that doesn't mean he won't hurt me. Bear's breath is heavy against the back of my neck.

"The fuck?" Kai growls, frowning at Bear. At least Kai still cares.

"Don't let him do this," I beg, and Kai's eyes soften for a second before they turn hard again, and he shakes his head.

"We're not getting a response from the supplier. We need leverage. Why not take something valuable to them?" Bear shrugs.

Kai studies the ground, then nods and softly says, "It's out of my hands." My chest squeezes.

Gage pulls out his gun at the same time as Kai and Zion, and I stand between them, placing my hand on Gage's heart, in the middle of the train tracks, with Bear's arm still firmly around me.

"Give her back," Lucas growls, stepping forward, and Bear's hand tightens around me.

"Talk to your father and give us the remainder of the weapons we paid for. Until then, she's ours," Kai says to Hazen before turning around.

"My father?" Hazen asks, his cheeks paler than they were a second ago. "What's he got to do with this?"

"Catch up, dickhead." Bear rolls his eyes dramatically. "Daddy dearest's been sellin' us weapons, but the last shipment was short. So we'll take this little weapon here"—Bear shoves me in the back, and I stumble forward before he catches me—"until you can provide us with the real ones."

"Like fuck you're taking her," Hazen says, his voice deep and gravelly.

"I won't walk away from you again," Gage says to me, and my pulse quickens. Those words hang heavily in the air, touching every single part of my heart. *He won't leave me. They won't.*

I've waited so long to hear those words from him—and now I have them. He loves me. He'll do anything for me.

And I'll do anything for him.

Which is why I have to stay. If I'm with Kai, I can convince him to stop this madness, surely.

"They won't hurt me. Just go," I plead, my voice coming out all raspy.

"No. Take me instead," Lucas says, stepping over the tracks.

"No, you idiot. They'll kill you!"

"He's right. We're taking him, not her," Kai says.

Bear presses a sloppy kiss against my cheek before shoving me forward, and Hazen pulls me into his embrace.

"No!" I yell, struggling against Hazen, but he wraps his arms around my waist, not letting me go.

They can't take Lucas. I'm safer with them because I know Kai won't hurt me, but Lucas? He wouldn't hesitate. Fuck. This can't be happening.

Bear grabs Lucas, snapping cuffs around his wrists before turning and walking away, leading Lucas as he goes. Kai and Zion follow.

"Don't you dare hurt him!" I yell, and Kai flips me off over his shoulder.

Hazen releases me and goes to follow, but I reach out, grabbing his uninjured arm and yanking him back over the tracks.

"You can't. We need you here," I say, and he rips his arm out of my grip and storms toward the car.

"Fuck!" he roars, and I stand there, frozen to the spot.

If Dominic gave the Daringhood boys weapons, then this changes everything. I came into this hoping for a way to end this war, and it just blew up in my face.

We are fucked.

Chapter 35

Hazen

I slam the car door shut. Anger roils inside me and my hands shake. Blood runs down my arm, and I lean forward, pulling off my T-shirt and fastening it around the knife wound. I can't fucking believe him. My father went behind our backs, behind The Brotherhood's backs, and gave weapons to our enemies. He betrayed us.

Dominic has always put The Brotherhood first. All my life, it's been drilled into me that they come before anything else—hell, even before ourselves. We don't exist as people; we are The Brotherhood. If what Kai said is true, then my father has broken our trust. Kai doesn't have any reason to lie about the weapons. Is my father that power hungry that he'd go against us?

Yes, he would. Fuck, why didn't Brax notice this? He's been glued to his ass, and now it's too late. We need to find out who else is involved in this and betrayed The Brotherhood, and we need to stop Dominic.

"That must be where the missing shipments have gone. Dominic has stolen them," Gage says from next to me in the driver's seat.

"Message Brax for an update on Dominic—does he have eyes on him? And call Duke. Ask him to review security footage to see if any of Dominic's men have been lurking around," I snap.

Gage taps away on his phone before bringing it to his ear. When he finishes, he places his phone in the center console. "He's on it, and Brax doesn't have eyes on Dominic. He lost him in traffic."

"Fuck!" I slam my fist down on the dashboard.

"What's the plan?" Freya asks from the back seat.

"We need to confront my father," I say, squeezing my eyes shut for a second, breathing in and out of my nose, trying to calm my racing pulse.

"No, let's just blow them all up. Fight to get our boy back," Gage declares.

I shake my head. "Then we'd be just as bad as them. We can't risk Lucas getting hurt in the crossfire. We need to see my father first."

"And how do we find him? Brax lost him," Gage says.

"Maybe Mia?" Freya suggests, and I quickly pull out my phone and press dial on her number. Why the hell didn't I think of her before? I've been too caught up in recruiting and keeping everything else afloat. She slipped my mind.

"Hello?" Mia answers.

"Where are you?" I ask, and Mia pauses.

"Why do you wanna know?" she asks, and I squeeze the bridge of my nose. I don't have time for her shit.

"Meet me in ten minutes at Ace of Hearts," I say, before hanging up.

We drive through town in silence. My knee bobs up and down; I'm itching to find my father. I need answers. Gage pulls up in the back of Ace of Hearts, and before he turns the car off, I'm out the door, stalking toward the back entrance.

This bar has been open for years. One of our guys took it over when it was a dive bar, and now it's an elite gentlemen's club for members only. I haven't been here in months.

I knock on the door, and it opens. Zeke stands there, frowning. "Man, didn't know you were coming here today. We aren't open yet, but come in." He steps aside, and I move past him.

"Sorry, bro, Brotherhood business. Meeting someone here," I say, moving down the dark corridor. Private rooms are on either side, all the doors shut, with neon lights indicating if the spaces are occupied or not. It's early morning, so no one is here yet, but when it's open, these rooms are always busy.

At the end of the corridor, the club opens up. The bar sits in the middle of the space, surrounded by dance floors, viewing docks, and luxe seating.

"Wow," Freya says from behind me.

I look over my shoulder, and her eyes are wide, taking it all in. "I'll bring you here one day when it's open. It's pretty cool."

Zeke puts on quite the show with his girls; it's like stepping into an award-winning circus but with sex.

I head over to the large black leather couch in the corner and take a seat. Freya sits next to me, and Gage falls into a chair opposite us.

"Can I get you any drinks?" Zeke asks, and I nod, listing off our order.

"We're expecting someone else," I say to Zeke, just as there's a knock at the back door.

Zeke disappears and comes back with Mia. Her high heels click against the floor. She flicks her straight, long hair over her shoulder as she stalks toward us.

I don't trust Mia; she's the reason my mother, brother, and sister left again. It's not the first time my mother's fled, either. Every time this happens, when she finds out about my father's affairs, she leaves, but she always comes back. He forces her to return to his grasp, and I hate him for it. They are better off away from here—at least I don't have to watch out for them that way. They are safe, and that's all I want.

"Martini, please," she says to Zeke as she moves past the bar.

"Mia," I say with a nod.

She smiles, taking a seat on a chair next to Gage's. "What can I help you with?" she asks, pursing her fake lips together.

"My father owes members of the Hood weapons that he's taken from us and promised them," I say, getting straight to the point. We don't have time to fuck around; they have Lucas. Who knows what they'll do to him while we try to recover their goods?

Zeke places our drinks on the table between us, and I thank him. I'm not worried about him overhearing our conversation; he's one of our most trusted men. He sits on the board and knows better than to gossip beyond here.

"Yeah, and?" Mia takes her drink and sips it.

"We need your help finding him."

Mia puts her glass back on the table, crosses one leg over the other, and leans back. "What's in it for me?"

Fucking hell, this bitch.

"What do you want?" Gage asks, and she looks between him and me, completely ignoring Freya next to me.

"I want power. To be the first woman councilor for The Brotherhood."

I laugh, grabbing my glass of scotch and downing it. "That's never going to fucking happen."

"You let Freya sit at the table and have power in decisions," Mia whines.

"That's different. She's one of us," I say with a small smirk. "You're not."

Mia's face falls, and she looks at Freya with a mixture of hatred and adoration. She wants to be her, but she never will be. There's only one Freya LeClair, and she's ours.

"Well, before she was Dominic's plaything, she was with my brother," Freya says, looking between Gage and me. "If she can help deal with Dominic, find her a role. This shit needs to be dealt with. It may help bring peace and stability, serving The Brotherhood, adding new perspective to the table."

The room falls silent. I ponder Freya's words. New perspectives aren't always bad—but they'd need to be from the right people. There's no way in hell I'd ever let Mia join The Brotherhood, but she doesn't need to know that. She just needs to think we will so that we can get to my father. The clock is ticking, and the more we fuck around with Mia, the less time we have.

"Fine, you've got yourself a deal," I say, and Mia grins. Gage makes a grumbling sound, but I ignore him. His eyes bore into my skull, but I'll fill him in after she's gone.

"He's set up base in Freya's old place," Mia says, and Freya sucks in a breath through her teeth.

"Over in Daringhood?" Freya asks.

Mia shakes her head. "In Daringville."

Freya's cheeks turn pale.

"How many men does he have?" I ask, desperate for more details.

"I-I'm not sure," Mia stammers.

"How many?" I repeat. "Take a fucking guess."

"Honest, every time I've been there, I've gone through the front door, messed around inside." She has the good grace to blush and not make eye contact, thank fuck. "Then left. All his men seem to work out the back in an extra garage."

"It'd be good to have more intel," Gage mutters. "That yard backs onto bushland. Could have five soldiers or five hundred."

"He wouldn't have that many." Mia scoffs. "And besides, you guys are The Brotherhood. You're going to take him down."

I stand. She's right. We fucking are.

How the fuck didn't Brax or Zeke discover this? Has he been there the entire time? Fuck me.

They say, *like father, like son*. Well, the joke's on Dad. No one knows him as well as I do, and while I've sought his approval for years, I've finally realized I'll never get it. Nor do I want it. He deliberately risked my life for his gain. If Kai hadn't let slip that he'd been supplying them with weapons, we could have lost Lucas or Freya—and all because of him.

The Brotherhood protects its own—but it seems Dad's forgotten that. Luckily, I haven't.

And I know just what to do about it.

"I've got a plan."

We're coming for you, Dad. I hope you're fucking ready.

Chapter 36

Lucas

The handcuffs rub against my skin as Bear pulls me along behind them like he's leading a horse around a barn. I'm fucking pissed off. Dominic gave them weapons. That explains the missing shipments at the dock. This changes everything. I knew he wanted us to fail, but this takes it to a whole new level. If what they are saying is true, Dominic's working with our enemy and supplying them with guns to kill his own people. What a fucking dog.

We head north along the train tracks. I'm so close to home, but if I run, they won't hesitate to put a bullet in my back. I have to play this smart. I'm leverage until I'm not. Until they get the rest of their supplies, apparently.

I couldn't let them take Freya. I knew if they did, she wouldn't come back. Kai wouldn't let his friend back into our fold. I have to save her, even if it's the last thing I do. Our hearts have been shattered into tiny broken pieces these past couple of months, but fuck, I'd still risk myself for her over and over.

Hazen must be losing his mind over this. The hate I feel toward Dominic? Hazen must feel it tenfold.

"Lost little puppy is now mine. Lost little puppyyyy," Bear sings, skipping as he pulls me along.

My fists curl, straining against the metal burning into my skin. Fuck, I hate him. He's got that look about him that screams *batshit crazy*. I've seen nutty before, but Bear's got to be mentally insane; he should be locked up in the Daring Asylum. Hell, he probably has been. He's unpredictable, and that makes it hard to guess what his next move will be. Or to guess what he's thinking, because fucking hell, I'd hate to know. One second, he's singing, the next, he's pulling out a knife, running the tip along his tongue and watching me with those fucking weird bright-green eyes.

We've been walking along the train tracks for ten minutes, and I fucking hope my brothers are getting answers. If I haven't heard from them in a couple of hours, I'll be fighting my way out and back to the safety of Daringville.

Freya wanted one last attempt at peace, and I was all for it, but this news threw it all under the bus. What else is Dominic hiding? What else has he done? Is this war against Daringhood all his doing? Was he responsible for the town hall explosion? I have no fucking idea, but it doesn't sound promising.

We stop outside of an old, abandoned train station on their side of the tracks. The windows are all smashed in, but the bars are still in place.

"This shall be perfect for my puppy dog." Bear drags me around to the front entrance. The door is already open, and we walk into a dark, open room. Chairs line the walls, half ripped up and sitting sideways or completely broken. The stench of dust and mold fills the air, and I wish I had a free hand to cover my nose.

Kai and Zion don't follow, leaving me alone with Bear. He brushes past me before shutting the door. Darkness surrounds me. He flicks on his phone light, aiming it at me.

"They only left one of you against me—you must be the expendable one," I say, taunting him.

The corner of Bear's mouth lifts, and he chuckles. "No. I'm just that good."

"Fair enough. You don't need me tied up, then, do you?" I say, raising my wrists.

Bear pulls out his knife, running the blade over his bottom lip. Blood drips down his chin, but he doesn't move his gaze from mine. "Tell me, Lucas, do you like the smell of burning flesh?" he asks, moving around me. I don't turn. I keep looking straight ahead, my pulse quickening.

"Ehhh, not particularly," I reply, trying to figure out where he's going with this. Who the fuck knows?

"I do. It smells divine—like burned leather mixed with sweat. And sometimes like burned steak on the grill. Fucking beautiful." Bear jumps right in front of me, and I stumble backward, the cuffs around my hands keeping me off balance.

He grins, his bright-white teeth on full display. I shiver, wanting to get the fuck outta Dodge. I've smelled burning flesh before, and it's fucking gross. The fact that he likes it says a lot about him.

"Tick tock, tick tock. The clock is running out," Bear sings and pulls me roughly forward by my cuffs.

I lose my balance and fall to my knees, the hard ground ripping my pants. Asshole. "Fuck you," I spit through my teeth.

"I'd fuck you in the ass until you bled, but I don't think we have time for that. Do you?" Bear grins, and a shiver runs down my spine. Creepy fuck.

"Stop being a little bitch and untie me, or are you scared I'll hurt you?" I ask, pushing out my bottom lip.

Bear's eyes darken before he smirks. "You can't touch me, little Lucas. I mean, look at you," he says, pointing down my body, then back at his. "You're weak. I'm strong. Maybe I will untie you so we can have a fair fight. What do you think?"

He peers past me at something in the corner of the room before he reaches into his pocket, pulling out the keys and unlocking the cuffs. They land on the ground with a clank, and I roll my wrists but don't otherwise move. I stay perfectly still, staring at Bear.

He starts hopping from one foot to the other, bouncing around with a lopsided smile. "Fight me, Lucas. You know you want to."

I shake my head. There's no way I'm waiting around in here with this lunatic, and I'm not taking the first swing.

"Aww, didn't our girl kill your mother? Ouch. That must have hurt."

I see red. Everything around us disappears until it's just Bear right in front of me. My fist flies straight for his nose, and he doesn't do anything to stop it. He takes the full hit, falling sideways. Blood shoots from his nose, and he grins. When blood runs down his lip onto his teeth, he licks them, his eyes rolling to the back of his head.

Before I have a chance to move, he's on me, tackling me to the floor. My back smashes against the hard floor, and a heavy breath leaves me. Pain shoots through me, and it takes me a second to move. Bear punches my stomach over and over. I kick and punch him back, grabbing a handful of his bleached-blond hair. I pull hard and smash my fist into his nose. It's bent, probably broken, but the look in his eyes tells me he's enjoying the pain.

In the next second, he leaps up, and I take a fistful of hair with me. He pulls out his knife, jumping onto my stomach, then forcing me onto my back. I kick and try to buck him off, but he's too heavy. He pins me down with his knees and brings the knife to my throat.

"Bye bye, little pup. I'll miss watching you be a good little boy for me," Bear says, and I spit, hitting his cheek.

He grins, and for the first time in my life, I think it's over. He's got me, and fuck, I don't want to leave this world yet.

Chapter 37

Freya

I n between staring at the plain-white ceiling of my bedroom, I check my phone for the third time, the cool glass smooth against my fingertips. It's been twenty minutes since Gage and Hazen left to get a team of new recruits together to infiltrate Dominic's home. Every minute that ticks by, Lucas could be beaten to a pulp. I can't stay here, not when the man I love is in danger.

I call Hazen, and he answers after two rings. "Hey."

"We need to go now," I say, and Hazen says something to someone on the other end, but I can't hear.

"We are moving as fast as we can, but these things take time. My father is dangerous."

"Then let me help." I sit up, moving back against the pillows.

"He will use you as my weakness—you're the only person I'd do anything for." Hazen's voice softens, and my heart skips a beat. He's right, but it doesn't help Lucas. Every second that goes by is another second without him.

"I'll see you soon," I say, before hanging up.

I need to do something, anything at all.

Five minutes later, the door to my bedroom opens, and Mia walks through.

"Anything?" I ask, shuffling to the end of my bed and dangling my feet over the edge.

Mia shakes her head, moving farther into the room.

"We need to do something," I say.

"I know. But what?" She slumps next to me on the comforter, and a light enters her eyes. "We could . . . sneak in."

"You think?" I ask, but a plan's already forming in my mind. "Like, to see how many men they have, so we can help the boys be better prepared."

"Exactly!" Mia agrees.

"We can't tell them, though. Otherwise, they won't let us go. They are already busy enough, arming up, planning, and gathering the men." I slide off my bed, shoving my phone into the pocket of my pants.

"We gotta go now. Everyone is out back." Mia heads out the door, and I follow closely behind.

Hazen and Gage will be pissed when they find out, but I need to contribute somehow, and it's either this or crossing the tracks to negotiate with Kai—and I'm pretty sure they'll like this plan better.

We walk through the front door, and one of the new guards standing by the door watches me closely.

"Approved by Hazen and Gage," I say, and he nods before letting us through.

"Let's take my car. I parked it down the road," Mia says, pulling out her keys from her bag.

The drive through Daringville is quick, and before I know it, we're parked a couple of doors down from my childhood home. My stomach churns with anxiety, a heavy feeling that intensifies as I shut the car door behind me. Maybe we should wait for the guys. But Dominic has fooled us all before. Any intel we can gather will help. We need to do this—for Lucas.

"Where are they going to be?" I ask Mia, and she turns around, taking my hand in hers and pulling me into the backyard of the house next door to mine.

It feels so fucking surreal, being back here and about to go into the house that holds so many good and bad memories for me. Of course, Dominic chose this place.

"The guards will be inside or out back in the garage," Mia says, and I squeeze her hand back.

I've never liked Mia much, but what she's doing for us gives her a little street cred in my books. She didn't have to tell us where Dominic was hiding out, but she did—well, with a little side deal. She is getting exactly what she wants in exchange for what she's doing, and I'd do the same thing if I were in her shoes.

That's exactly why I currently trust her.

The plan is simple: we'll check on Dominic, see how many men the guys are going to deal with, and report back to them. They'll come with the new recruits and get the weapons back and save Lucas, and then we can hopefully sort out some kind of peace agreement between the Hood and the Ville. I hope this works.

"Let's go," Mia says, releasing my hand, and she moves through the bushes of the neighbor's yard. She looks left and right.

Something catches my eye, and I reach out, grabbing her arm, pulling her back into the leafy scrub. A couple of guys walk past us, coming from my old backyard. They are dressed in all black with rifles strapped to their backs, looking like they are ready for war.

"What the fuck?" I hiss, and Mia shakes her head, pressing her finger to her lips. Voices carry through the afternoon air, and Mia moves through the bushes, going deeper into the neighbor's yard. I peer through the bushes, and all the blood rushes to my ears.

In my old backyard are at least fifty men, all dressed in black. Some are sparring against one another; others are pulling out guns from wooden crates. Holy fucking shit. We knew he'd have men, but this many? It's next level. He's creating an army for something. But for what?

"We need to call Hazen and Gage," I say, and Mia presses her lips together before nodding.

I crawl out of the bushes, but my hand lands on a hard black boot. Fuck.

"Leaving so soon?" a voice that sounds all too familiar asks. My gaze moves from the boot up into Dominic's blue eyes.

Mia brushes past me, gets to her feet, and runs, but Dominic is faster. He grabs her by the throat, and her eyes widen.

"Don't hurt her," I plead.

Dominic scoffs. "Shut the fuck up. Both of you are coming with me." He nods his head toward Mia. "And you're a traitorous bitch."

He grabs my shoulder, forcing me to stand. As he digs his fingers in, tightening his grip, I grit my teeth.

Mia struggles against his hold, and it takes everything in me not to fight back—it's not worth it. We wanted to talk to him, and now we can, though this isn't the way I intended.

"This place should be familiar to you, Freya," Dominic says.

I bite into the inside of my cheek. If I give him anything, it'll be exactly what he wants.

Dominic shoves Mia inside the house first, then me, and I stumble in. Bracing my hands on my knees, I push myself up and my eyes widen. Everything's changed, yet everything is the same. The dark floorboards I've walked on a million times before. The white walls with light-blue floral wallpaper. The only difference is the swarm of soldiers inside the house, moving around. Some of them look familiar, men I recognize from The Brotherhood, and I know the guys are going to be pissed that they turned on them.

I move toward the living room, clutching the door as memories invade my mind.

Alec chasing me around the room before tackling me onto the rug. Playing board games until the early hours of the morning. Mom cuddling us to sleep on the couch, telling us stories. Tears fall down my cheeks as I'm taken back to the best memories of my life, before everything changed. Before the ground was ripped from under our feet, all thanks to Nadine. For giving Mom the drug that changed everything.

Dominic's hand lands on my shoulder, his breath lingering as he moves in close, but I don't dare move. "Aww, Freya, is this all too much for you, doll?"

I take in a deep breath and exhale before rolling my shoulders and barging past Dominic. I'm done playing his games; I need answers.

Wiping away the tears staining my cheeks, I face him. "Shut up and tell me what you're planning here," I snap.

The corner of Dominic's stupid fucking mouth lifts. "I always loved them feisty, and here she finally is." Dominic grins, and I roll my eyes. "Mia, lead the way to my office, won't you, darling?"

Mia's throat bobs before she turns and walks down the corridor, her hands shaking. I follow her, watching Dominic closely over my shoulder. One wrong move, and we won't make it out of here alive. We have to get back to Lucas. As much as I love Kai, I don't trust that he won't hurt him. They hate each other more than anything, and with Lucas left under Bear's wing? Who knows what fucked-up things are happening to him.

My fingers run along the familiar white-and-blue floral wallpaper. Pieces crumble in my fingers, and I have to look away. I remember helping Mom put the wallpaper up on the walls; we had music blaring, and she had no idea what she was doing, but she did it. I passed her the pieces and watched in awe as she worked. She sang, laughed, and gave me treats. I'd almost forgotten about those days—the good days. When everything turned to shit, I tried to hold on to those good times, but they eventually vanished.

I follow Mia to the last room down the hallway and stop just outside the door. My fingers grip to the doorframe, my pulse quickening and my breaths coming out in short bursts. My old bedroom. Where my single bed once stood, with my red-and-black checkered duvet, now stands a dark wooden desk.

Heat hits my back, Dominic's breath tickling my neck, and I want to move away but I can't. My feet won't budge. They're planted to the ground.

"When I took over this place, I just knew this was going to be my favorite room," Dominic whispers in my ear.

He grabs my shoulder, and I've had enough. I stumble forward, out of his reach, moving next to Mia. She stands, looking between Dominic and me, her face neutral, showing no emotion.

I breathe in and out through my nose, picturing all the ways I want to kill him. Rip his heart out and stomp on it for everything he's done to me, to my mother and the guys. He's a monster, and I can't stand being in his presence any longer.

"You sold weapons to the Hood. How could you betray your precious Brotherhood?" I ask, pushing down the bile rising up my throat and locking down the old memories that want to resurface. We need to survive.

Dominic laughs, moving into the room and stopping right in front of us. "That's a big accusation, Freya—something that could start a war."

I cross my arms over my chest. "Just admit it and hand the guns over before it's too late. They have Lucas."

He scoffs. "Even if I did, what makes you think I'd be happy to pay my dues just to save one of the boys who betrayed me?"

"Well, what are you gonna do? Kill your own son?"

"No." Dominic grins. An evil glint flashes in his eyes, and my heart skips a beat.

Two guards move through the doorway, carrying automatic rifles, and block our exit.

Dominic steps forward, and I retreat until my ass hits his desk.

He licks his lips, his gaze moving up and down my body. A shiver rolls through me.

Shit, maybe this wasn't such a good idea after all.

Chapter 38

Gage

We've gathered fifty of our old and the best of the newest recruits. Now, we're grabbing the last of our weapons. With the last shipment being low, thanks to Dominic, we don't have what we need.

"Get the transport ready, and I'll get Freya and Mia," I say, grabbing my phone and keys from the office table.

"Freya shouldn't come, it's too dangerous," Hazen says.

I shake my head. "You know our girl. She won't let us leave without her. We need her with us, to know she's safe."

He releases a loud exhale. "Fine. Meet you out front in ten."

I leave, moving out of the office, then through the training center, keeping my head down, staring at my boots. I'm worried about Lucas, and the longer it takes us to sort this mess out, the more my chest constricts. We need to make sure we have enough manpower to confront

Dominic, just in case he did anything reckless. He's unpredictable, and we can't afford any more losses.

Stepping back inside Hazen's house, I take the stairs two at a time and storm down the hallway. The door to Freya's room is open. I take one step inside and my heart sinks. Where the fuck is she? I move through the room and into the bathroom, but it's empty.

There's a knock on the door, and one of the new guards clears his throat.

"Where the fuck are the girls?" I ask.

He frowns. "Freya and Mia left about twenty minutes ago. They said you approved it."

"They what?!" I yell, and his face pales. Of fucking course she left. Fuck me, this girl.

"Where?" I ask, barging past him, and he shakes his head. I raise my gun and pull the trigger. As he falls to the ground, I storm past him. Fucking useless.

The front door opens and slams shut. I run down the hallway and stop at the top of the stairs. Mia's standing on the landing, her face red, eyes wild. I'm down the stairs and off the bottom step in seconds. I reach her, grabbing her by the shoulders and shaking her.

Hazen comes through the door, his gaze moving between us.

"Where's Freya?" I ask Mia.

She shakes her head, her brow furrowing. My grip tightens, and she winces, but I can't pull away. If anything's happened to Freya, I'm going to kill the motherfucker who caused her pain.

"He's got Freya," Mia sobs, and I'm frozen, unable to move or breathe. Everything turns dark, and I can't see straight. Mia's face blurs. "You have to come. I managed to escape, but we don't have much time."

A hand lands on my arm, and it takes a moment for my vision to come back into focus. I release Mia, and she stumbles backward before spinning around and running toward the door. We follow her out and all pile into my car.

My foot hits the gas. The security gate opens just in time for us to fly through. I'm not stopping for anyone. My girl is in trouble, and if anyone walks in front of the car, I'll run them over without remorse. My fingers grip the steering wheel so tightly it feels like I might be able to rip it off.

I pull the car to a stop a few houses back from where Dominic is holed up, my tires screeching. I'm out the door, running after Mia and Hazen. The smell of burned rubber fills the air.

"Where is she?" I ask, and Mia stops at the house next door. I want to scream at her for coming here with Freya alone, but now isn't the time.

There are at least a dozen guards patrolling Freya's old house, and I recognize most of them; they are members of our Brotherhood. What the actual fuck? I should just pull out my gun now and shoot them because they are dead to us anyway. You betray your brothers, you pay with your life.

"We have to go through the secret passage. Dominic uses the old underground passages that connect Daringhood and the Ville. I've used this one to escape a few times," Mia says, moving onto the porch of the house next door.

"Do we need backup?" I ask as we step into the house.

Mia looks over her shoulder, scrunching up her nose. "You guys can't handle a little trouble?"

"You know we can, but I still think we should alert someone. Message Ronald and tell him Freya's been kidnapped and to send out the men," I say to Hazen, and he nods.

I pull out my own phone as we follow Mia deeper into the house and tap out a message to Amirah.

Me: Freya's been kidnapped. Be on alert. Don't do anything stupid or reckless. Stay put.

I hope to fuck Amirah listens for once. I can't lose her or Freya. It's not an option.

We follow Mia down a flight of stairs into a dark basement, the stairs creaking under every step. Hazen flicks the light on, and there's nothing in here, apart from a little door in the middle of the wall straight ahead.

If Mia fucks with us now, I'll lose my mind.

The stale, musty air clings to my nose the longer we stay down here. Mia stops in front of the wooden trapdoor. She opens it, and I peer inside. There's nothing but darkness ahead.

"Give me one good reason to trust you," I demand.

Mia snorts. "You're giving me exactly what I want—more power. So why would I fuck that up?"

She's right, but still, I don't trust her.

"You first," I say, and Mia shrugs, kneeling and crawling through the hole.

I wait a couple of seconds before following her in. Hazen comes in behind me, leaving the door open. I shine my phone light ahead while my knees and hands sink into the hard dirt. The air closes in around me, and I want to get out of here as fast as we can. It feels as though the walls are getting smaller, closer, like I've got nowhere to go.

If I die in here, I'll be fucking pissed. It's no way to leave this world, in a closed-off dirt tunnel. No way in hell.

Mia suddenly stops, and I bump into her ass.

"What the fuck? Give me some warning before I'm sniffing your butt," I snap.

"Shut up," Mia whispers. "I'm about to open the door, and I don't know what'll await us on the other side."

She twists the handle. The door creaks before light fills the tunnel. She sticks her head out and then opens the door fully, sliding out.

"Ready?" I ask Hazen, and he pushes my back without saying a word. That's a good enough answer for me.

I grab my gun from its pouch. The cool metal rests in my palm, and I follow Mia out, exiting into an empty, brightly lit bedroom. The floorboards creak under my feet.

"Where is she?" Hazen asks, moving toward the closed door.

"In the room next door. Follow my lead." Mia brushes past Hazen and opens the door slowly. She waves us through, and we move into a quiet corridor. Voices carry from the front of the house, but no one seems to be back here.

I push past Mia and run to the next room. The door is open, and anger rages through my blood. Freya is tied to the chair behind the desk, her eyes wide and her mouth covered in tape. Hazen moves quickly, reaching her before I do. He starts untying the rope from her bound hands and legs.

She looks at me, her eyes wide, and I fall to my knees in front of her, my hand caressing her cheek. She's yelling something behind the tape. I rip it off as gently as I can.

She licks her dry lips. "It's a trap!" she screams, and before I can find my feet, footsteps slap against the floorboards.

"Well, well, well. Look who finally decided to show up and rescue their little pet." Dominic's voice sounds like nails against a chalkboard.

I stand, pulling Freya up, trying to keep her behind me, but she rips herself free from my grasp and stands between me and Hazen.

Mia is gone. Has she betrayed us, or did she get lucky and escape? I don't know, and right now, I don't care—we have bigger issues at hand. Four guards fill the room, and Dominic stands in the doorway.

With a smirk, he snaps his fingers together. "Finish them!"

"Would you really order the murder of your own son?" Hazen asks, and Dominic steps inside the room, within reach of us.

"You're still welcome to join me." Dominic reaches out, landing a hand on Hazen's shoulder. When he winces, I fist my hands at my sides. "Remember how things used to be, son, how we were a team." Dominic pauses and releases a heavy breath. "I've taught you so much—you need me."

I scoff, and Dominic looks at me, the corner of his mouth lifting. "That goes for you, too, Gage. You're like a son to me. We can all lead together."

"Not a chance," I say, and Dominic steps back, putting some distance between us.

"Son?" Dominic looks back at Hazen, and he shakes his head.

"We may have a common enemy, but we won't be giving up our leadership to a man who's made so many shitty decisions," Hazen says.

Dominic's lip curls. "You had your chance, and since you're not leaving this house alive, I'll admit to one last thing." His gaze focuses on Freya. "The town hall wasn't the Hood's doing—it was mine."

Someone gasps and my ears ring. Everything around me closes in. I can't breathe. I can't see straight.

He disappears through the door. "Kill them!" he yells, before slamming the door shut.

Everything comes back to me, and we're closed in the room with four guards.

"You really want to turn your back on The Brotherhood and work for him? Someone who took all those innocent lives?" Hazen says, taking a step forward and shoving his gun into its holster, raising his hands up in surrender. He's offering them a peace treaty.

Fuck that—they betrayed us the moment they traded sides and chose to work for *him*. They don't get a second chance in my books.

"He was our leader first," one of the older guards says, and I recognize him. He's always been a soldier, never moving higher up the ranks.

"Wrong answer," Hazen says, before he charges forward and chaos erupts.

I turn to Freya. "Leave through the door at the first chance you get and run."

She shakes her head. "No. We fight together."

I open my mouth to argue, but a fist lands against my cheek, knocking my head backward. Ringing pierces my ears, and it takes me a second to get my bearings before I release havoc.

The only way we are getting out of here is by killing these dogs.

Chapter 39

Lucas

Images of Freya and my brothers flash in my mind. Watching Freya come apart below me, the way her dark-pink lips part and a soft moan falls from her lips.

We've been through so much heartache together, and there's no way I'm leaving this world now. Even after she broke my heart and took my mother from me, I couldn't walk away from her. I choose Freya, to be by her side through everything life throws at us. I won't allow someone else to force us apart again. I'll fight until my dying breath—for her, for them, and for us. Sure, I don't believe in happily ever after, like in those stories I read to my sister when we were kids, but I do believe in forever with them. So that's what I'll fight for.

The blade of Bear's knife digs into my neck. Warm blood trickles down my skin, and I decide his too-white teeth need knocking out.

"You really want to be a bitch and win this fight without giving me a chance?" I ask, raising my eyebrow.

Bear's eyes narrow into slits before his tongue slides between his lips. "You're a smart little pup, aren't you?" he teases, pulling the knife back slightly. "You want a treat for being a good boy?"

I hold back my smart-ass reply before nodding. I'll play his game, if it means giving me a chance to get out of here alive.

"Woof like a good boy for me, pup," Bear says.

I bite into my bottom lip, shaking my head. No way in hell I'm doing that.

He smirks. "No treat for you, then." He hums a tune, closing his eyes, and I take my chance.

I buck my hips. Bear loses his balance, falling sideways. He sits on the floor with a thud, and I jump up and ease backward. Bear laughs, getting to his feet, the knife in his hand.

"Fuck, I think I love you, my naughty little pup," he says, and I roll my eyes.

"Drop the knife and fight me like a man."

Bear brings the blade to his bottom lip, watching me closely, and I'm ready to bolt. My gaze shifts to the exit, and Bear follows my line of sight before dropping the knife on the floor between us.

"On the count of three, the first one to get the knife wins. Then it's a battle to the death. May the best dog win," Bear says, and before he starts to count, I move. Fuck him and his games. I'm taking charge.

I jump forward, grabbing the knife. As I grip the leather handle, Bear's blood stains the blade from earlier.

"Naughty little pup. Such a bad, bad boy." Bear purses his lips together. "You're my new favorite. Wanna fuck?" Then he grins.

I charge at him. He doesn't move as the knife plunges into the side of his stomach. He doesn't fight or show any emotion. He just watches me. And then his eyes turn from bright green to dark in one blink.

Bear shoves me hard, and I stumble, falling on my ass. The knife is still imbedded in his stomach, blood oozing out, painting his white T-shirt red. He pulls out the knife without even an ounce of pain evident on his face. He brings the blade to his lips and licks off the blood, his eyes rolling closed. I need to move now, but I can't. I'm stuck to the floor, watching this lunatic taste his own blood like it's a drug.

His eyes glaze over. "You just stabbed me, and I still want to shove my dick in your ass."

"You are batshit crazy," I say, getting to my feet.

Bear drops the knife over his back, and it lands on the floor with a *clink*. He pulls his T-shirt over his head and drops it at his feet. Blood gushes out from his side, and at this point, I'm wondering how he's still standing. Is he even human?

"I may be crazy, but you're still my little bitch. Wanna come lick Daddy's wounds, pup?"

He stands between me and the exit, and his gaze is locked on mine. But I need to get out of here—now. I'm done with him.

"I'm outta here," I say and head straight for Bear. He doesn't move.

"What? You going to see your little girlfriend who killed your parents? You'd rather her over me?" Bear snorts. "Such a sad wittle puppy."

I jab my shoulder into his, and before I take my next step, his arm whips out, gripping me around the throat, cutting off my air. He pushes me backward until my back hits the wall. Pain shoots through my spine, but I keep a neutral expression.

"You've made Daddy very sad. Choosing her over me," he says, and white-hot rage pulses through me. I'm so done.

I push into his grip, wriggling to try to free myself, cutting off even more of my own air supply in the process.

Bear punches me in the eye, and my head snaps sideways. I can't breathe. I manage to use the last piece of energy I have left to push my fingers into Bear's wound. His grip loosens, and I take that moment to pull free, dodging his arm aiming for me, and I run. I run without looking back.

My breath wheezes through my throat as I rush through the door.

"This isn't the end. I'll come find you!" Bear yells, his voice following me outside.

Kai and Zion are nowhere to be seen, so I bolt, placing one foot in front of the other until I'm well over the tracks, and I come to a stop in front of our neighborhood gates. The sun's setting and it'll be dark soon.

I brace my hands on my knees, catching my breath. My lungs burn hot, and not enough oxygen is getting through me. One of my eyes is swollen shut. The gate opens, and I look up. Amirah's pink Bentley stops in front of me and the passenger door opens.

"What the fuck happened to you?" she asks from the driver's seat, eyeing me up and down.

"Long story. Where are they?"

"Get in," Amirah snaps, and I jump in. Before I even shut my door, she shoots off.

"Dominic has Freya, the guys are there, and shit's fucked up," Amirah explains.

Fuck. We can't get to them quick enough. I didn't go through all this shit to lose them.

Amirah pulls up out the front of Freya's old house and gets out.

"Go back home, Amirah. I've got it from here. The first lady of The Brotherhood can't be out on the streets unprotected. Shit's about to explode, and you can't be in the middle of it."

Amirah shakes her head. "No."

I round the car, then push her back into the front seat. "Go the fuck home. Now!" I growl, and she huffs but doesn't fight me. I never get angry at her or raise my voice, but we can't have her out here. I have no idea what I'm about to walk into and can't look after her too.

She drives off, and I roll my shoulders back. Cars arrive. Our men storm out, covering the streets.

It's time to find my woman and my brothers.

Chapter 40

Hazen

My fist smashes into the traitor's nose. A loud crack pierces through the room, and it's like a lullaby to my ears. Fuck these assholes. I need to get to my father and finish this; he's gone too far this time. An uncontrollable fire flares to life inside me, the flames burning through my heart until I feel nothing for him or anyone who gets in my way.

After taking over The Brotherhood, I wanted to change things, to gain control of Daringhood again and make things peaceful. Look at how well that's turned out, all because my father doesn't want to let go of the power. He wants to hold on to what our ancestors created for us. If he just allowed us to lead, then none of this would have happened. We wouldn't be fighting so hard with the Hood. Our brothers wouldn't be forced to pick sides between us and Dominic. Lucas wouldn't be held hostage. Freya wouldn't have been taken.

Everything is at the hands of the person I call my father, but he's as good as dead to me now.

All my life, I wanted him to respect me. I sought his approval and did everything I could to make him proud. Pathetic, when I think about it, but I didn't know any better. Now I realize how much heartache he's caused for me, for us, and I'm done being his son.

One soldier drops to the ground. Blood pours from his unrecognizable face, and I should feel bad. I don't. He deserves it for choosing Dominic over us. We are the leaders now, and if you aren't with us, then you're nothing but gum to my boot.

The man lies on the ground, unconscious. One down. I look around the room. Gage has killed one guy, leaving two more. He's fighting against one, and the other is closing in on Freya. Oh, hell no.

I stalk toward them. The soldier goes to punch her in the jaw, but before I can get there, she ducks and kicks her leg out, bringing him to the ground. Warmth fills my body for a split second. I storm up to her and claim her lips in a red-hot kiss. I want to fuck her right here on his desk, but with so much chaos going on around us, it'll have to wait.

Freya is pulled away from me. The soldier has his hand wrapped around her hair. Freya screams, and I see red. I wrap my hand around his throat, hard. He releases her hair, his eyes widening. When he tries to speak, I squeeze harder until his eyes almost pop out of their sockets. He takes his final breath before I release him, and his lifeless body falls to my feet.

Freya slides up next to me and spits. It lands on his cheek, and the corner of my mouth lifts for a split second before I remember what's at stake and what I have to do next.

A loud pop fills the room, and Gage keeps his gun out, aimed at the door. All four guards are dead.

"Let's find Dominic. He can call this off," I say, moving toward the door.

Freya and Gage follow me out into the corridor. I take my gun out of its holster and keep my finger on the trigger, waiting for someone to pop out of a closed door.

Voices carry from the front of the house, and the closer we get, the louder they sound. I stop just outside the living room doors. They are open and I peer inside. My feet freeze to the spot. There, with Dominic, is Ronald, one of our most trusted councilmen, and a bunch of the older soldiers. They're standing around Dominic like they are worshipping a god.

"We're going to withhold the weapons from the Hood—create a war, and who will save the precious citizens of Daringville by blowing up the Hood, other than yours truly? It won't be long before the Ville will be mine again," Dominic says, his voice getting louder with each word. They cheer, and I use the opportunity to move into the room. Raising my gun to the roof, I let off one round, then another.

Silence fills the room, and all eyes are on me. I move through the crowd, coming face to face with him. He's not my father. He just fucked my mother and came inside of her and she had me. He doesn't deserve the title.

"You'll have to get through us first," I say, and Dominic throws his head back and laughs. My hand shakes as I move the gun around in my grip.

"You're weak. You let women sway you." Dominic steps into my gun. The metal presses against his dead, cold heart. He looks behind me, his lips curving into a half smile. "I mean, I get it, son. She's got a nice, tight cunt. The way it—"

He doesn't get to finish as chaos erupts around us. Somebody shoves me forward. I lose the grip I had on my gun, and it falls to the ground.

Gage starts fighting against Ronald, and Freya punches a guard in the face. I grip on to Dominic's shirt as he stumbles backward, falling to the ground, and I straddle him. My fist smashes into his cheek, and he grins, blood staining his teeth.

"Aww, did I hurt your feelings?" he asks, pouting his bottom lip.

Everything around us disappears until it's just us. The guy I spent so much time trying to impress, lying beneath me, his eyes the same blue as mine. I used to love that we had the same color eyes, but now I hate it.

"I hate you," I spit.

He chuckles. "I knew you'd disappoint me, eventually. I wasted too much time on a good-for-nothing little boy."

Something smashes into my side, and I fall down, hard. It takes me a second to get my bearings, but before I can, Dominic is on me. He punches me in the stomach repeatedly. My ribs burn, and I struggle to breathe. He grabs something from the ground—my gun is in his grip. I lunge forward, but he dodges and moves behind me, then wraps his arm around my throat, pinning my back to his front. I slam my foot down on his, and he leans forward, but his grip doesn't release. He gives me just enough room to breathe.

The coolness of metal presses against my skull. I look around the room, my gaze locking with hers. I mouth, *I love you*, and she says it back.

"Even if you kill me, my brothers—they will fight," I say, watching as Gage brings Ronald down, and he surrenders to him, raising his hands up in defeat. Gage doesn't finish him; he offers Ronald his hand, and he takes it.

"It'll be worth it. You're not my son," Dominic whispers into my ear, and I expect to feel something, but nothing comes.

"And you're not my father," I yell.

Grabbing his arm, I flip him over my back, and he crashes against the floor. He scrambles to his feet, the gun lying between us. He looks from me to the gun, then we both move at the same time. I dive for it, but he grabs it first. I roll onto my side, finding my feet again.

He holds up the gun, aiming it right at Freya. My heart thuds, and I'd gladly step in front of her to save her. She's got so much more life to live—this can't be it for her. I won't allow it.

My gaze locks with Gage's. He throws his gun to me. As it sails through the air, Gage runs, tackling Freya to the ground. A gunshot goes off as my fingers wrap around the Glock. I aim it at Dominic and pull the trigger. The bullet hits him in the heart.

He looks down as blood oozes through his shirt. He drops to the ground, and his head hits the floor with a loud thud. His heart will stop any second now. He's gone, and I don't feel any remorse. My family is who I've chosen—not him.

Footsteps slap against the ground. A familiar mop of blond hair moves into the room. "What'd I miss?" Lucas asks, and I ignore him, moving to Freya and Gage.

If she's dead, that's it for me. Fuck The Brotherhood and fuck everything else. Without her, there's nothing left.

Gage is crouched over her. I pull him away, and Freya looks up at me with her bright-blue eyes and smiles. "Is he dead?"

I nod. "He can't hurt you anymore," I say, and she wraps her arms around my neck, pulling me to the ground.

Her lips clash against mine, and a wave of relief washes through my veins.

It's done. Now it's time to reunite our men and prevent a war.

Chapter 41

Freya

I pull back, resting my hands on Hazen's chest. It rises and falls at the same pace as mine. We're okay. Dominic is gone. Hazen's right—he can't hurt me or us again. Everything is right in the world. The asshole is dead. I smile, teeth and all.

Arms wrap around me from behind. I look up into Lucas's shining eye—the other is practically swollen shut—and squeal. He lifts me and my hands tangle around his neck.

"Is it good to see me, little thorn?" Lucas asks, and I chuckle, pressing my lips to his and putting everything into the kiss. He's safe—well, apart from the swelling and a few bruises on his cheek and nose. Bear did a number on him.

I pull back and Lucas slaps my ass.

"Let's celebrate our reunion later. We've gotta take back control of our town now that he's dead," Hazen says, getting up off the ground.

"Where's Mia?" I ask. Last time I saw her was in the office, then she disappeared.

"No idea, who cares?" Gage moves in front of Ronald, and he gets to his feet. The rest of the men have left. "Before we round up and kill all those who aren't with us, we need to deal with the elephant in the room." Gage clears his throat.

Ronald is in the corner, holding his bleeding nose, watching us closely. I glare at him, the traitorous bastard. He should be dead for choosing Dominic over us.

"Why did you betray us, Ronald?" Hazen asks, towering over the older man.

He raises his hands in surrender. "I didn't want to. Dominic had shit on me from my life before The Brotherhood. He threatened me, said that he'd use it to ruin my marriage. I couldn't afford to lose Meredith." His voice drops at the mention of his wife, and part of me feels sorry for him.

"You could have come to us about this, and we would have fixed it," Gage says.

Ronald nods solemnly. "I know, and I'm sorry. I'll spend the rest of my life making it up to you boys. You are the true leaders of The Brotherhood, and I want to be part of that."

Silence fills the room. Lucas takes my hand and squeezes.

"Fine. You are on probation. One wrong move and you are done. Got it?" Hazen crosses his arms over his chest, and my stomach flips.

I'm going to lock these men up in my room later and let them control me like this. My cheeks burn, and I try to think of anything but fucking them. Seeing them be all bossy drives me crazy.

Ronald nods.

Hazen steps aside. "Gather up all the traitors and bring them to us."

Ronald scurries out of the room, nodding at Lucas on his way past.

"What about the guns that the Hood are apparently owed?" I ask, dreading the answer. Either way we act, it won't end well for us.

"Why give them more power?" Hazen asks.

I press my lips together. "If Kai gets his guns, he'll have more power to use against us, but if he doesn't, he'll be pissed and use that anger against us." I sigh.

Hazen scratches the back of his neck. "Let's leave some cars from my father's estate for them and give them a night to cool down."

"It's something," I say. "We'll ask for a meeting—they need to know Dominic was behind the town hall bombing too. Let me text Kai and get one of your men to drop them off at the park."

Hazen nods and I text Kai.

"We'll try to broker an agreement one last time for a new future, where we can work together. If that doesn't work, then I'm sorry, Freya, but we can't stop the inevitable," Gage says.

I nod. He's right, and I just hope to fuck we can come to some kind of agreement before it's too late.

I've said it time and time again—I refuse to choose between my best friend and the men I love. If my brother is looking down on me now, which I know he is, I have one request: *Please make this all right. Get Kai to accept peace and allow everything to be good, not go back to the way it was, because that wasn't right either.* I've lived in Daringhood; we have to make it better for everyone.

Five minutes later, the backyard of my childhood home is full of Dominic's soldiers. The majority were once The Brotherhood's men, and the others came from God knows where.

"There are only two ways you are leaving here today," Hazen yells, staring around the crowd of at least two hundred men. "Dead, or by pledging your allegiance to The Brotherhood. What will it be?"

At least twenty men run before gunshots ring through the air, and they all drop to the ground. The rest of the crowd falls to their knees, dropping their weapons. I stand next to Lucas, watching in awe as more men bow down at their feet. If it were up to me, I'd make them do more than just submit, but I'm not in charge of The Brotherhood. Nor do I know what else they have planned for them. That's up to the guys, and I have enough going on in my head—I don't need more responsibility.

"Over the next week, you'll be put through hell. We'll be testing you and your loyalty to The Brotherhood. You'll wish you ran," Gage yells, and another ten men run for it. Their lifeless bodies fall to the ground. Red rain splatters over a few of the men standing near the edge of the crowd. The backyard is becoming a bloodbath.

Mia appears, followed by an army of Brotherhood soldiers. Mia makes her way over to us, and the others crowd around the backyard. She stands next to Hazen, her head held high, staring down at the soldiers with a smirk on her lips. She thinks she got exactly what she wanted.

"We need to take back control of our town and the Hood. Who's with us?" Hazen roars, and the crowd goes crazy with cheers.

"Victory is ours! Brothers before all else!" Gage shouts, his voice rumbling through the crowd of people.

They all look at Gage, Hazen, and Lucas with respect and admiration.

Well, shit. I think I just came.

Chapter 42

Freya

The three of them, Hazen, Lucas, and Gage, lie naked on my king-size bed. Each one of their arms is bound to the head-board, and they're unable to move. Sex toys are laid out in front of them. Fuck, I need to take a picture of this. All of them boast matching tattoos—*DB* under their hearts, and down their stomachs they have the words *Daring Brotherhood* at the top of an hourglass with three skulls inside it. They need to add one more for me because I'm theirs and they are mine.

We've been through so much together, and our story isn't over yet—there's still so much to figure out, but for the next hour or more, none of that matters. I'm going to devour each of these men, one by one, until we can't move or speak.

I take a photo with my phone and shove it back into my pocket.

"Freya, take off your clothes. Now," Gage demands.

I cock my head to the side. "You're not in charge today—I am. So, shut up or I'll bite off your tongue," I snap.

Lucas chuckles. The corner of Gage's mouth ticks, and I can tell he doesn't like me being in charge of him. He wants the power, but I'm not giving it to him. I need this, and he'll just have to bend over and take it like a good boy.

"I'd love to see you bite his dick off instead," Lucas says, and I glare at him. He pinches his lips together, and it takes everything in me to keep a straight face.

Pulling my phone out of my back pocket, I hit play on "To My Bed" by Chris Brown. As the music fills the room, I close my eyes, moving my body to the beat. I can feel their gazes on me, tracking my every move. It feels so powerful, knowing I've got my three men tied to my bed and that I'm in control of them. They are at my mercy.

I pop open the fly to my jeans, lower the zipper, and turn around. After hooking my fingers into my pants, I pull them over my butt, taking my sweet-ass time. A deep animal-like groan comes from behind me, encouraging me to put on a show for them. Their wish is my command.

My pants pool on the carpet, leaving me in my black lacy thong, my curves on full display for them. I take off my shirt, and it hits the ground. The coolness of the ceiling fan hardens my nipples, despite the black lace protecting them. I drop into a squat, glancing over my shoulder. My gaze goes to Gage first. He licks his lips, and I slowly rise, jiggling my butt as I do.

"Fuck," he growls out.

Lucas lies in the middle of them, watching me intently with gleaming eyes that seem to wonder what I'll do next. Hooking my fingers into my bra straps, I release my breasts, and my hard nipples spring free. The song changes to "Sex With Me" by Rihanna. After running my fingers down my chest, I cup my boob, flicking my nipple.

"Lucas, run your hand up and down your hard cock. Nice and slow for me," I say without breaking eye contact.

Lucas doesn't have to be asked twice. He grabs his hard cock with his free hand and does exactly what I asked.

"Gage and Hazen, do the same, and keep up the same pace as Lucas," I demand, flashing them a wicked grin.

My gaze moves between the three men, all of them with their hands on their beautiful dicks. It takes everything in me not to pounce on the bed and have them. I want to take my time and play, but my body is aching to be touched. Wetness pools between my thighs.

"Touch yourself, Freya," Gage says on a groan, and I glare at him.

I jump onto the bed and straddle him, my hand wrapping around his throat. His hard cock presses into the outside of my panties. He pulls against his restraints, pushing farther into my grip.

"What did I tell you about talking?" I ask, raising an eyebrow.

He glares at me in challenge. "You know you want to fuck me. For me to tear that thong to shreds and bury my cock deep in your soaked pussy."

Jesus. He's right—he's so right—but no. Fuck him.

"This is my game, my rules, and those who go against me will be punished. Hazen, pass me that ball gag," I say, never taking my eyes away from Gage's.

It lands in my hand, and I place it over Gage's head.

"Open wide, princess," I say, and Gage growls before obeying. After pushing the ball into his mouth, I lean back, smiling at my handiwork. The nipple clamps sit on his chest. I lift them, and Gage shakes his head wildly, but I ignore him, clipping both of his nipples before turning around and shoving my ass in his face. He pulls against his restraints.

"Lucas, make sure he doesn't touch, okay?" I ask, and Lucas nods, his hand still running over his own cock.

Gage's cock stares me down, the veins almost bursting. Licking my lips, I take in his tip before taking him whole.

"Fucking hell, little thorn. You're something else," Lucas huffs out.

I can feel Gage's hot exhales on my pussy, and I'm regretting the gag. I want his mouth there. As if hearing my silent demands, Gage's free hand shoves my thong aside, and he buries a finger inside me. I jolt forward, his cock hitting the back of my throat. I breathe through my nose to avoid gagging, but fuck. He strums my cunt like a guitar, adding another digit. I moan, my teeth running up his shaft.

Lucas groans beside me, his cum hitting my cheek. A low growl rumbles from my chest before Gage's hot release shoots down my throat. I sit back, slipping his cock from my mouth, and push farther onto Gage's fingers, riding them. He hits exactly where I want him again and again until I'm screaming out his name. My belly explodes, my thighs clutching around his hand.

I slow down, riding out my release before crawling over to Lucas and grabbing his hand. I place it over my cheek, wiping off his release. "Naughty boy. What am I going to do with you?"

Lucas's eyes sparkle. "Sit your pretty cunt on my face."

I shake my head. "You just came on my face. You don't get rewarded. You get punished," I say, and Lucas shrugs, leaning back against the pillow, clearly waiting for it.

I stand, pulling down my underwear, then I step out of my lacy thong and bring it over Lucas's head, covering his eyes so he can't see what's about to happen.

"No touching or talking. Got it?" I say, and Lucas nods eagerly, moving his hand behind his head.

I kneel down, lining his hard shaft up with my soaking, still-needy pussy. He fills me fully, and it takes me a moment to adjust to his size. Bracing my hands on his chest, I bob up and down to the rhythm of the music, slow and steady. Lucas's chest rises and falls at the same rate as mine.

"Hazen, I need something else inside me. Untie yourself and give me what I want." My voice comes out all croaky. I close my eyes and hear the sound of metal against metal while silently praising Hazen for doing as I asked.

Hazen's hands brace my hips. The sound of something clicking open and closed hits my ears before wetness is rubbed around my asshole. Fuck me, he's not even inside of me yet and I'm done for.

Gage mumbles something against his gag, and my eyes shoot to his.

"Hand on your cock, watch and imagine I'm riding you," I say, and Gage's eyes turn dark green.

Hazen slips his thumb into my crack, in and out, and eventually, I feel his tip sliding into my ass. As my cunt squeezes against Lucas's cock, he groans. They both fill me, stretching me to my limits. Hazen takes his time as my ass adjusts to him.

I'm completely full, and I have no idea how long I'm going to last. It feels so good, and I'm climbing higher and higher. Gage bites into his gag, the clamps bite into his hard nipples, and his hand gripping his cock moves to the same rhythm as us.

It takes everything in me not to finish. I want this to last, but fuck, these men are making it near impossible. Hazen's fingers dig into my hips, holding me in place.

Lucas grabs my wrist, forcing my hand around his neck. I squeeze, applying just enough pressure. My breathing picks up, a low pressure builds in my stomach, and I'm about to give in.

Hazen pulls out, his hot cum shooting across my back. I let go, riding out my orgasm until Lucas finishes inside me. I collapse onto Lucas's chest, resting my head on his heart.

We lie there without saying a word.

These men complete me, and I complete them. Each of us is fucked up, but somehow, together, we fit. We complete each other, and that's more than I've ever wanted.

Chapter 43

Freya

It takes an hour to clean ourselves up. A dull ache sits between my legs, reminding me of what we just did. I'll never get sick of fucking these guys.

My phone vibrates on the bathroom vanity. I pull my hair out of the towel and run my fingers through the knots. It's probably Amirah—I haven't heard from her or seen her since everything that happened with Dominic, but I've been a bit occupied these last few hours. Gage said he told her to stay put at home.

I open my phone and my hand shakes as I read the message from the unknown number.

Unknown: You may have won the battle, but you still won't win the war. What's a kingdom without its princess?

What the fuck is that supposed to mean?

"Uh, guys?" I yell, and all three men come storming into the bathroom.

Gage snatches the phone from my grip. He frowns before showing Hazen and Lucas.

Lucas snorts. "Our princess is right here. What's this lunatic talking about?"

"They are just playing games. Ignore it," Hazen says, and I nod, but it doesn't shake the sick feeling in the pit of my stomach.

"Party at Gage's house. We need a release before meeting with the Hood," Lucas says, and I don't argue. I need to see Amirah, anyway.

We arrive at Gage's thirty minutes later. Music booms from inside, cars fill the driveway, and we all look at Lucas. He shrugs.

"What? I just wanted the party to get started before we got here. I called ahead and told our Brotherhood it was time to let loose."

I roll my eyes, moving through the front door and walking straight up the stairs, heading for Amirah's bedroom. I need to change, and she has the best clothes for occasions like this.

Her door is halfway open, and I kick it the rest of the way. Darkness meets me, and I flick on the light. "Amirah?" I sing out, but I'm met with nothing but silence.

I move farther into her room. Her bed is a mess, the duvet all tangled to one side. She must be in the bathroom. The lights are on in the en suite, so I slowly make my way there.

"You in here?" I say, before pushing the door open.

I scream, covering my mouth with my hand. Broken glass is scattered all over the floor. There's so much blood, and in bright-red letters, scrawled on the mirror, are four terrifying words:

The princess is mine.

The End

T he End

Want more?

Discover what happens when the war between the Ville and the Hood really heats up in Deadly Little Pawn—Amirah's story.

Also by Jenna Daring

Tens series

The Invitation

Mafia Princess of Roxbury Prep

Reclaim

About Jenna Daring

Jenna Daring is a dark romance author living in Melbourne, Australia with her high school crush and their golden retriever Coop. When she's not writing strong female characters or alpha males, she's dreaming up the next thing, coaching or reading.

Join her readers group on Facebook – The Daring Den

www.ingramcontent.com/pod-product-compliance
Lightning Source LLC
Chambersburg PA
CBHW070548120726
47909CB00007B/2278